Disturbing the Peace

Disturbing the Peace

Nancy Newman

AVON BOOKS
An Imprint of HarperCollinsPublishers

Grateful acknowledgment is made to reprint the excerpt from "Desert Places" from
The Poetry of Robert Frost edited by Edward Connery Lathem.
Copyright 1936 by Robert Frost, © 1964 by Lesley Frost Ballantine. © 1969 by
Henry Holt and Co. Reprinted by permission of Henry Holt and Company, LLC.

HarperCollins books may be purchased for educational, business, or sales promotional
use. For information please write: Special Markets Department,
HarperCollins Publishers Inc., 10 East 53rd Street, New York, NY 10022.

FIRST EDITION

Designed by Glen M. Edelstein

Library of Congress Cataloging-in-Publication Data

Newman, Nancy, 1944–
    Disturbing the peace / Nancy Newman.—1st ed.
        p. cm.
    ISBN 0-380-79839-5 (pbk.)
    1. Birthmothers—Fiction. 2. Mothers and daughters—Fiction. 3. New York
(N.Y.)—Fiction. I. Title.

PS3614.E63 D57 2002
813'.6—dc21

2001053577

02 03 04 05 06 RRD 10 9 8 7 6 5

For my husband, H.H.E.,
with love

They cannot scare me with their empty spaces

Between stars—on stars where no human race is.

I have it in me so much nearer home

To scare myself with my own desert places.

—ROBERT FROST

Acknowledgments

I want to thank Lynda Sturner Traum for generously sharing her knowledge of and experience with the adoption search process.

My husband Henry's unwavering confidence in me has meant more than I can express.

I am grateful to the following friends and family members for their loving support over the years: Joanne Berghold, George Blecher, Laurel Blossom, Kristin McDonough, Donald McDonough, Nora Eisenberg, Tom Engelhardt, Steve Kroll, Pat Laurence, Liz Levy, David

Nemec, Barbara Newman, Sydell Newman, Nancy Tanner, Leonard Todd, Jerome Traum.

My sons, Adam, Justin, and Ben, have given me invaluable criticism, technical advice, and inspiration.

Special thanks to my extraordinary agent, Anne Edelstein, for her acumen, wise counsel, and loyalty.

Last but not least, I want to thank my HarperCollins editor, Lyssa Keusch, for her guidance during the publication process.

Disturbing the Peace

Prologue

This time, it was the pale hand that got me going, a hand that looked identical to mine: long thin fingers, spatulate nails, a large freckle on the wrist. My heart whacked madly in my chest as I leaned forward on the escalator to see more of her face, sure there was something familiar about her features, sure we were connected. Hadn't I always known I'd recognize her?

My mother.

I followed her off the escalator, past a few mannequins, down an aisle that led us into the lingerie department. When she stopped to examine some nightgowns, I ducked behind a metal clothes rack

1

so I could keep an eye on her. We looked exactly alike: same bony frame, light skin, leonine hair. (My adoptive mother and I had looked nothing alike—had been nothing alike.) I gazed at the lines etched onto her face, the deep furrow in her brow, wondering if this was how I would look in twenty years. But was this woman really my mother? Then she reached for a pale green nightgown—my favorite shade of green—and I knew it had to be her.

I stepped out from my hiding place and edged closer. Just then, she took off again, walking briskly now as if late for an appointment. I followed her down the aisle and out of the store, keeping a safe distance between us as she crossed the street and entered a towering office building. By the time I pushed through the revolving door and scanned the clusters of people in the lobby, she had already entered one of the elevators. I dashed across the floor and managed to wedge in next to her a split second before the door closed. Our eyes met. I smiled expectantly, but her face registered nothing.

When the door opened and she stepped off the elevator, I hesitated for a moment, then trailed after her down a long, winding corridor to a medical laboratory. Watching her enter the office, I felt a stab of grief. Was she seriously ill? Did she have an incurable disease? I pictured her lying in a hospital bed, emaciated and weak, embracing me for the last time.

Why had I waited so long to find her?

I grasped the knob and opened the door. A sharp medicinal smell assailed me as I glanced around the waiting room. The woman I'd been following stared at me quizzically. My cheeks flamed with embarrassment. Was I mad? Of course this stranger wasn't my mother. I mumbled something about having made a mistake, backed out of the office, and fled . . .

Part ☆ One

Chapter One

The night I stopped in at the Happy Carrot, my friend Ann's organic health food store—a place I never ventured when hungry—I was not in the perkiest of moods for several reasons, one of which was that my thirty-fifth birthday loomed ahead on the calendar like a great menacing behemoth. And unlike all the birthdays I'd managed to ignore by telling myself these were only the practice years, this one insisted on being noticed.

Ann was working the juice bar at the back of the store when I came in. Petite, pretty, with huge dark eyes that seemed to absorb whatever you told her and then some, she was a good listener even when you weren't talking. True to form, she picked up my mood as soon as I settled myself on a rickety wooden stool at the counter.

"You look half-dead," she pronounced, taking my hands between her two smaller hands and rubbing them vigorously. Ann staunchly believed that skin contact maximized health, and whenever I got sick, she maintained I wasn't having enough sex. "You need something with a real kick—maybe a lentil burger with squash and spinach dumplings—"

"Don't bother, I'm not hungry," I said quickly, trying for tact. I loved Ann's good company but was no fan of her food. In truth, she'd been a junk-food addict when we'd roomed together in college but had since married into the health movement and now had the zeal of a convert. I admired her newfound knowledge of herbs and devotion to vitamins, but wasn't crazy about her soy patties, tofu stews, and seaweed snacks. And right then, I really wasn't hungry because I always lose my appetite when I'm nervous or upset. My overweight friends say they envy this, but bony isn't better than blobby despite what the fashion magazines say; hipbones sticking out of flesh, minibreasts, a flat ass are nothing to envy as far as I'm concerned.

"What's up?" she asked, giving me a penetrating look. "No, wait, let me guess. Another student proposed marriage to you tonight and you didn't want to hurt his feelings so you said yes." She started laughing but broke off when she saw my expression.

"Doc Chin's driving me crazy," I said glumly.

"The creep in your class who's always following you around?"

"I never said he was a creep, I said he gives me the creeps. He insists that we're soul mates."

"Pooh, you're too involved with your students," she said, slapping a shivery piece of tofu onto a slice of bread and handing it to me.

"Not true," I protested, pretending to nibble on an edge of the bread. "I bend over backwards to keep my distance."

"Yeah, well, sometimes I have the distinct feeling you're bending in the wrong direction."

I laughed. "Now you sound just like Stoddard."

"Impossible. Your boyfriend talks the language of the next generation. I feel like his goddamned mother. 'Chill out, Annie,' " she said, imitating Stoddard's Texas drawl.

"Come on, he's only six years younger than us."

"Only? Sarah, he was in seventh grade when we were in college. Okay, so he's real cute and the sex is great and you hardly ever get sick. Big deal. There's always kyolic or astragolis or even penicillin. You're almost thirty-five—"

"And so are you," I cut in, "so if we're going to do Stoddard and me right now, we're also going to talk about why you're still baby-sitting a bunch of vegetables instead of going back to California to finish your course work and dissertation—"

Ann looked so stricken, I worried I'd gone too far. We'd been arguing over each other's lives for years, but I knew she took her vitamins and minerals very seriously.

"That's him!" she whispered conspiratorially, looking over my shoulder at the door.

I turned and saw an unshaven man wearing an elegantly tailored pin-striped suit, grubby T-shirt, battered cowboy hat, and highly polished wingtip shoes with no socks. A lawyer out for a ride on the range? Park ranger turned banker? At 10 P.M. in the East Village, the possibilities were dizzying. "Who is he?" I asked, genuinely curious.

"The guy I've been telling you about . . . the one who'd be great for your book."

"Thank you, but I'm not interested," I said, giving her a canny look. Ann was very underhanded and very persistent when it came to enhancing my social life, and I didn't want to give her any encouragement.

"But he's got this extraordinary rags-to-riches story," she whispered. "Came from Romania around twenty years ago with absolutely nothing and is incredibly successful. Sh-h-h-h! He's coming."

A moment later, Mr. Rags-to-Riches sauntered over to us, slid onto a stool next to me, kissed Ann hello, and took off his cowboy hat.

"Alex Astor, this is Sarah Bridges," Ann said, beaming at the two of us. "Sarah's the friend I've been telling you about who's doing a book on her immigrant students."

He turned in my direction and studied me carefully while rubbing his woodsman's chin stubble. I now noticed that his curly black hair was threaded with gray. I also noticed that his face had a sort of biblical intensity that seemed at odds with his mischievous smile.

"So. Ann tells me you're enshrining immigrants in this book of yours," he said after a moment.

"I'm not enshrining them, I'm simply documenting what

it costs people to come to America," I answered, bristling at his sarcastic tone.

"And what would an all-American woman like you know about this particular subject?" he asked, cocking his head to the side.

"Sarah's been teaching English as a second language at the New York Association for Foreign Students for eleven years," Ann explained as she stuffed a handful of grass into her juicer and turned the machine on.

"Ah, NYAFS," he said, nodding. "That's the program run by the gentleman who always looks like an unmade bed."

Ann laughed. "You've been known to take quite a few fashion risks yourself, Alex," she said, eyeing his odd outfit.

He looked down at his frayed T-shirt and smiled. "This was all I had in my gym locker."

"Well, in any case, looking chic isn't what NYAFS or Al Falcone are about," I told him.

"See? I knew you two'd have lots to talk about," Ann said, filling two tiny glasses with chartreuse-colored liquid and handing them to us.

I eyed the drink with suspicion. Ann was capable of some pretty wicked concoctions, and I knew from experience that this neon number was one of her deadliest. "No thanks," I said firmly.

"But it'll launder your system, and the nausea'll only last ten, fifteen minutes."

Alex lifted his glass and toasted me. "As the Chinese say, sometimes you have to eat bitter to taste sweet." He swallowed the green slime and shuddered slightly.

"Thanks, but my life's so sweet, I don't need anything

bitter." I slid the glass back over to Ann. She shrugged and then swallowed the stuff down herself, shuddering exactly as Alex had.

"Well, I guess I'd better get going," I announced, standing up and grabbing my briefcase before the conversation could start again. "I just stopped in to say hi, Ann, but I've got a million papers to correct tonight." I pecked her on the cheek, nodded in Alex's direction, and made for the door.

It had been a nasty, drizzling, pinching cold day, the kind of late winter weather that always invites me to stay in bed, which is exactly what I'd done all afternoon. (Many of the things I liked doing best could be done in bed, alone or with company, and it wasn't unusual for me to hole up with a stack of books for days at a time in crummy weather.) But now the rain was really taking itself seriously, and gusts of water were blowing across the sidewalk. I huddled under the awning trying to work up the courage to head for home when I suddenly felt a tap on my shoulder. I spun around and saw Alex standing behind me, holding the lapels of his suit jacket closed.

"May I provide you with transportation?" he asked.

"No thank you," I responded, thinking that the last thing in the world I needed just then was to have to make polite conversation with yet another emigré.

"You have no umbrella."

"This is true. I have no umbrella." I sneezed hard and then again.

"My car is right here," he said, pointing to the Checker cab parked in front of us.

"Thank you, but I can't afford a taxi habit. Anyway, I love walking in the rain."

"In this weather? Like hell you do." He held the door open for me.

I hesitated, torn between my desire to stay dry and my aversion to making small talk. As I stood there shivering and thinking about all this, he ran around to the driver's side and got in. I sneezed again and climbed in next to him, consoling myself with the thought that I'd be home in about three minutes.

"Damn! I stepped in a puddle up to my knees," he muttered, pulling off his shoes and tossing them into the backseat. He studied the dashboard for a moment, then toyed with a few different knobs. "Sorry, it's going to take me a moment to figure out how to get the heat going. My driver became ill this evening, and I had to drop him off at his home . . ."

He continued talking about the car and driver, but I was only half listening as I stared down at his naked feet, aware that a small kernel of desire was heating up my center—a complete surprise. For one thing, there was my boyfriend, Stoddard. For another, I tended to fall in lust with angular high-strung men, the kind who could be cast to play Sherlock Holmes, and this man definitely wasn't my type. And also, he was a cabby, which in itself wasn't a turnoff—I knew lots of smart, well-educated emigrés who drove taxis when they first got to New York—but which was suspicious in light of the fact that according to Ann, he'd been in New York for twenty years and spoke terrific English,

which meant (despite Ann's claim that he was very successful) he was either uneducated, lazy, stupid, or crazy, or
maybe all of the above. Someone to steer clear of even if I
were interested in finding a replacement for Stoddard.
Which I most definitely was not.

"Would you mind reaching into my gym bag to see if you
can hunt up a pair of dry socks?" he asked as the engine
came to life. "I played squash earlier, so ignore the sweaty
clothes."

"Great detectives never ignore anything," I said under
my breath as I reached for the bag, mentally switching into
my Nancy Drew mode, a secret habit—a sort of nervous tic
that grew out of my childhood addiction to Nancy Drew
mysteries.

*Girl detective Sarah Bridges opened the zipper and pulled
out damp tennis shorts and a jock strap that had seen better
days. Digging deeper, she unearthed a set of miniature
tools, a Christie's auction catalog, a silk scarf with a
Givenchy label, and a small tape recorder—a very suspicious mix of objects . . .*

—THE CASE OF THE MYSTERIOUS CABBY

I stopped my little interior narrative and announced that
there were no socks. Then I pulled one last item, a small
textbook, from the bag.

"The Theory of Sound," I read out loud, riffling through
pages of mathematical formulae that looked like hiero-

glyphics. "Where are you taking a math class?" I asked, adjusting my opinion of him one notch higher. Cabby or not, he was obviously trying to improve himself.

"I'm not taking a class."

"Oh? Just doing some light reading?"

"That's right. Actually, Lord Raleigh's book is more history of sound than mathematics. It's a classic in the field."

"I see," I lied, stuffing the objects back into the bag as I worked up a theory about him. He might be an athletic mathematician with an interest in art, a con man with expensive taste, an intellectually curious drug dealer, or, Ann's penchant for kooky men notwithstanding, your normal, run-of-the-mill New York lunatic. I slid my hand over to the door and rested it on the handle in case I needed to make a fast exit.

"So, how long have you known Ann?" I asked, trying to sound nonchalant.

"About six, seven months. I've gotten into the habit of stopping in at the store whenever I'm downtown. But she's told me so much about you, I feel like I've known you for years."

"Really?" I said uneasily.

"Oh, yes. I know your whole life story. . . . Let's see, your father was a well-known Civil War scholar. You grew up in a small town in Connecticut. You ran track and played the oboe in high school. You studied theater in college and married an actor—I'm afraid Ann doesn't think too highly of your ex-husband, by the way," he added, smiling slyly. "And then, after your divorce, you came to New York to work in the theater but ended up teaching English. You're utterly devoted to your students and work long hours in a run-down school for almost no remuneration—"

"Thank you for the sympathy, but it's misplaced. I happen to enjoy my work enormously," I told him briskly, the words coming out sharper than I'd intended. To soften them—after all, it wasn't his fault Ann had me pegged as a martyr—I asked where he'd learned his excellent English.

He gave me a sidelong glance and laughed. "I know you're working hard to pigeonhole me, Sarah, but I'll save you the effort by dispelling your notion that I'm a pigeon."

To cover my embarrassment, I leaned forward and rubbed fog off the window with the cuff of my raincoat, craning my neck to see why we'd come to a halt.

Alex stuck his head out the window for a moment, then pulled back in, his face glistening with rain. "A garbage truck's blocking the street." He shut off the engine and leaned back in his seat happily. "Now you'll have an opportunity to correct my English while we wait it out."

"You don't need any correction. Your English is perfect."

"My grammar is correct and I've worked hard to lose my accent, but somehow people can still tell I'm foreign-born. Actually, it mystifies me," he added, drumming his fingers on the steering wheel. In the dim light from the streetlamp, I noticed jagged purplish marks on the backs of his hands, but I couldn't tell whether they were scars or shadows. He caught me looking at his hands and abruptly pulled them away.

"This is a great car," I said to lighten the mood. Though I usually enjoy floating on undercurrents in casual conversations, something about this conversation was beginning to make me edgy.

"Checker taxis were part of the Hollywood image I had of New York before I got here, and I try to keep it up."

"The cab or the image?"

"Both, I guess—though it must sound pretty foolish to you," he added, throwing me a quick glance.

"Not really. You're just suffering from what the Brazilians call *saudades*."

"Saw-what?"

"*Saudades*. It's a form of nostalgia—sort of the blues—for something that may never even have existed. It's what Ralph Lauren capitalizes on—our fantasies about the past. Most emigrés suffer from it in spades when they first get here."

He looked at me without saying anything, then broke into an appreciative smile. "You know, Ann's been trying to introduce us for months, but I've been avoiding you. From her description, I thought you'd be a cross between Mother Teresa and Margaret Mead. Frankly, I'm surprised that you're so . . . somehow, I'd think a woman as attractive as you—an actress—would get restless teaching grammar year after year."

"First of all, I've never been an actress. I was just a theater major—you know, the shy girl in the wings whose name no one could ever remember. And secondly, I teach a lot more than grammar."

"Such as?"

"Forget it," I said with a wave of my hand. "It'll just bore you. People always get a glazed-over look in their eyes when I talk about my students, so I don't."

"Try me," he said, crossing his arms on his chest.

I shrugged. "Okay. But don't say I didn't warn you. . . . Well, most of my students are wrecks by the time they come into my class. They've gone through hell to get away from home, feel completely disconnected from their families and friends—from everything familiar—and live in an emotional limbo because of the language and culture gap. So, along with teaching standard English, I try to spruce up their cultural skills, limber up their slang. I show them things like how loud or soft to speak, how close to stand next to someone, how to apply for a job, even how to ask for or reject a date so they can get their lives going again."

He let out a low whistle. "I wish I'd had such a dedicated teacher when I first arrived."

I narrowed my eyes. "Are you being sarcastic?"

"Not at all."

"Well, it's not selfless dedication. As I said before, I love my work. I feel like I'm throwing lifelines out to people who are drowning, and when I can haul someone to shore it's very satisfying."

"Interesting," he said after a long pause.

"What is?"

"Your fervor. You sound positively evangelical when you're talking about rescuing your students, and I've always been fascinated by evangelists—by what motivates them."

"Why? Do you think it's weird to care about other people?"

"I didn't say weird, I said interesting. Especially in light of your particular background—"

Just then, the garbage truck in front of us started up with a terrible roar. I waited for the noise and my irritation to die down, and then turned toward him and gave him a tight smile, silently cursing myself for allowing so much intimacy to spring up between us, the result, no doubt, of being stranded together in a car on a rainy night. "Maybe I can give you some advice about your English after all," I said, switching into my most teacherly voice.

"Yes?"

"The tip-off that you're not native-born is your occasional use of textbook English. For example, when you offered me a ride home before, you said 'May I provide you with transportation?' instead of Want a ride or Can I give you a lift. You also used the phrase, I'll dispel your notion, when something less formal would have done just as well. It's the choice of words—the formality of your syntax— that marks you as a foreigner, you see. I'm afraid that if you want to be taken for a native-born American, you're going to have to sound a bit sloppier. . . . And now, since the traffic's moving again and it's getting late, would you mind making a right at the next corner and then your third left and I'll be home."

He revved up the engine and we took off. My curt criticism produced the desired effect; he hardly said another word until we pulled up in front of my building. I thanked him and offered my hand.

"Your hand's ice cold," he said, clasping it tightly.

"Chilled from the rain," I answered, quickly disengaging myself and glancing up to the fourth floor, surprised to see my lights on. Either Stoddard had gotten more depressed than usual by his friend's opening or he was out of hot water again at his place.

"Do you ever do any private tutoring?" Alex asked.

"Yes, lots of it, but I don't have time to take on new students right now."

"Too bad . . . You know, it's quite dark in your hallway. Would you like me to accompany you inside?"

I was tempted to correct his overformal English again but thought better of it and just thanked him for the ride and got out. It was still pouring, and no one was in sight except street people and wackos. I took a few steps, then noticed two skanky-looking men loitering in my lobby. I made a quick U-turn back to the car.

"Maybe I'd better take you up on your offer after all," I said somewhat sheepishly.

Alex put on his shoes and followed me inside the vestibule and up the staircase. Although he didn't say anything, his silence somehow seemed more expressive than words. It struck me as we approached my landing that he exuded a kind of sexual-availability-without-aggressiveness I'd known in men who genuinely liked women, and I found myself growing edgy again. When we got to my doorway, he reached out to wipe away a droplet of water from my cheek with the back of his hand, a gesture that was at once so casual and so startlingly intimate, I felt a warm flush spread through my body.

Well, I thought.

To avoid his gaze, I busied myself by fiddling with the lock, but he must have accidentally leaned on the buzzer just then because all of a sudden I heard the thunk of the dead bolt and the door swung open and there was Stoddard wearing nothing but a striped towel, his shoulder-length hair tousled and dripping. From the startled look on Alex's face, I realized Ann had failed to mention Stoddard in her little narrative about me.

"Hey, Sar, you're almost as wet as me!" Stoddard exclaimed, kissing me enthusiastically and throwing a damp arm around my shoulder.

"Stoddard, this is Alex Astor, Ann's friend. Alex was kind enough to give me a lift home in his cab—one of the last Checkers," I added, as if that explained everything.

The introduction hung awkwardly in the air for a moment as Stoddard took in Alex's getup—the business suit and wrecked T-shirt, the absence of socks, the cowboy hat—without reacting. He was what I liked to think of as a New Age man and was very nonjudgmental.

"That sure is a frog strangler out there tonight, isn't it?" he said, absently smoothing down the pale clump of hair on his chest.

"Pardon me?" Alex said.

"Texas lingo for a sudden heavy rainstorm," I translated.

"Want to come in for a drink or somethin'?" Stoddard asked. "Y'all still got that wine I left here, Sarah?"

"Thank you, but it's late," Alex said, bowing slightly and

turning to go. Then as an afterthought, he paused and pulled out a business card, which he pressed into my palm. "Just in case you find time to do some tutoring."

"Got to hand it to you, Sarah," Stoddard said after Alex disappeared down the stairs. "You do one hell of a job. That new student of yours speaks better English than me."

Chapter Two

I'd met Stoddard at a friend's party some three years earlier, and when he told me he was an artist who painted murals in homes and restaurants to support himself, I was charmed. On a whim, I hired him to paint a garden on my bedroom wall. He'd virtually camped out in my bedroom for a couple of weeks while he'd worked on it, but I hadn't found his presence intrusive, which surprised me since I usually enjoy spending great stretches of time alone.

One of the first things I'd noticed about Stoddard was that we looked enough alike to be taken for brother and sister, both of us being sandy-haired and lanky and pale-eyed, though Stoddard's eyes are blue and mine are a sea green, my most singular and commented-upon feature. And while he sketched out the flowers he was going to paint on my wall, I discovered we also shared similarly traditional upbringings in small towns, although we just skittered across our childhoods, he because of feeling painfully out of place in his conservative Texas family, and I because it was a subject I didn't like thinking about. He explained that he lived on a small trust fund left by a grandmother who'd died before he'd grown up to be an embarrassment to his family of bankers, adding that by living penuriously and taking on an occasional mural job as a supplement, the tiny but secure inheritance allowed him the freedom to paint.

I'd listened to all this with a vague awareness that his country-boy accent, his gentility and openness, and the fact that he was twenty-six to my then thirty-two made me feel very easy, something I'd never felt with my ex-husband, Eric. And though Stoddard looked painterly with his long hair and baggy paint-spattered overalls, there was something wholesome and responsible about him. Strange as it sounds, Stoddard even smelled like home to me. So when he'd finished his mural and started packing up his brushes, I had mixed feelings about his departure but wasn't sure whether I should reveal them. For one thing, he hadn't mentioned any women in his life, and I wasn't sure about his sexual proclivities or romantic attachments. For another, I'd spent so many years lurching from relationship to relationship, I was hesitant about starting over again with someone new.

"You satisfied with your garden?" he'd asked, stepping back from the wall to eye his final product, which wasn't easy in my bedroom. It was a wonderful room—splashed with sunlight, sometimes even moonlight—but my antique brass bed occupied most of the floor space and stacks of books crowded every surface.

I studied the decidedly erotic arrangement of roses and peonies and daisies on my wall, taking in the fact that each individual flower looked like a male or female genital or some combination thereof. "It's very ... exciting," I answered, choosing my words carefully. It was then, I think, that I recognized the full nature of my attachment to Stoddard.

"I've got to confess something," he said, looking distressed. "No matter whatall I paint, it always comes out lookin' like a cunt, a prick, and two balls. Even happens when I do murals in babies' rooms. If you want, I can white it out and try again. I won't charge you any extra, of course. Truth of it is," he added shyly, "I really like being here with you, talkin' and all, so I wouldn't mind starting the whole thing over again."

I automatically registered the fact that he pronounced *thing* as "thang," but what I was really focusing on was the thick mat of blond hair covering his ropy forearms and the question of whether he was equally blond all over. "No apologies necessary, I think it's just right," I assured him. Then I added: "You see, when I was younger, I thought sex was serious but not very important. Now I think it's important but not very serious."

He'd laughed and sat down on my bed and I'd sat down

next to him and one thing led to another and then quite naturally and without a great fuss or any pronouncements, I began spending most of my days and some of my nights in his loft, which was situated over a commercial bakery on Great Jones Street. Soon my clothes, too, took on the wholesome smell of freshly baked bread.

I'm not sure what first attracted Stoddard to me because, as I said, I was considerably older than he and not really his romantic type. (He admitted early on that tiny women with large breasts populated his fantasies.) I suspected that my availability in the daytime coupled with my financial stability—two qualities that rarely hang together—were what turned him on. And, of course, there was also the fact that I was quite determined to leave ours an undefined and, for the most part, diurnal relationship.

As for myself, Stoddard offered me a peaceful haven after the havoc of my divorce from Eric Powell, Northwestern University drama department's leading egomaniac, and the series of checkered affairs that had followed. I'd been involved with an almost-divorced writer, an environmental activist who'd wanted me to move out to Wyoming with him, and a forty-three-year-old Indian poet.

By the time I'd met Stoddard, I was weary and wary of strangers' beds, and felt ready for a relationship that would neither be marriage nor freelance fucking. I hungered in equal parts for freedom and companionship and had little interest in delving deeply into my own or a lover's inner workings. Maybe it was because my parents were so emotionally distant, maybe it was the result of my disastrous marriage to Eric, maybe it was an instinctive self-protectiveness. Whatever the cause, the bottom line was that too much intimacy made me feel the way I did when I sat too close to the stage in a theater: I needed some distance in order to hold on to the illusions I'd unwittingly created for and about myself.

But as I said, around Stoddard, something in me relaxed. I took pleasure in his generosity of spirit and playfulness—he loved to lark around—but, when his work was going badly, I got out of his way. I carefully observed and monitored his moods but didn't try to change him, much the way a meteorologist charts the weather without interfering with its course. And when his brooding silences turned into angry outbursts, I took off to my place until one or both of us cooled down.

Since Stoddard suffered from claustrophobia and had a minimalistic attitude about possessions—he elevated impermanence to an art form—he had very little furniture in his loft. There was an oak dresser he'd rescued from the street, a big, rollicking sofa he'd bought at the Salvation Army, and a couple of tables made from telephone-wire spools. But when I started spending most of my days at his place, I needed a desk, so he took one of the loft's few remaining interior doors off its hinges and set it on wooden sawhorses for me. I never told him but I liked to think of that unhinged door as a metaphor for our affair; for though we spent most afternoons together, we often separated in the evening. Off I'd go to teach my night-school English classes at Washington Irving High School on Seventeenth Street, or to meet friends for dinner, or to some off-off-awful Broadway performance—I periodically gorged on theater the way others gorged on food. Or I would simply go back to my place to work on my book or practice my oboe or just read, whereas Stoddard spent his free time hanging out with other painters in run-down bars or went to art openings I found noisy and boring. I didn't much care for his painter friends because they talked an affected, gobbledygook language of art theory I didn't understand and were fiercely competitive. In turn, Stoddard wasn't interested in the psychosociological bent of my friends' conversations or in going to the theater, so we kept chunks of our social life quite separate. I trusted Stoddard and was sure he didn't see other women—we were both paranoid about AIDS—but we assiduously avoided talking about the M word. To sum up, we were very good friends, in and out of bed.

And in bed, we were something else as well, which I probably should explain.

I've always been afraid of speed, height, deep water, and dark places but have fought hard against my cowardice, so hard, in fact, that when childhood friends scrambled up fences, leaped across rushing streams, or jumped off high-diving boards, I gritted my teeth and forced myself to keep up with the bravest of them, earning over time something of a reputation for being a daredevil. Although, as I said, Stoddard and I resisted talking about our childhoods in great detail—there was a line of privacy past which we didn't venture, our mutual intention being to prevent our lives from merging in any serious way—I suspected Stoddard of harboring similar fears about himself which he hid by initiating feats of sexual daring. Naturally, I felt compelled to take him up on his challenges, so early in our relationship we quickly worked our way past the standard new-relationship sex (on elevators, in friends' bathrooms during parties, in odd places like sleeping bags and hammocks) to more interesting and original experiments on mountain ridges while hiking, in a variety of vehicles, and once, on a particularly dark night, on our rickety fire escape. Discussing this last feat afterward, we admitted that the fire escape had not only been spectacularly uncomfortable, it had been dangerous as well, and made a pact at that point to tone down our antics. And after our almost three years together, we no longer had so much to prove to each other.

"Don't you all keep anythin' to eat around here 'cept peanut butter?" Stoddard drawled when he emerged from his shower a second time. The heaviness of his accent was not a good sign. It tended to increase with the blackness of his mood and was always at its most exaggerated after a competitor's opening.

I turned and studied Stoddard's freshly shaven face, pink and innocent as a baby's, and just then his innocence and country-boy accent thoroughly annoyed me. "I don't see how you can complain when you weren't even supposed to show up here tonight."

"Good Lord, don't get into a hissy fit. I'm not talkin' about a four-course meal."

He looked so injured, I quickly explained that I'd had a difficult evening and still had to call a bunch of students to tell them how to get to East New York, New Jersey, for the

TOEFL exam in the morning, leaving out the fact that I also had to hunt up a decent living place for Gyung Toa, a Tibetan journalist who was temporarily housed in a shelter.

"Well, at least that pesty Chinese guy won't be in your class again next term. Then maybe you'll stop having so many bad dreams."

"That's not definite yet," I said faintly, opening the cupboard and standing on my tiptoes. Stoddard was referring to Doc Chin, my most troublesome and troubling student, who not only had been trailing after me all term for advice and consolation, but who had ignited such combustible feelings in me that I'd been having nightmares about him. "Maybe there's some tuna up on the top shelf—"

"Sweet Jesus! Al's got to get Doc Chin off your back. I swear, that sonofabitch boss of yours treats you worsen' a migrant worker."

"Al's trying his best, but classes are packed. He's going to hire more staff when our grant situation stabilizes."

"Wake up and smell the coffee, will you?" he said, lightly rapping the top of my head with his knuckles. "Your boss has been feedin' you the same bull crap for ten years. I'm tellin' you, he's never going to get his hands on any real money 'cause he's got the personality of a vacuum cleaner. He makes a lot of noise and is filled with hot air."

"Hey, Al's the first to admit he's a terrible fund-raiser. That's why I'm going to help write up the new set of grant applications."

"Oh, great. Now you can put in an extra million hours a week you don't get paid for."

"I happen to owe Al a lot. If he hadn't given me part of

the Diamond grant to finish my book, I'd still be tutoring like crazy to make ends meet."

"He didn't do it for you, dummy; he thinks your book's going to be great publicity for him."

"Not for him, for NYAFS," I corrected.

"Well, I don't buy it. I still think he's like my brother Robert—a con man with a briefcase."

"How come everyone you don't like reminds you of your brother?"

He flicked his hair off his face with a jerk of his head, a sign that I'd hit a chord. Stoddard was very touchy about his brother Robert, who was eleven months older than him and exactly what his parents had expected Stoddard to be—a macho banker with a wife, two kiddies, and a Mercedes.

"So how was the opening?" I asked, steering the conversation away from my job, which was our major source of friction.

"Mark can't paint worth a pig's ass," he said, slamming the cabinet door so hard the glasses inside rattled.

I sighed loudly. "See? I knew you'd be in a foul mood tonight. That's one of the reasons I came back here instead of going to your place."

"Me in a foul mood? You're the one who's been jumpin' down my throat lately. I don't know if it's 'cause you're working such long hours or your birthday's coming up or you're worried about your book, but whatever it is, it's eatin' both of us up."

I opened the refrigerator and made a great show of studying its contents, not an easy thing to pull off since there was only a shriveled carrot, two wizened apples, and a now-wilted red cabbage I'd bought because of its lurid color. Stoddard was right, of course. I was in a horrible prebirthday mood. To make matters worse, I'd just received my eighth book rejection and was beginning to think I'd never get my manuscript into print. Four years of hard work down the tubes, all my students' stories lost forever.

"I don't get it," I said, scowling at the dead carrot and tossing it into the garbage. "All the editors who've read my manuscript say they love it, but no one'll buy it."

"I told you why—it's too woeful."

"But that's the whole point—how much it costs people to emigrate."

"Yeah, but who wants to read about a little Vietnamese girl getting raped on a raft, and that guy from East Timor—the one whose parents got chopped up by soldiers. And what about that Guatemalan lady whose baby died of rat bites when they hid in a tunnel. Shit, the whole book's nothin' but a catalog of misery. Can't you lighten it up—give one of the chapters a happy ending or something? Otherwise, you're never goin' to see any money on it."

"You know I'm not doing it for the money."

He rolled his eyes. "I love you to pieces, Sarah, but you're such a jerk sometimes. You want the book in print, right? You want people to read it? So you have to get them to buy it."

Before I could respond, he grabbed my arms and knocked one of my legs out from under me, taking me down to the floor with him. Stoddard had been an avid wrestler in high school and liked practicing his favorite holds on me. I tried some of the escape moves I'd learned, but he had me pinned solid.

"Can't we have a moratorium on your book for just one night?" he pleaded, nibbling on my ear and working his way down my neck.

I laughed and went limp as he moved south of the border. But as soon as he loosened his hold on me, I wriggled out of his arms and sprang to my feet. Snatching the towel from his middle, I ran into the bedroom and flung it as hard as I could. He let out a battle cry and made a dash for it, and by the time we both tumbled onto the mattress, I could hardly remember why I'd been so annoyed at him.

When Stoddard left the next day, I began brooding about my book again, thinking back to all the interviews I'd done in the past few years. As my students' faces floated before me, I remembered their sad stories. Each of them was unique, yet they all had one thing in common: Scratch their shiny new personas and just beneath the surface lurked despair, depression, loneliness.

Reaching for my jar of Ann's homemade peanut butter—my version of Valium—I ate a couple of spoonfuls and stared absently at the picture of the raffish dog Stoddard had drawn and taped onto the refrigerator door to remind me to buy some food. The dog's mouth hung open expectantly as if he were waiting for a juicy bone, just as my book was waiting for—what? I took another large spoonful of peanut butter and chewed slowly, thinking over what Stoddard had said. Maybe the book did need an upbeat ending of sorts, a snappy final chapter absolutely reeking of success. . . . Suddenly, Alex Astor popped into my mind. Ann had said he had a classic rags-to-riches story. Also, he was articulate, confident, and outgoing—in short, the perfect subject.

Excited about the prospect of interviewing him, I started hunting for his business card. I sorted through the papers on my desk, checked wastebaskets, fished through a couple of drawers, and finally found it in the kitchen garbage pail, crumpled up and stained with tuna oil. Humming "The Star-Spangled Banner" under my breath, I wiped it dry and dialed.

"Astor Place," a woman answered breezily. I heard something clang in the background; people were arguing loudly, phones were ringing.

"Is Mr. Astor in? This is Sarah Bridges."

"Yes, but he's unavailable, Ms. Bridges."

Then I heard a clicking noise, and to my surprise, Alex was on the line. "This is—"

"I know who it is, Sarah. Did you find time to fit me in for some tutoring?"

"Um, not yet," I said in a nervous voice. "Actually, I'm calling because my book needs . . . well, as it turns out, I need one more interview with someone who's very . . . who's been in New York a long time."

"Sorry, I don't do interviews," he said in a clipped tone.

"Are you asked that often?"

"Would you mind hanging on a moment? This place is a madhouse today."

While I was on hold, I envisioned the seedy taxi office—the floor littered with discarded Styrofoam coffee cups, the walls covered with tacky calendars, one of which would have a picture of a blond Jesus wearing a pageboy that would make him look like a transvestite. I took another spoonful of peanut butter and was still chewing when Alex came back on the line.

"Actually, I *would* like to see you again," he said, "but I'm leaving on a business trip in the morning. Why don't we plan to get together after I return."

"When will that be?"

"In a couple of weeks. I'm not exactly sure."

I thought it over. He sounded singularly unenthusiastic about being interviewed and could easily change his mind by the time he came back. Instinct told me not to risk a delay.

"The thing is, I'm already past my deadline," I told him, raising my voice so he could hear me over the din. "I don't mean to be pushy, but is there any possibility you could fit me in before you leave? It won't take very long, I'm pretty experienced at this. I could zip over to your office for a quick on-the-job sketch, or catch you at home later—whatever's easiest for you." I held my breath, listening to the sound of papers rustling.

"I suppose I could cut my last appointment short," he said as if thinking out loud. The voices in the background were growing louder and more insistent, someone was calling his name. "All right," he agreed. "Why don't you come up to my place for an early dinner tonight."

"No dinner, just the interview," I said quickly, wanting to make my intentions perfectly clear.

"Fine. I'll send my car to retrieve—*retrieve* isn't quite right, is it? A bit too formal. You see, I've already started practicing what you suggested. My driver will pick you up at six sharp."

"Don't bother. A car's not necessary, the subway is fine," I said. But the phone line was humming and I realized I was talking to a dial tone.

Chapter Three

I hung up in a sweat and started thinking hard about how to deal with Alex. I knew from experience that these interviews could be gut-wrenching and treacherous, my approach had to be flawless. Even a single emotional outburst could prove fatal to the evening, and if I messed up tonight, I might never get a second shot at him.

I dialed Ann to get some background information but couldn't reach her at home or at the store, which meant I'd have to go in blind—a great disadvantage. In any case, I had to make sure I didn't seem jittery, since anxiety was contagious and could damage the flow of a subject's memories.

I headed into the shower to cool off, telling myself to stop worrying. The man was hardly a delicate flower, and I'd done over a hundred interviews, most of which had gone smoothly. Even when my subjects had fallen apart, I'd dealt with them well enough to get through my list of questions. All I had to do was watch out for telltale signs of discomfort—knuckle cracking, fingernail biting, eye twitching—and change direction if things heated up. Like a surgeon, I'd get in with my sharpest questions, carefully remove his memories, and get out before complications could set in.

But as steam continued to rise up around me, I flashed back to our conversation in the taxi—the way he'd enjoyed catching me off guard. And there was that odd mixture of objects in his sports bag, and the strange scars on the back of his hands, and his seductiveness . . . No, I decided, stepping out of the shower and patting myself dry, for all his charm, Alex Astor was not going to be an easy subject.

Annoyed the rush of hot water hadn't soothed my jangled nerves, I glanced at the clock. Time was rushing by; his driver would be arriving soon. I hurried into my bedroom and began rummaging around my closet for something suitable to wear, not an easy task since most of my clothes had migrated to Stoddard's. I pulled out a black turtleneck and black slacks but decided they were too clingy. The Indian skirt and embroidered blouse were too ethnic and hokey. The green-velvet jumpsuit looked too unprofessional. All that left me with was a funereal black suit and prim white blouse—more conservative than my usual clothes but the best of the lot.

I finished dressing and dropped to the floor to hunt up a decent pair of shoes—a snag. The tattered sneakers I'd worn over from Stoddard's weren't a possibility and the only other choices were green suede boots, flip-flops, and a pair of whorey-looking sling-backs I'd bought at a thrift shop to wear to the mythical New Year's Eve party Stoddard and I always planned but never got around to throwing. I was still crawling around the apartment in the hopes of finding a sensible pair of flats under the furniture when the downstairs buzzer rang. In a panic, I stuck on the slutty high heels, grabbed my briefcase, and loudly click-clacked down the staircase, almost skidding to my death on the first-floor landing.

To my relief, the driver, whose ill-fitting suit and morose expression made me suspect he'd recently arrived from Eastern Europe, wasn't the least bit interested in making conversation. Left with my own thoughts, I sank into the plush leather seat and noted that the car was as it had been the night before—immaculate, gleaming, luxe.

Or was this a different car? Perhaps Alex operated a whole fleet of luxury Checkers, maybe an upscale private car service. I pressed what looked like a window switch, and to my surprise, the door on the wooden box in front of me slid open, exposing a small but elaborate sound system. A *very* upscale car service, I decided as I opened my notebook and began listing questions to ask him.

"Mr. Alex very good man, very generous," the driver announced as if I'd just asked him a question.

I looked up and saw him leering at me in his rearview mirror.

"Not only give time and money for Romanian peoples who come, but have donate many big science scholarships. Also very saxy. Many womens like for date. You like for date."

"This isn't a date, it's a business meeting," I said crisply, irritated by his assumption and irritated that it bothered me.

He smiled with obvious disbelief and continued listing his employer's charms, but I was not amused. Had Alex also made the wrong assumption about the evening? I'd only had one such misunderstanding in the past, but it had been extremely unpleasant. The man, a priest from Lagos dressed in full clerical garb, had been quite decorous at first, but an hour into the interview had suddenly asked: Do you fuck? Yes, I'd answered coolly, but only with my boyfriend. Even so, I'd had to dodge his octopuslike arms and punch him fairly hard on the shoulder to get my message across. An incident of this nature with Alex would be doubly awkward because of his friendship with Ann. . . . But as the driver continued snaking the car through rush-hour traffic, I decided a misunderstanding wasn't a possibility. I'd been brisk and professional on the phone, and he'd met a nearly naked Stoddard at my apartment. He wasn't stupid; he'd add it all up.

Having disposed of this worry, I went back to my list of questions and continued working on it until we came to a full stop. I looked up, jarred by the fact that we were parked in front of a posh building on Central Park West. Had Alex borrowed a wealthy client's apartment just to impress me (it had happened several times before when students were ashamed of their homes) or did he live with a rich lover—an eccentric heiress, perhaps—who got off on blue-collar men? As the doorman escorted me inside, I imagined Alex in bed with a society type. His earthy sex on her designer sheets . . .

"Mr. Astor left instructions for you to go right in, miss," the elevator man instructed, his white gloves glowing in the dim light like the phosphorescent charms I'd collected as a girl.

I thanked him and stepped into the foyer. The front door was wide open, but I hesitated in spite of instructions and rang the doorbell. A faint voice called out a greeting, so I made my way inside and found myself standing in a vast entrance gallery with a vaulted ceiling and white-marble floor. I gaped at the oriental rugs, the massive collection of paintings and drawings on the wall, the enormous crystal vase filled with flame-colored lilies. I'd been in some fancy uptown apartments for the annual NYAFS fund-raising dinner, but never one this palatial.

"Beat you here by two minutes," Alex said, emerging from an interior doorway wearing red-satin running shorts and a matching shirt. Now that he was clean-shaven, he looked younger and much less formidable than I remembered, and somehow, his body gave the impression of being in motion even when he was standing still.

"Just did a quick lap at the reservoir on my way home," he said, wiping sweat off his forehead.

"Swimming or jogging?" I inquired, refocusing my attention on the conversation.

He laughed. "The latter. You're a runner, aren't you?" he asked, giving my body a speculative look.

"I used to be, but now I only run to catch buses. My work's sort of taken over." I rested my briefcase on a tapestry-covered bench that had long passed shabby and gone on to irreplaceable.

"Perhaps I can persuade you to jog with me one evening. The skyline's particularly wonderful at dusk. Mind if I take a quick shower? Hang up your coat, make yourself at home. I'll only be a minute. Want something to drink?" Without waiting for answers, he disappeared.

Sweat trickled down between my breasts. I took off my jacket and hung it in the hall closet on a polished wooden bar next to the collection of men's coats. Suede jacket, cashmere overcoat, down ski parka, tweed sports coat—I stopped and stared at the ripped and battered Army jacket, so forlorn and out of place. A souvenir from Alex's past? The uniform of the Romanian mob? The closet was definitely Nancy Drew territory, I noted, shutting the door quietly and ambling down the hallway. I stopped to sniff the sweet-smelling lilies, then peered into a room so filled with audio equipment, it resembled the cockpit of an airplane. At the other end of the gallery, I stood in front of a series of watercolors that depicted writhing figures of indeterminate sex, all the while thinking: gigolo or drug dealer? But how had he talked his way past the snooty co-op board?

"What's so puzzling?" Alex asked, appearing out of nowhere and mimicking my furrowed brow. He'd changed into jeans and a sweatshirt and was carrying two large glasses and a container of orange juice.

"Oh, I was just . . . wondering about these paintings," I stammered, pointing to the watercolors.

"It's always hard to tell whether Schiele's people are in agony or are having orgasms, isn't it? That's what I find so interesting about his work—the tension between extremes. What do you think?"

I studied the pictures for a moment. "I admire them, but I think I'd find them hard to live with."

He grinned. "That's exactly what my ex-wife used to say. Of course, she said it about me, too, but that's another story. . . . How come your nose is all yellow? Oh, it's pollen from the flowers," he said with a laugh.

Flustered, I took a few swipes at my nose before following him into the elaborately paneled living room. He sank onto the couch and gestured for me to sit next to him, but I walked over to the window instead. I'd obviously gotten things very wrong about him and needed time to rethink my questions.

"Incredible view," I murmured, looking out at the park. "It's straight out of one of those thirties movies where the man in white tails says to the woman in the slinky satin gown, 'This is my town, baby. Stick with me and I'll make it your town, too.' "

"But it's not the thirties and it's not my town, it's yours," he responded in an odd tone of voice.

I turned and looked at him in surprise. "This part of town's hardly mine. Uptown's like a foreign country to me."

"That's not quite what I meant."

Some instinct told me not to ask what he did mean, so I ignored his comment and began studying the group of small objects on a nearby table. I picked up an ornate silver frame and examined it closely. Both the photograph and the woman in it looked ancient. "Your mother?" I asked.

"My aunt. Vera Ida Popescu. A very important person—to me, at any rate. I lived with her after my parents died."

"Did she come to New York with you?"

"No, she couldn't get out of Romania."

"She's beautiful."

"She was a famous actress before the war, but had to become a laundress in order to survive. It's a pity she never made it to New York. She'd have loved it here."

I put down the picture. "Have you lived in this apartment long?"

"About eight years."

"Do you ever go home?"

"This *is* my home."

"I meant Romania," I quickly amended.

"I've only gone back once, about a year after Ceausescu died. I wanted to see how things had played themselves out."

"How long did you stay?" I asked, debating inwardly about getting hold of my tape recorder. I didn't want to lose any good material but was afraid of scaring him off by pushing too hard. I decided to stay put.

"I'd planned on staying a week, but it didn't work out that way."

"What happened?"

He frowned. "The first night I was there, I got together with a bunch of former school pals—people I hadn't seen in a decade. They'd always been a wild bunch—not mean or ugly, just exuberant. But as soon as they started bragging about beating up union organizers, gypsies, reporters, gays—anyone they could get their hands on who was the least bit different from them, I could see they'd changed. They sounded just like the Securitate—Ceausescu's secret police. I guess it was some sort of delayed reaction to the regime's repressiveness. All their bottled-up rage was exploding in crazy directions. Anyway, it scared the hell out of me, and I left the next morning."

I walked across the room to take a look at the African masks on the mantel. Alex was watching me so intently, I felt like I was crossing a minefield. One false step and *kaboom!* it'd be all over.

"Do you collect African art?" I asked, gazing at a mask with a particularly devilish expression.

"I enjoy some of it."

"But you're obviously a serious art collector—"

He put down his glass with a bang. "Listen, Sarah, I know you're trying to be tactful and I appreciate that, but we don't have all that much time. Why don't you just say what's on your mind and get it over with."

"Excuse me?"

He smiled and shook his head. "It's fortunate for you that

you're a teacher and not a politician, because everything you're thinking is plastered all over your face. Looking at you is like reading a newspaper."

"Okay, what am I thinking? Or, rather, what do you think I'm thinking?"

"Don't be embarrassed. I meant it as a compliment. It's one of your most attractive qualities. . . . Go ahead and ask me anything you want without using euphemisms, so we can get on to something more interesting than my money."

"Well, I'll admit I'm a bit . . . confounded by all this. I mean, Ann told me you were successful, but I didn't expect you to be this—" I stopped, leaving the sentence hanging.

"Rich? You can say it. It's not a dirty word—at least not in my vocabulary. I know intellectual Americans find money-talk embarrassing, but that's because you people have grown up in such a comfortable world, you don't realize how brutal life can be without money. And in any case, you shouldn't be shocked by my wealth. You told me you're an expert on the subject of emigrés, and we both know anything's possible in America."

"Are you being facetious?"

"About the American experience or yours?"

"My experience is irrelevant, yours is what we're after tonight," I said, trying to sound playful as I strode over to the couch and sat down. I reached into my briefcase for my paraphernalia. His combative tone did not bode well, and I wanted to get started.

"Why the box of tissues?" he asked, looking amused.

"I'm sure some of your past will be . . . difficult to talk about, and I like to be ready for all situations."

"Is that why you've slicked your hair back like that and put on a camouflage uniform?"

"In a way, yes. My goal is to fade into the background."

"Well, don't fade too quickly. We need to talk before we start the interview."

"The talking *is* the interview," I said, trying to ignore the fact that one of his muscular thighs was very lightly touching mine. I moved away a fraction of an inch, but if he noticed, he didn't let on.

"So," I said, clearing my throat and sitting up straighter, "it certainly looks like you've got quite a story to tell, judging by how you're living. Is Astor your real name, by the way? It doesn't sound Romanian."

"It was Popescu. I changed it a year after I got here."

"Why?"

"Because Ceausescu's people were harassing me—opening my mail, phoning at two, three in the morning, that sort of thing. So I moved to a new apartment and found another busboy job. I took my new name from the Astor Place subway stop because it was so easy to spell. Funny thing is, I didn't find out who John Jacob was until a couple of years later."

"Was that your first type of work in New York, busing in a restaurant?" I asked as I switched on the tape recorder.

Alex quickly leaned forward and switched it off.

I searched his face, wondering if he was more nervous than I'd realized. He didn't seem shy, but one never knew about these things until the actual interview began.

"I can take notes by hand if the tape recorder bothers you."

"The machine isn't bothering me, it's that we're moving too fast. I need a better sense of who you are before I begin."

I looked at him in surprise. "I thought Ann told you my whole life story. What do you want, a formal résumé?"

"No. I'd just like to talk for a few more minutes."

"I think we'd better save the chatting for after we've finished."

"Oh, this isn't just a chat. I need to get a few things straight about you before we start."

"Like what?"

"Like how you're going to use the material I give you."

"You know I'm writing a book," I said, straining to keep my smile steady.

"Yes, but I also know how facts can be distorted. That's why journalists are not my favorite people in the world. They can be hard-nosed, unscrupulous. Perfectly capable of lying if it'll spice up the story. Not that I'm accusing you of such behavior," he added. "In fact, I'd guess you're the exception to the rule, which is one of the reasons I agreed to meet with you. But as I said before, I'd feel more comfortable if I got to know you a little better before we started."

I hesitated, trying to decide whether he was stalling out of nervousness or was propositioning me. His tone was casual, but I sensed a reservoir of feeling beneath his words. "Let me see if I have this right," I said cautiously. "You're worried I might . . . compromise your integrity. So before you begin, you want to make sure I'm a—" I paused, trying to come up with the correct description. "A good friend."

"Something like that. As you said before, talking about the past can be difficult, so this is only going to work if we can make certain arrangements."

My smile wilted. "What kind of arrangements?"

"A simple agreement between us."

"Don't you trust me?"

"Sure I trust you. I trust everyone. But when I was nineteen and alone in New York, I was taken advantage of so many times, I picked up a little habit that's come in very handy over the years."

He stood up and went over to the massive French armoire in the corner of the room. Expecting him to unveil some meaningful pictures or documents, I reached for my notebook and pencil.

"Care for something to drink?" he asked, opening the cabinet's carved doors and taking out a small bottle.

"No thank you."

"This is wonderful Romanian plum brandy."

"I don't drink."

"You mean on the job?"

"I mean ever."

He mumbled under his breath in what sounded like Romanian and poured himself a hefty drink. "I know you're not going to like this," he said, rotating the glass and sniffing the liquor before taking a sip.

"No, go right ahead if it'll help you relax. Just don't get too drunk to talk."

"I don't mean the brandy. I was referring to my habit—the one I mentioned before. You see, if I don't know someone very well, I like to have a signed piece of paper saying who's supposed to do what. Just in case memory fails."

"You want me to sign a contract?" I asked, taken aback.

"Don't get excited until you hear me out. No lawyers, nothing complicated. I'll jot down a few simple ground rules and you'll sign the paper before you turn on the machine."

"I've interviewed a hundred people and no one's ever asked me to sign anything."

"That's other people's business. I'm only interested in my business."

"And what exactly *is* your business, by the way? Obviously, you're not just a cabdriver."

He looked perplexed for a minute, then threw his head back and exploded into laughter. When he recovered, he took another sip of his drink and shook his head, still laughing. "I've been accused of many things in my life but never of being a New York cabby."

"But . . . I mean, you were driving a taxi last night."

"True. But I distinctly remember telling you I'd dropped my driver off because he was ill."

"You mean the Checker's your personal car?"

He nodded. "I used to have a standard stretch, but it was too ostentatious. The Checker gives me more privacy."

"I see," I mumbled, feeling like an idiot. I bent over to pick some imaginary lint off my skirt, wondering how I'd managed to miss all the signals. Of course he wasn't a cabby!

"As to my business, it's a bit difficult to describe," he went on. "I was trained as an engineer, but I've always been interested in music. A few years after I came to New York, I became enthralled with computers and eventually combined all three interests. At this point, I'd have to say I'm primarily an inventor."

"An inventor," I said, trying not to sound skeptical. "Uh, what sort of things have you invented?"

"Various sound-related computer parts that wouldn't mean much to you. The only patent you might have heard of is cycle-acoustic cuing, because it's gotten so much attention in the press. In fact, I've even been attacked for developing it."

"Why?"

"A professor at Yale wrote a book decrying the fact that American technological talent is being squandered on inessentials—hi-tech toys he called them—and he used my work as one of his prime examples. He said someone with my particular set of skills should be working on important humanitarian projects. He's probably right, too—at least in theory."

"But?"

He shrugged. "I guess it has to do with my childhood. Conditions were terrible in Romania. Everything was in short supply—food, fuel, clothing. In order to get hold of even the barest necessities, we had to spend a great deal of our time doing useful things. Just like animals. So, when I came to America, I was determined to do something that wasn't like an animal at all, something only a human being would do. . . . But we can talk about my work later. Right now, I'd like to get back to our agreement. My first condition is quite simple. I get to read the interview in its final form and have the right to withdraw it if I don't like what you've written. That's nonnegotiable, by the way."

He came back over to the couch, took the pencil and pad out of my hands, and scribbled a few sentences.

I stared at what he'd written, struggling against the urge to tell him to take his contract and stuff it. I was vaguely insulted he didn't trust me, and more than a little annoyed by all this rigmarole. But I had to admit that what he'd said so far was interesting, and I suspected that if I could just pin him down, I'd end up with an interview that would knock some editor's socks off.

I signed the paper.

"What's the second condition?" I asked warily.

"I want to know why you're doing the book. This part doesn't have to be in writing, by the way."

"You already know why—so my students' stories will become part of American history."

"That's what they get out of it, but that's not my question."

"Okay, I'll probably get a few thousand dollars and a book with my name on the cover. Chalk it up to ego gratification . . . I don't see what difference all this makes."

"Oh, it makes a great deal of difference to me. Frankly, the only reason I agreed to this meeting is that I'm curious about you."

I looked at him uneasily. "I'd prefer to leave my psyche out of this. As I said before, I'm completely irrelevant to this interview."

"No you're not. You came here to find out about me, so I'm trying to describe a reaction I've had to you—or rather, your voice."

"My voice?"

"That's right. It evokes in me a feeling of...I don't know quite how to explain.... It's the way I felt as a kid whenever there was a big snowstorm. My friends would throw snowballs and build snowmen and forts, but none of that interested me. I preferred digging beneath the snow to see what had been covered over. Strange, isn't it? I'd forgotten all about it until I heard you talking so fervently about saving your students."

I smiled thinly, trying to disguise my anger. "You know, if this didn't come up so often, I'd almost think it was funny."

"What is?"

"Your suspicion about my so-called evangelistic tendencies, as you put it."

"Have I hit a raw nerve?"

"It's just that I hate when people make certain assumptions about me. I mean, if I came from an ethnic background, you'd probably assume I was a very compassionate person and leave it at that. But since I look sort of WASPy, you figure I must have a screw loose.... Well, you go ahead and stereotype me as a masochistic kook if you like, but the label's your problem, not mine. I'm only responsible for my behavior, not my genes."

"Whoa, take it easy, I wasn't accusing you of anything," he said, holding up his hands defensively. "I'm sure your motives are absolutely pure. It's just that I find it a bit curious that a bright, attractive, quintessentially American woman—a woman who could be a doctor, lawyer, Indian chief, who could be married and have a couple of kids by now—would spend years working nights for a pittance and be baby-sitting that kid—what's his name, Studly?"

"Look, Alex," I said, throwing down my pad and pencil, "if you're not interested in doing the interview, say the word and I'm out of here."

"Why are you so indignant? Keep in mind what you're asking me to talk about—how those Communist pigs wiped out my family. How I was forced to eat garbage on the streets in order to stay alive. What it felt like to spend two days nearly suffocating in a stinking beer barrel to escape from Romania. If there hadn't been a hole in the bottom of the cask and beer hadn't leaked out, I'd have drowned for sure. That was twenty-three years ago, and I still can't stand the smell of beer."

He reached for a tissue and wiped a small rivulet of perspiration from his forehead. "I know how anxious you are for me to describe how it felt to arrive in New York completely alone. What it was like to spend twelve hours a day unloading crates from the back of trucks on Orchard Street—not that these scars let me forget for very long," he said, holding up his hands and studying them for a moment before letting them drop onto his lap. "Journalists are so bright-eyed and bushy-tailed when it comes to asking other people questions, but when you get asked a couple of questions, you become outraged."

He broke off suddenly and rubbed his temples as if trying to wipe away his thoughts. "Believe me, I'm not trying to be difficult. I know you aren't the kind of person who drops to her knees each night praying for wretchedness and perversion so she'll have something juicy to write about. It's just that I've got this prejudice against journalists—the way they feed off other people's lives, turn tragedies and disasters into commercial entertainment. A bomb goes off. There's an earthquake, a flood, a revolution. Whee! What fun! Read all about it in the newspaper. Turn on the TV and watch the news for a thrill. If it's too bloody or not bloody enough, shut it off and leave someone else with the pain."

He got up again and went over to the window, staring out at the sky for a long moment before closing the curtains and facing me. "I love this country, Sarah, and I love a lot of people here, but I've never gotten used to the way you Americans see life."

"And how's that exactly?"

"As if it's a—I don't know—a made-for-television movie. Everything's supposed to be pleasant and happy. Have a nice day! It'll all work out! If it's ugly or frightening, you refuse to deal with it. You people cling to your mental virginity as if it's some sort of national disease."

"Oh, come on—that's a ridiculous generalization!"

"Maybe so," he said, returning to the couch and sitting down next to me, "but it's the way Americans are perceived around the world. One of my Japanese clients phrased it beautifully the last time I was over there. He said Americans can set a pretty table and fix a good meal, but they hate like hell to clean up their mess afterward. That's why I think interviews like this are a complete waste of time. It's futile for me to try to describe my past to someone like you—someone who hasn't suffered the kind of losses most people in the world—"

"Wait a minute," I cut in. "Just because people don't go around shouting about problems doesn't mean they've been partying their whole lives."

"It's not a question of partying. I'm talking about something else, something much deeper. . . . Look, let's take you, for example. I'm sure you've had your share of romantic disappointments, financial squeezes, career setbacks—that sort of thing. But there's another level of experience someone like you doesn't know the first thing about."

"God, I can't believe your condescension! I know it may come as something of a surprise to you, Mr. Astor, but you Europeans didn't invent suffering, and you certainly haven't patented pain. Just because I'm not a member of the Third World and haven't personally lived through war, revolution, or famine doesn't mean I can't feel deeply for people who have."

"But it's all there on your innocent face—in your voice when you're talking about saving your poor, pitiful students."

"What is?"

"That you get a real rush from listening to your students' tragic stories. Come on, be honest. Admit it's as exciting as watching a TV show. And when you've had enough, you can turn off your tape recorder and run home safely to Mommy and Daddy."

I stiffened. "I wouldn't make too many conjectures about me if I were you," I warned in a knife-edged voice. "You don't know a damned thing about my life."

"I know that you grew up in a safe little family in a safe little town. Connecticut, wasn't it?"

"So?"

"So it's not exactly holocaust country."

"How do you know I haven't had my own personal holocaust?"

"Meaning?"

"Suffering. Loss."

"Right," he said with a dismissive half laugh.

"Don't you dare laugh at me!" I exploded, suddenly so enraged that I felt almost deranged.

"I don't need any lectures on how it feels to lose a family. I know all about that. My father is dead, and I don't have brothers or sisters. I was adopted by my stepmother when I was a baby, but she's also passed away, and I've never met my biological mother—I don't even know her name—" I stopped, stunned by what I'd heard myself say.

Alex waited for me to go on, but I was completely frozen. I'd never told anyone that Ruth wasn't my real mother—not a single friend or lover. I didn't even like thinking about it.

"Are you okay? Here, maybe you'd better have some of this," Alex said, shoving his brandy glass into my hand.

I took a gulp of the liquor and felt it sear a path from my throat to my stomach. A second swallow clouded my mind, made me feel like I was floating. I leaned back against the sofa and closed my eyes, drifting far away. Then the grotesqueness of what I'd done—told an absolute stranger the secret I'd never even told my ex-husband—hit me full force. It was absurd. Ridiculous! Laughter burbled up from my chest and burst from my throat, contorting my features out of shape. Tears streamed down my cheeks, but I wasn't sure whether I was laughing or crying.

I grabbed a fistful of tissues and tried to hide my collapsed face while the spasms continued. I was a mess. One part of me was trying to catch up to my crazy outburst, another more rational part was trying to figure out the fastest way to escape.

"I—I've got to go," I mumbled, grabbing my tape recorder and stuffing it into my briefcase.

"Isn't there some way of tracing her?"

I snapped my briefcase shut without answering.

"There must be records somewhere—"

"I never talk about this," I said sharply.

"But you just did."

"A mistake—an accident. It was stupid. Unprofessional. I don't know why I brought it up."

"Obviously, your adoption disturbs you."

"No it doesn't! I'm not even a real adoptee. My father was my real father, and I had a terrific stepmother, so there's never been any reason to mess up my life thinking about—whatever she is. My biological mother. The subject doesn't interest me."

Alex sprang to his feet. "You see?" he said, looking exasperated. "This is exactly what I was talking about before—what drives me so crazy about you Americans."

He squatted in front of the fireplace, wadded up a few sheets of newspaper, and stuffed them under the logs, his back muscles rippling with tension. "I know I should be used to it after all these years here, but I still find it phenomenal."

"Adoption's hardly a phenomenon."

"I'm not talking about adoption. It's the way you've written off your mother because—how did you put it? Because you don't want to *mess up* your life. What I don't get is how an intelligent person like you can possibly construct any kind of authentic future without knowing the past—or at least getting the facts right. The amazing part is you're not even self-conscious about it. . . . I guess what they say is true—everything in America really is disposable. Styrofoam packaging, diapers, razor blades, buildings, mothers. The rest of the world mourns for lost relatives, but you, who might have a mother alive somewhere, say it's inconvenient to think about her. Well, now I understand why you enjoy collecting your students' stories. It's so much easier than dealing with—"

I stormed out of the room before he was finished. By the time he caught up with me, I was in the vestibule, ringing for the elevator.

"Sorry, sorry, sorry," he said, raking his fingers through his hair. "I always get a little crazed when I talk about Romania, and I haven't had much sleep this week because of my trip. . . . Don't run off. Come back inside. I swear I won't ask you another question."

I threw him a murderous look and stepped into the elevator. "It's quite obvious that you have nothing but contempt for me and my book, so let's quit while we're behind."

He was still apologizing when the door slid shut between us.

Chapter Four

By the time I got home, my head was throbbing so viciously, I felt like slamming it against the wall. I knew Stoddard was expecting me to spend the night at his place, but I didn't feel like talking to anyone just then, not even to myself.

Still seething with anger, I gulped down a couple of headache tablets and lay down in bed without bothering to take off my coat or undress. I shivered and curled up into a ball, but my feet felt like two chunks of ice and my head continued to pulse horribly, the sure sign that a migraine headache was on its way. In an effort to relax, I squeezed my eyes shut, but my mind flipped right into instant replay, and I cringed inwardly as I watched myself on my mental screen.

What had all that hysteria been about? Ruth was the only person I'd ever thought of as my mother. . . . Or was she? I wondered, rolling onto my back and staring up at the crisscrossed bars of light on the ceiling.

I'd always told myself that my adoption didn't bother me—that I had no interest in my biological mother—but how could that be true? I must have thought about her sometimes, must have been curious about her when I was growing up. . . . I struggled to remember how I'd found out Ruth wasn't my birth mother. Had I been told when I was very young or had I figured it out on my own? Because, somehow, I'd always known that I had another mother, known, too, that my parents had suffered some terrible grief because of her.

As I lay in bed thinking about all this, my eyes fell on the framed picture of my family that I kept on the top shelf of my bedroom bookcase, almost out of sight. The picture had been snapped in our front garden when I was about five or six. I was standing between my parents, squinting into the sun, holding my father's hand. Ruth, a tiny woman whose hair was always kept in a tight bun, was wearing one of her typically utilitarian outfits—plain white blouse, dark skirt, and heavy shoes. Her dowdy clothes and severe expression were a sharp contrast to my father's elegance, his windblown hair and easy smile. They were an odd match, and neither of them had seemed particularly happy to be together.

There had been so much hidden sadness in our household, yet out of habit, I'd rarely let myself focus on it. Suddenly, I was enraged at Alex all over again. Why had I let him bait me like that? Why hadn't I cut him off the moment he started attacking journalists?

Then guilt swooped down on me for having told Alex— a virtual stranger—something I'd never told Stoddard.

My head pounded as I got out of bed and took a cab down to Stoddard's place. When he didn't answer the door, I let myself in and found him sprawled facedown across his mattress fast asleep, his arms spread as if he were flying. I lay down next to him and slid my hands beneath the blanket to stroke him awake.

"Stoddard, I need to talk to you," I whispered, feeling my throat constrict.

He opened one eye.

"It's about my mother."

He groaned. "Hey, you're not startin' in on her now, are you? I know she Betty Crockered you to death, but I've got to get up real early tomorrow."

"I don't mean Ruth. She wasn't really—"

"Oh, listen, before I forget, Doc Chin and Maria Goncha-something-or-other and Thin Thang or Thang Thin called. And there's another message, something about an emergency from—wait a minute, I wrote the name down here somewheres." He clicked on the lamp and shuffled through some papers on the night table. "I swear it's got half the alphabet—Here it is, Vilawan W-u-t-t-h-i-d-e-t-g-r-a-i-n-g-g-r-a-i, if that's possible. What kind of name is that?"

"Thai. He's the student in Bellevue psychiatric."

"Yeah, well I'm gonna end up in Bellevue with him if you don't stop givin' out my number to every Juan, Dick, and Harry," he said, burrowing into the pillows and pulling one over his head. "These calls are driving me batty," he added, his voice so muffled I could barely hear him.

"You know what they say—home's the place you get messages," I said, lifting the pillow off his head.

"Well, now you got 'em, so shut the light."

"Wait—I have to tell you something. . . . Stoddard? Are you listening?"

"No. I'm trying to sleep."

I threw a pillow at him and sat up. "How come you always cut me off when I get serious?"

"You used to say it's why we get along so well—because I don't let you get too serious."

"Maybe just getting along isn't enough."

"It's enough for me, especially when I've got to get up at 5 A.M. for a mural job, and if you don't know that by now, you don't understand me at all." He switched off the light and turned his back to me.

Tiny needle pricks of pain shot up and down my spine, I was too wired to sleep. The floor creaked as I got out of bed and began prowling around the loft aimlessly, finally ending up in front of Stoddard's most recent work, a massive painting of computerlike creatures devouring one another. Fangs were bared, blood dripped from their claws, but the painting wasn't charged with the terror I knew Stoddard intended. If anything, it looked like a cartoon, not a damning portrait of modern life. Studying it in the near-dark, I was struck with the unwelcome thought that what made Stoddard so appealing as a man was exactly what flawed him as a painter. His work was charming and amusing but lacked real depth.

Pained by my disloyalty, I turned away from the painting and stretched out on the couch with a book on my lap. I closed my eyes for just a minute, but I must have fallen asleep instantly because when I opened them again, the loft was flooded with light and Stoddard was whistling loudly in the bathroom. A mossy taste clung to the roof of my mouth, my neck hurt from the odd position I'd slept in, my head still ached miserably.

I stood up and staggered into the bathroom trying to look better than I felt. Stoddard was big on sickroom drama but I hated being fussed over, the residual effect, I suppose, of my mother's belief that getting sick was a form of self-indulgence. I stared into the mirror at the web of burst capillaries in my eyes, my swollen lids and blotchy skin. I looked like I'd spent the evening in hell, which wasn't far from the truth. To revive myself, I ran a washcloth under the tap and slapped it onto my face, wincing as water dribbled down my neck and under my collar.

"I'll fix breakfast—maybe some flannel cakes," Stoddard offered in a conciliatory tone as he slathered soap onto his cheeks. He didn't have much facial hair but made up for it by turning shaving into a major ritual each day.

"No thanks," I answered, nearly gagging at the thought of food. "I'm going back to my place this morning. I need to be alone for a while."

"Oh, the privacy thing," he said, his mouth knotting in annoyance. "Look, I know you want me to put up some more walls in here, but it'll make me feel like I'm painting in a chicken coop."

"I wasn't complaining. I'm just a little headachey."

His expression shifted into concern. "What do you mean headachey? You having one of your migraines? Maybe you're comin' down with that bug I had last week. Where'd you put the thermometer?"

"I'm not sick. It's probably just a hangover."

"You, a hangover?" he guffawed. "From what, soda pop?"

I shook my head, a mistake. My skull felt like someone had taken an ax to it. "I had some Romanian plum brandy last night when I was doing the interview—I was trying to loosen the guy up."

"Oh, yeah, how'd that go, anyway?"

"It didn't. He was so paranoid about being interviewed, he made me sign a contract before we started. Then he launched into this diatribe against Americans and I sort of lost it and told him—" I stopped mid-sentence as a wave of nausea washed over me. It was bad enough I'd told Alex about my mother, but at least I wouldn't have to see him again. If I told Stoddard about her, she'd exist in a way she hadn't before and I couldn't handle that. ". . . so I got fed up and told him to forget about it." I slithered past Stoddard and out of the bathroom before he could ask any more questions.

After I got dressed, I tucked a set of student essays into a dog-eared manila envelope, disturbed to find myself thinking about a similarly battered envelope—the one my parents' lawyer had given to me after my mother's funeral. "Pandora's box," George Horton had warned when he'd handed it over, his badly fitting false teeth clicking in his mouth like castanets. "Get involved in this, young lady, and you'll never have a moment's peace."

I'd been thoroughly shaken by his words and his fierce tone. Even in the best of times, Horton had struck me as a menacing person despite his sugarcoated vocabulary, and I knew he was serious about this warning. But along with fear, his threat had also elicited a rebelliousness in me that didn't often surface.

It's my life, not his, I'd reminded myself while he was still talking to me. *I can do anything I want.*

As soon as he'd left I'd ripped open the envelope and pulled out one of the legal documents. My pulse raced as I stared at my birth certificate. But the name listed next to *Mother's Name* was Ruth Pym Bridges.

I'd stuffed the yellowed paper back into the envelope as if it were contaminated. Later that same day, I rented a safe-deposit box in a bank and put all the documents away. Out of sight, out of mind, I told myself.

Case closed.

When I got back to my place, I forced myself to sit down and look over the essays on American holidays that my prospective students had submitted with their NYAFS applications ("Ghosts on Hallowin selibrate with many surprising trix and tasty treets!") but my stomach started doing flips and my head ballooned to the size of a parade float. I finally faced up to the fact that I wasn't getting any work done and called one of my colleagues to ask her to cover my class that evening. I put on a ratty old nightgown, crawled into bed, and fell into an uneasy sleep that lasted until a school bell began ringing. I struggled to open my eyes but didn't have the strength to lift my lids. By the time I surfaced from my dream, my answering machine had clicked on, and I was listening to Alex's voice. He was calling from the airplane, he said, because he felt terrible about our evening and hoped I'd give him a chance to apologize in person when he got back from Japan. He was leaving his hotel number in Tokyo in the hopes that I would call him collect so we could set up another meeting.

Despite my nausea, I climbed out of bed, sat down at my desk, and wrote him a terrifically nasty note that ended with a scathing assessment of his character. (*You're not only smug and eccentric, your cultural observations are moronic, to boot.*) But after I finished, I remembered he was Ann's friend, so I ripped the letter up and started over. *Dear Mr. Astor, unfortunately I will not be able to meet with you now or in the future, as my calendar is fully booked.* I signed it with a flourish and went back to bed.

"Happy birthday!"

Stoddard stood in my doorway holding a jar of Ann's

peanut butter in one hand and a long-stemmed rose in the other. I stared at him groggily.

"I hate to disappoint you, Stoddard, but my birthday's not until the end of the month."

"I know, I know. But this is a surprise party. You hate birthdays so much, I thought maybe if you eased into it gradual-like, you wouldn't get into such a funk this year." He put the jar down, stuck the rose between his teeth, and waltzed me into the bedroom.

"Get dressed, we're goin' out for dinner," he said, twirling me toward the closet.

I groaned and leaned my head down on his shoulder, dizzy from all the movement. "Sorry, but the only place I'm going tonight is back to bed."

"Sounds good to me," he said, waggling his eyebrows and pulling me down onto the mattress. Just then the phone rang and I reached across his belly to answer it.

"Bambina, where you been all day?" Al asked in his raspy voice.

"Sleeping. I think I've got some kind of virus." *It's Al*, I mouthed silently to Stoddard. He grimaced and made an obscene gesture at the receiver.

"Well, take something for it and get your ass down here. Tonight's very important."

"I know it's the first night of the new semester, but Roz said she'd cover my class."

"Forget Roz, I need you. The big honcho from Ford Foundation said she might drop by, and we've got to razzle-dazzle her. I'm counting on you, babes."

"Listen, Al, I'm really not up to it. I feel like a truck hit me."

"Give her a break, you slave-driving sonofabitch. She's got the flu!" Stoddard yelled into the phone.

"Oh, so you've got a little company in bed. Now I get it."

"Stoddard came over to nurse me."

"Yeah, sure he did. Tell him he can minister to you later—after you come back from school."

I hung up without another word. Al was like a she-lion protecting her cubs when it came to NYAFS, and there was no point arguing with him. I got out of bed and slipped off my nightgown.

"You're not going to work, are you?" Stoddard said, looking at me in amazement.

"It's an emergency."

"I don't believe this," he said, clasping his hands beneath his head and staring up at the ceiling. His breath made a loud whooshing sound that filled up the room.

"Al says—"

"Al says, Al says," he mimicked angrily. "What's goin' on with you lately? It's like we're playin' now-you-see-her, now-you-don't. Mostly, you don't."

I finished dressing and ran a comb through my hair, watching his reflection in the mirror. "I promise I won't be gone long. It's just a class, no office hours."

"That's not the point."

"Oh, come on, Stoddard, stop sulking. You sound like a four-year-old." The minute I said it, I knew I'd made a mistake. Stoddard was extremely sensitive about our age difference, especially because he knew my friends thought he was much too young for me. When his face darkened, I could see we were headed for the kind of argument I didn't have time for. I grabbed money from my bureau and dashed out of the room before he could blow up.

"I promise I'll be back as fast as I can," I called to him from the front door.

"Don't bother rushin' home on my account. I'm goin' to party without you!"

Chapter Five

That night, my class was so jammed, I couldn't fit all my students into my regular classroom, so I moved them to the oversize basement room I'd always avoided because of its bubble-gum pink walls, a color trying to be optimistic but which made me feel like I was in a giant stomach.

I perched on the edge of my desk and scanned the eager, anxious faces—some new and others quite familiar—as students entered the room singly or in pairs, carrying Styrofoam coffee cups and brown paper bags. The air was redolent with the hot dogs and french fries, burgers and potato chips that served as dinner for those who had no break between work and school; the room felt almost cozy. I chatted with Kurash Hassan and Nill Namiz about the garish pink walls, helped Mimosa Ingan fill out a late registration form, and looked at pictures of Surenglin Tumutsuren's hometown in Mongolia. Everything was humming along until I noticed who had slipped into his regular seat in the back row. My blood froze as our eyes locked for a moment.

The dreaded Doc Chin.

Trying not to look spooked, I stood up and launched into my usual introduction of the course, explaining that I was going to teach them much more than textbook English. "The point is," I said, while drawing two stick figures on the blackboard, "until you've learned how to express your deepest feelings in English without shame or embarrassment, you won't be able to create new lives—new *American* lives—for yourselves." With a flourish, I drew a thick line connecting the stick figures, and as always happened at this point in my introduction, the class burst into wild applause.

Avoiding Doc's solemn gaze, I went on this way for a while longer, then asked students to take turns introducing themselves to the class.

"Is correct I should say only Boris, or Boris plus final name in this instant?" a large Russian man asked.

"Using both names would be appropriate in this instance," I answered, writing *instant* and *instance* on the blackboard. "By the way, Americans refer to their family names as last names. My first name is Sarah. My last name is Bridges. . . . Now, before we go on, can anyone explain the difference between the two words on the board?" I looked around the room as several hands shot up.

"Instant is very fast, like instant coffee. Instance having to do with standing," a Korean man answered from the front row.

"You're right about *instant*," I said encouragingly, "but you're confusing *instance* with this word," I explained as I wrote *stance* alongside the other words on the board. "*Instance* means an example of something. A stance is a physical or intellectual position. These are complicated and subtle vocabulary words, so before you get discouraged, I want to explain that difficult words will not be part of your assignments in the beginning of the term. But I will write interesting words on the board and explain them as they come up in class discussions so that you can see them spelled correctly and hear their meanings. If you wish to create a special vocabulary list for yourselves, you can copy the words into your notebooks. This is entirely your choice. You won't be tested on them, but you will be given extra credit if you can use them in your writing assignments."

Students began introducing themselves, some speaking with great difficulty, some with tremendous flair. There was a good mix of backgrounds but Asians and Latinos dominated, followed closely by Russians. When everyone had taken a turn, I asked them to sign up for conference appointments at my office on Houston Street. As people clustered around my desk, I pretended not to notice Doc circling the group like a shark, but all the while, I was plotting my escape.

When the bell rang, I excused myself and made a beeline

up the stairs toward a little-used exit. Doc's nasal voice called my name, and in a moment of unreasonable panic, I ducked into the girls' bathroom and scurried into one of the stalls, slamming the door behind me. I sat down and stared at the graffiti on the metal door, struggling against the urge to take out my red pen to correct the misspellings. The faulty but daring "kunnlingious" was forgivable but the "fok yu" was every English teacher's nightmare. Footsteps approached, I picked up my legs and scrunched my body into a ball. . . .

Worried Doc Chin would follow her into the washroom, detective Sarah Bridges glanced up at the window over-head, wondering if she could escape by wedging her slender body through the small opening . . .

—THE CASE OF THE CHINESE STUDENT

I uncoiled my legs but stayed put, afraid of an ambush. Doc was timid and shy, but ever since I'd interviewed him for my book the previous semester, he'd been dogging my heels, fixed on the notion that I was the only teacher in the program who could fully empathize with his plight (father and mother executed in China, little brother drowned while escaping, no relatives in America). Nothing I said or did disabused him of the notion that we were affiliated in some way, and by the second half of the term, I'd found our encounters so unnerving that I'd begun treating him with an uncharacteristic impatience that left me feeling both ashamed and guilty. I had even tried to extract a promise from Al that Doc would be assigned to another teacher for the spring term. Yet there he'd been in his usual seat, chewed-up pencil in hand, pleading, innocent, mournful eyes riveted on me as if I were his last and only hope. And here I was slinking around school again like a fugitive on the lam.

I wasn't even sure what it was about Doc that was so maddening. He was a gentle, generous man, eager to volunteer for extra class work, quick to share his food or supplies. True, he was lonely and emotionally needy, but so were most of my NYAFS students, which was why I often consulted psychologists, social workers, doctors, lawyers, and government bureaucrats in order to help them solve their problems. And there were other students who were in far worse straits than Doc due to physical disabilities or overwhelming family responsibilities or financial pressures. At least Doc was young and healthy, able to support himself, and essentially free from the burdens of family life. Yet none of my other students had ever gotten under my skin quite the way Doc had. None of the others had made me feel as distressed and inadequate, and, if I really wanted to be honest with myself, irate.

To distract myself from these unsettling thoughts, I studied my green suede boots, surprised at how shabby they seemed under the sharp fluorescent light. I loved those boots and felt almost magical in them, but hadn't really looked at them in a long time. They'd been too expensive for me, of course, but their flamboyant color and Robin Hood fringe had made them irresistible. And now they were stained and balding, like a Robin down on his heels. (I confess to a passion for shoes and a theory that all sorts of subliminal sexual signals are sent by the presence or absence of laces and bows, buckles, zippers, soft slippery surfaces, and shine, and by what I call toe cleavage. Religious leaders have always known this, which is why old-fashioned nuns wore those clunky brown oxfords. What I've never been able to figure out is why weirdos on subways favor slip-on sneakers.)

I looked at my watch; it was getting late. If I didn't get out of the bathroom soon, I'd be locked in with rats, roaches, and whoever else called the school home—a sobering thought. And besides, I reasoned as I stood up and gathered my things, it was bizarre and ridiculous to have panicked when I'd spotted Doc, a man who reached only to my shoulder, a pitiable, skimpy, trembling mouse of a man whose skin was so pale, it seemed almost translucent. *Be firm*, I instructed myself as I emerged from the bathroom, *patient but firm.*

I glanced over my shoulder to make sure the coast was clear, tiptoed down the corridor, and pushed on the exit door.

Nothing happened.

I pushed harder but the door wouldn't budge. Trying not to panic, I cushioned my briefcase against my shoulder and crashed against the door with all my might. It gave way with a sullen creak and I was suddenly catapulted into the dark night and down the three steps onto the sidewalk, where I slammed directly into Doc Chin.

"Ah, teacher Sarah!" he said, reeling backwards. "Doc have wait long but think you go."

He was dressed in his standard outfit: black high-top

sneakers, blue-polyester slacks, and the infuriatingly thin cotton jacket he wore even in the snow. His narrow shoulders were hunched against the raw weather, against all his misery.

"Uh . . . excuse me, Doc, I have no food at home, so I've got to get down to the supermarket before it closes," I said, taking a few small steps. It was beginning to drizzle; I turned up my coat collar and shivered.

"Room you got Doc share with Swoye Obirika very good," he said, keeping up with me as if we were a dance team. "Lawyer Oscar Reilly you give have also very help. Now must discussing job—"

"I've been trying to find you a new job," I said, picking up my pace. "I called Wing Lam at the Asian Society twice, and Jenny Zeng at the Chinese Workers Association . . ."

While I was still giving him my litany, feeling all the while like a candidate for the Bitch of the Year Award, he stopped walking, gently, almost reverently, placed his books on the ground, and clasped his bony hands in front of his face as if in prayer. I tried to ignore his chapped lips and skinny neck, the spiky black hair standing up in heartbreaking cowlicks, that maddeningly thin jacket. When he gave me one of his brave, twitching smiles, I felt like strangling him.

"Teacher Sarah only one understanding how Doc Chin feel one hundred percent alone person because you have same."

"I don't know where you're getting that from," I said in exasperation. "Our circumstances are entirely different."

"But you say in class you having no parents, no sister, no

brother, no husband, no childs. Same like Doc Chin. No alive family," he added, a look of anguish washing over his face.

"It's true that I don't have a family in the strict sense of the word, but my friends are another sort of family. I'm sure you'll eventually have this kind of family, too. New York's such a big place—"

"Every student know Teacher Sarah best at understand New York is *lu fen dan, biaomian guang*. Shiny on outside like donkey droppings."

To avoid his gaze, I bent down to pick up his books. The holes in his sneakers were even larger now than they'd been the previous term, his frayed laces were held together by a long series of knots.

"Doc work hard in class for you," he was saying in his singsong voice. "Do good cleaning work at fish store. Owner say—"

"Yes, I know how hardworking you are," I said crisply as I handed him his books. "But all I can do is write you another letter of recommendation."

I turned abruptly and strode away, hating him for his sorrow and loneliness, hating me for my callousness, hating Al for not keeping Doc off my back. Thinking about all this left me so flummoxed, I walked all the way up to Twenty-third Street before realizing I was headed in the wrong direction. Cursing out loud, I spun around and ran the rest of the way down to the Food Emporium, managing to get there just as the pock-cheeked manager was locking up for the night.

I tapped on the glass to catch his attention, clasped my hands together in front of my face as if in prayer, and mouthed *please*. He shifted his toothpick from one side of his mouth to the other and finished locking the door.

I was sure Doc would have done better.

Stoddard was still fuming when I got hold of him in the morning, but neither of us brought up the previous evening's incident, probably because it was too explosive a subject for a phone conversation. What he did tell me, in a pointedly cool tone, was that my friend Sam had called with the news that his wife Nina had just given birth to a baby girl.

"Want to come to the hospital with me?" I asked, knowing that he'd decline my invitation. He hated hospitals and avoided them like the plague. True to form, he told me he'd pass.

After I hung up, it occurred to me that I shouldn't visit Nina either, since my body was still out of whack—I'd been downing antimigraine and antacid tablets every few hours. I called Nina at the hospital a couple of times but couldn't reach her, so I finally gave up and left a short message on Sam's office tape explaining that I wasn't feeling well and would visit Nina and the baby when I'd fully recuperated.

Then things got frenzied at my office. Two staff people were out sick and I had to cover their classes. Grant deadlines were hanging over our heads like guillotines, and we had to shape our final proposals. To top it off, I had to make a series of unexpected and time-consuming appearances at the Immigration Department for Achmocat Joulloull, who was having trouble getting a job because of a misspelling of her name on her visa. Before I knew it, several weeks had flown by, and I still hadn't seen Nina and the baby.

"We thought you'd decided to wait till the kid turned twenty-one," Sam growled when I finally called their apartment.

"Didn't you get my message? I've been sick," I explained nervously. Sam wasn't one to mince words, and I knew he was going to give me a hard time, which was why I'd hoped Nina would be the one to pick up the phone. "Listen Sammy, I'm on a break between classes and can only talk for a minute—"

"Yeah, yeah. Cut the shit, Sarah, I know you haven't been here because you think babies are boring. And don't deny it. I've heard you say it a million times."

"Maybe I've said *other* people's babies are boring, but not yours. Did you get my flowers?"

"Yes. And the teddy bear. Very cute, thanks a lot. But it's your company Nina needs."

"Can I come up tonight after class—or will it be too late?"

"As far as I'm concerned, it's never too late to see you."

Chapter Six

Sam and Nina still lived in Sam's old bachelor apartment on Ninety-sixth and Riverside, which is where he was living when I first met him. Back then, he was studying at Julliard in the mornings and teaching with me at NYAFS at night, and we'd taken an instant liking to one another. For a while, our relationship teetered between friendship and romance, but when we'd finally tumbled into bed one night, pretending to be more stoned than we actually were, something hadn't clicked for me. Sam was funny and sweet and wonderful and I loved him—but not in a sexual way.

When I'd confessed all this to him, using my then-recent divorce as an excuse, things got pretty sticky. Without telling me ahead of time, he quit teaching at NYAFS and took a job as a sound engineer at RCA. After that, I didn't see much of him until after he'd met and married Nina. But once they settled down, we'd settled back into a comfortable friendship, and I now considered both of them my closest friends.

"Hey, Sarah!" Sam said, opening the front door and giving me a sloppy kiss on my mouth. Sam was a tall bearish man with a mop of dark frizzy hair he called his Jewfro. He'd put on a considerable number of pounds since the old days but the weight hadn't made him less appealing. He just seemed more Sam-ish somehow.

"Nina, Sarah's here," he called out. "Finally," he added under his breath, smacking my rear as we climbed over plastic toys and made our way around a baby swing that took up most of the entryway. Pacifiers, bottles, cloth diapers, baby blankets were strewn around the living room, and a new smell hung in the air, a mixture of baby powder and piss.

"Place is bursting at the seams," he said, kicking a box of diapers off the couch just as Nina emerged from the bedroom. I could see from the dark circles under her eyes and the careless way she'd tied her red hair into a ponytail that the baby had taken its toll on more than just the apartment.

"Come here, quick," she said, grabbing my arm and pulling me into the bedroom.

The three of us leaned over the bassinet to peer at Jesse, who was wearing a yellow nightgown with lambs printed all over it. She looked pretty much like all the other tiny babies I'd ever seen except for the fact that she'd inherited Nina's wonderful red hair. But I didn't say any of this because Nina and Sam were staring at her with new-parents-rapture, an expression bordering on madness.

"I wanted you to see her before she fell asleep," Nina whispered.

"Say hello to your Auntie Sarah," Sam said, as the baby flailed her arms.

"She's still moving the way she did in my womb," Nina said, absently rubbing her belly and exchanging a private look with Sam.

"Want to hold her, Sar?" Sam offered, as if worried I'd feel left out.

"No, thanks. I don't know anything about babies. I've never had that female nurturing urge—"

"Nurturing is not gender-related," Nina corrected.

"Hey, don't waste your time proselytizing Sarah about babies," Sam said as he scooped Jesse into his arms. "She thinks anything that can't talk is boring. Plants, dogs, cats, accountants."

I laughed. "I just haven't had much experience with babies."

"But isn't she wonderful?" Sam asked, nudging me with his elbow. "That's a rhetorical question, by the way."

"I assume you mean me, sweetheart," Nina said wryly.

"Jealous, Mom?" Sam said with a wicked laugh.

"Would you stop calling me 'Mom.' I'm not your mother. And don't swing her around like that or she'll get the hiccups."

"She says it's worth it," he answered, nuzzling Jesse's belly. "Umm, she smells so good."

"Sam, she'll never fall asleep if you get her all excited."

"I have to warn you about Nina's shitty mood," Sam said in a stage whisper. "Her afterbirth blues have turned into a torch song."

"Okay, *you* get up four times a night to feed her and let's see how you feel," Nina snapped.

"Fine, if you put in eighteen hours a day at the studio."

"You don't have to work that many hours, especially now that Jesse's here—"

"Time out for a toast, gang," I said, retreating into the kitchen so they could finish their spat without a witness. I opened the bottle of champagne I'd brought for them and got some glasses down from the cabinet.

"Finished fighting yet?" I called out.

"Who's fighting," they answered simultaneously.

"Sam's driving me crazy, that's all," Nina said when I joined them in the living room.

"Of what crime am I now being convicted?"

"Listen to this, Sarah, and you be the judge: The baby's got some sort of stomach problem. I've been up and down with her every hour or two for days. You can see for yourself I'm a mess. I'm fat and puffy, my hair looks like a rat's nest, my breasts look like my grandmother's. I feel just like a goddamned cow. Moo. All I do is feed her."

"It's your own damn fault," he protested, turning toward me to plead his case. "She won't let me give the kid a bottle. She thinks if Jesse tries a bottle once, she'll get addicted and won't nurse anymore."

"So last night," Nina continued without looking at him, "having been up for most of forty-eight hours, I'm at my breaking point. It's five in the morning and Jesse wakes up to eat. I bring her into bed to nurse and she throws up. So now we're sitting in a pile of spit-up, and milk is spurting from my breasts like a fountain, and Jesse is screaming her little head off, and it's so horrible, I think I'm going out of my mind. And do you know what your friend Sam says? 'Isn't this wonderful?' Totally ignores reality, totally ignores my condition—"

"Honey, I know it's been rough on you," he said, putting his arm around her and pulling her close, "but we're boring the shit out of Sarah. . . . So tell us what's new and different, Sar," he said, popping a cracker into his mouth and crunching it loudly. "How's Alberto doing?"

"Oh, he's his usual frantic self. Our major donor dropped out, so he's in another funding panic."

"Nothing new about that. And how's the cowboy? Still pretending he's a painter?"

"Just tell me one thing, Sam. Why do you hate Stoddard so much?"

"I don't hate him. I just think he's a juvenile, mindless redneck."

"Okay, so he's a little laid-back—"

"Laid-back? No-no-no-no. He just wants to *get* laid."

"Cut it out, Sam! You're as bad as Ann—she even tried fixing me up with one of her customers. . . . Hey, have you ever heard of acoustical cuing or cycle cuing acoustics, something like that?"

"You mean cycle-acoustic cuing?"

"Yeah, that's it."

"How could I not have heard of it," he said, flicking a crumb off his belly. "It's one of the hottest things in the music industry. I'd kill to get my hands on the equipment, but my studio's not big enough. What about it?"

"Ann's customer invented it."

"Sure he did," he scoffed. "One of Ann's California hippie-dippy friends invented a major breakthrough in the music business. Believe me, Alex Astor has better things to do than hang around Carrotland guzzling her ginko drinkos."

"How do you know Alex Astor?"

"Know him? Only in my dreams. I'm such small potatoes, I can't even get through to his secretary. Sony bought his last patent for—what was it, Nina?"

"Six-something. Maybe sixteen. Maybe sixty."

"Sixteen what?" I asked.

"Million bucks. Now start over again. What did you just say about him and Ann?"

"Ann introduced us at her store."

"And?"

"And he gave me a lift home."

"Come on, come on, keep going," Sam said impatiently. "We want details."

"Well, he seemed kind of interesting, so I called the next day and asked if I could interview him for my book."

"And he agreed?" he said in disbelief.

"Sort of."

Sam whooped loudly. "Holy shit! We're talking about a man who's so publicity shy, no one even knows where his lab is. He's the J. D. Salinger of the music business."

"What's he like?" Nina asked.

"I'll tell you what he's like," Sam said, leaning forward in his seat. "He's a fucking wizard, a genius. He figured out how to evoke otoacoustic emissions in computers by interfacing the—"

"Talk English, Sam," I said, waving my hands in the air. "You know I have new-technology dyslexia."

"Okay, okay. It's like if you're watching a jungle film, you'd ordinarily hear all the sounds coming from the screen. But with Astor's gizmo, you might hear the rustle of bushes from behind you and the lion panting in front. In other words, you can position each sound at an infinite number of points in the room even if you've only got two channels. See, the brain deduces a sound's location from minute acoustical cues, and Astor's found the mathematical equations for describing codes embedded in a computer processor—"

"The baby's crying," Nina said, jumping to her feet.

They both dashed into the bedroom. Left on my own, I mulled over the disturbing news that Alex Astor wasn't a crackpot after all, which was how I'd classified and dismissed him. A rich crackpot—a comforting thought in light of my bizarre behavior during the interview.

"Here, hold her for a minute," Sam said, reappearing with the baby in his arms and plopping her onto my lap.

"I—I can't!" I protested, looking at her in panic. "You know I'm no good with babies."

"Come on, Nina's in the loo, and I've got to check on the eats."

"But what if she starts crying?"

"Oh, relax and give Nina a break."

Still feeling panicky, I held Jesse so stiffly that my neck and shoulders cramped up. Babies terrified me. I didn't know what to do with them, how to talk to them. She stared up at me as if trying to figure out who I was. "I'm nobody," I whispered to her. "Nobody you'd be interested in. All you want is your mommy. . . ."

"Hey, don't look so worried—she'll be okay. It's me you should be worrying about," Nina said with a laugh as she sat down on the arm of my chair. "Boy, am I glad you're here, Sar. Conversation with Jesse's pretty limited, and Sam's working nutty hours. I don't know where I got the stupid idea babies sleep all the time, but let me tell you, they don't. I'm busy all day diapering or nursing or burping or bathing her. By the time she finally conks out for a nap, I'm so frazzled and I have so much to do, I end up blowing the time reading short stories in *The New Yorker*—and I hate those stories!" She laughed and shook her head. "To think—I was so smug before she was born. I was going to be Supermom—I had it all planned out. I was going to spend every spare minute of my time off preparing for my new course—I told you about it, didn't I?"

"Which course?"

"Motherhood in a Patriarchal Society. Here's the stuff I'm using," she said, pointing to a huge stack of books on the end table. "You've got to take some of these home with you. It'll blow your mind when you see how paternally oriented we are in this country. I never realized that our whole legal system's been designed for fathers. That's why impregnation is legally more important than nurturing—

because American men think of babies as their property. It's so different in other cultures. Like in Africa, relatives are people who have a uterine connection. . . . Anyway, I'm supposed to be plowing through all this stuff and taking notes for my lectures, but I can't concentrate. It's weird, but on some primitive level, the baby is the only thing I care about right now."

As if on cue, Jesse began whimpering. Nina gently picked her up out of my arms and carried her over to the rocking chair, unbuttoning her blouse and offering her breast. The baby rooted around the dark purple nipple for a while, and when she finally latched on, a tremendous look of satisfaction came into Nina's face.

"Want some privacy?" I offered, glancing away.

"Privacy?" Nina said with a laugh. "Are you kidding? Privacy's a luxury I've long forgotten about. This kid's been Velcroed to me since— Ouch! Boy, she's got strong gums. . . ." She sighed and stroked a tuft of the baby's hair. "You know, it's sort of funny in a way. I knocked myself out interviewing nannies and setting up elaborate child-care arrangements so I could get right back to work as soon as she was born. But now that she's here, I can't bear the idea of abandoning her."

"Leaving her a couple of hours a day is hardly abandoning her, Nina."

"See? I told you I'm not thinking rationally."

"It's just the sleep deprivation. I'm sure you'll be okay once her schedule levels out."

"No, I swear it's more than that. I've been zapped by these primitive feelings I didn't even know I had. When she cries, the sound cuts right through me as if I'm crying. When she's not crying, I still hear her in my head. I'm so goddamned weepy all the time, I even cry when I'm reading the newspaper."

She glanced toward the kitchen and dropped her voice to a whisper. "We weren't going to get pregnant until the studio was on its feet, but my diaphragm must have had a hole in it or something. I never told you, Sarah—never told Sam, either—but when I first found out I was pregnant, I seriously thought about an abortion. Every penny we've got is in that studio, and Sam needs time to get set up. But I was nearly forty-one and I kept thinking, What if I abort her and can't get pregnant a second time."

"You could have . . . I guess you could have . . . adopted a baby," I heard myself say, feeling the lump in my throat thicken. "I mean, if you'd had to."

She screwed up her face and looked at me as if I were crazy. "I don't even want to *talk* about that."

"Why not? I'm sure you'd have loved an adopted baby as much as you love Jesse."

"It's not a question of love. It's just . . . well, it wouldn't have been the same."

I chewed on the inside of my cheek nervously. It was the perfect moment to tell her about my mother's disappearance. But what was there to say? I didn't know anything about it.

"Uh . . . Nina—how would you have felt if you'd had to . . . give Jesse up after she was born?" I asked, trying to keep my voice steady.

"What a horrible question!" she answered, shuddering

slightly. "What's with you tonight? You thinking about adopting a baby?"

"No, I was just—I'm curious because . . . one of my students is pregnant and is considering giving up her baby for adoption and I was wondering if it would be so . . . hard. I mean, it's not like you knew Jesse before she was born—"

"Are you nuts? She was inside me for nine months. We're in such perfect sync, my milk comes in exactly when she starts crying. It's hard to explain, but when she's sleeping, I physically ache to get my hands on her. You'll understand when you have your own—" She stopped talking and studied my face. "Hey, you're really upset about this student of yours, aren't you? Listen, if she's giving the baby to good people, it's not such a tragedy—"

"Chow time!" Sam called out, emerging from the kitchen with a steaming bowl of pasta on a tray. "Why so glum, you two?"

"I'm feeling a little . . . emotional about seeing your baby," I said truthfully. I got up and slipped into my regular seat at the table, smiling so they wouldn't know how upset I really was.

"Enough already with Jesse. I want to hear more about Astor," Sam said, piling a mountain of linguini on my plate. "When are you going to see him again?"

"You mean when can I introduce the two of you?"

"What a great idea," he said with mock innocence. "Hey, kids, it's so crazy it just might work."

"Forget it."

"Why?"

"Because like you said, he's a very private man."

"So invite him for a quiet dinner, and we'll drop by."

"I can't, Sam."

"What's the big deal? If you're too busy to cook, we'll bring the food."

"It's not the food. I'd be embarrassed to call him."

"Since when are you shy, especially when it comes to your work?"

"I'm not shy. I just don't want to see him again."

"But an interview with him would guarantee you a book contract. He's a real buccaneer—"

"I don't care."

He stared at me for a minute, then cunning crossed his features. "Oh, I bet I know what's going on here. Astor's got the hots for you, and you're scared shitless."

"Don't be ridiculous, Sam. It's nothing like that. In fact, we ended on a very chilly note."

"Was that before or after you kicked him in the balls?"

"Stop bugging her, Sam," Nina said. "She's got enough on her mind already. . . . Now you two keep eating while I put Jesse back into her bed."

The minute Nina left the room, Sam put down his fork and spread his hands on the table, smoothing the tablecloth as if ironing an invisible wrinkle. "Things ain't going too well at the studio. I know it's a real long shot, but making contact with Astor might make a difference."

"Sammy, you know I'd love to help you out, but I really can't call him. I'll ask Ann to introduce the two of you. She knows him a lot better than I do."

"Didn't you tell me Ann's moving back to California?"

"I said they're talking about moving."

"Well, in any case, I'd feel much more comfortable if you made the introduction, Sar. I barely know Ann. . . . Look, he couldn't be all that repulsive. Anyway, I'm just talking dinner, I'm not asking you to sleep with the guy. That'd be great, of course—just joking, don't get mad. How about inviting Ann and that health-nut husband of hers and Astor to dinner. Stoddard'll be there as your chaperone. What's the big deal?"

"The big deal is he was very provocative and I got angry and, well, I said things I shouldn't have and left in a huff."

"So you had a fight and got huffy. I still don't see—"

"And then afterward, I wrote him a note saying I never wanted to see him again. Now do you get it?"

"Yeah, I get it."

I wound pasta around my fork, pretending not to notice Sam's expression. "Okay," I said finally, slamming down my silverware. "What's the matter?"

"This isn't the first time you've done this, you know."

"Done what—refused you a favor?"

"No, run away from a man."

I rolled my eyes. "I know you don't like Stoddard, but I am virtually living with him, so would you please stop pretending he doesn't exist."

"He doesn't exist if you compare him to Astor. Astor's in a whole other league."

"Who cares? I like the league I'm in. Anyway, even if I agreed to call him, it wouldn't do any good. He hates being interviewed and hates journalists."

"That's because the newspapers ate him alive when he married Christie Winters."

"Who?"

"Christie Winters. As in the Winters Foundation and the Winters wing at the Met and the Winters pavilion at New York Hospital. Even those of you without television must have heard of the Winters family."

"He was married to a society girl?"

"Yep. The amazing thing is that he'd just gotten to New York and was a garbage man or janitor at the time. That's why it made such a big splash in the papers. Don't you remember reading about it?"

"No, but that's beside the point. The bottom line is, I don't want to call him."

"Yeah, right, because you're too busy diddling around with the Pepsi generation. And who was it before Stoddard—the Indian poet who was supporting half his village. And before that was the married writer.... You know, Sarah, every goddamned time you meet a man who's a viable possibility for a serious relationship, *poof*, you're gone. I've seen you do it a half-dozen times." He leaned forward, throwing a quick glance toward the bedroom. "As you may remember, I've got some firsthand experience on this subject."

"Oh shut up, Sam. That was a million years ago."

"Right, and this is now. You're what, around thirty-five? Don't you want to get married and have a kid someday? Here's an opportunity to do me an incredible favor while getting to know a brilliant man. And he's obviously got his head screwed on right or he wouldn't be interested in you."

"Who said he's interested in me?"

"Believe me, if he agreed to an interview, he's interested."

I scowled at him. "I hope you realize you've ruined my appetite. And you're the one who's always telling me I'm too skinny."

"You are too skinny. You're verging on Olive Oyl."

I laughed and moved food around on my plate, thinking about all the extra jobs Sam and Nina had taken to save money for the studio, remembering all the times they'd offered me money when I was strapped. It had been Sam who carried my furniture up the four flights when I'd moved. Sam I'd called when there'd been a mouse running through my apartment at three in the morning. And it had been through Nina that I'd met Stoddard. They were the closest thing I had to family.

"Okay, okay," I said after a minute. "If I run into him again at Ann's store—"

"That'll be too late," he said grimly. "I haven't told Nina yet, but we're about to go belly-up. The shitty thing is, I'm really on to something big now—a decoding chip with a digital filter that'll give a CD much better resonance."

"Oh, Sam, I'm sorry. I didn't realize how serious it was—"

"It's not your fault. Just forget it. I shouldn't have laid it on you like this. We'll figure something out. Here, have some garlic bread."

"No, wait. I'll ask Ann to call Astor—Oh, the hell with it. I'll call him myself. So he'll think I'm a fruitcake, so what?"

He looked at me doubtfully. "Are you sure?"

"This is a full-service friendship," I said, squeezing his hand. "But listen, don't get your hopes up too high. He's probably going to hang up on me."

"Oh no he won't," Sam said with a knowing look. "Not if he's half as smart as he's cracked up to be."

Chapter Seven

In the morning, I stared at the phone with a mounting sense of panic. How could I possibly ask a favor from Alex now that I'd sent him that nasty note?

Unable to envision any conversation beyond "Hi! This is the woman who flipped out while interviewing you a few weeks ago," I kept stalling. I vacuumed the loft even though it was Stoddard's week to be maid, did an unnecessary load of laundry, marked a set of papers, even cleaned out my purse. Finally, my conscience got the better of me and I dialed his home number.

A muffled grunt answered my hello, then the phone slammed onto some hard surface. Delighted he'd hung up on me, I was about to put the receiver back into its cradle when I heard his voice again.

"Sorry. Dropped the phone," he mumbled, sounding only slightly more civilized. "What time is it?"

"Twelve."

"Day or night?"

"Noon."

"I'm still jet-lagged. Just got home. Why didn't you call me back?"

Until then I wasn't even sure he'd recognized my voice.

"Well, I don't know if you got my note, but I've been really busy—"

"Oh, that's right. You're booked for the rest of your life."

I felt myself color. "Actually, you see—" I stopped and cleared my throat. "Listen, I think it's only fair to tell you this is a business call."

"Let me guess. You're fund-raising," he said with a slight edge to his voice.

"No no, it doesn't have anything to do with NYAFS. I just want to talk to you about a friend of mine."

Silence.

"He recently started a sound studio and needs some advice," I continued, pretending I didn't notice his negative vibes.

"I've never liked mixing business and pleasure," he growled, sounding wide-awake now.

"Well, since this is all business, there's no problem on that score."

"Okay, Sarah, I know you're angry about what I said, but would you stop it with the all-business bit."

"You enjoyed watching me make a fool of myself, didn't you?" I blurted out as my anger flared again. "You set me up and baited me and had a good laugh when I fell apart."

"That's not fair. I wasn't trying to upset you. . . . Listen, I'm not working today. Why don't you come uptown this afternoon so we can straighten this out."

"No thank you," I said frostily.

"Why? Because you're embarrassed you told me your deep dark family secret?"

"I knew it was a mistake to call you. I'm just going to tell Sam it didn't work out."

"Don't do that. Maybe I can help him. Come on, meet me on the steps of the Museum of Natural History later—say, around two. I promise it'll be strictly business if that's how you want it."

"Are you trying to bribe me?"

"I'd prefer to think of it as a negotiated settlement."

My skin had a yellowish cast, my hair needed washing, and I was still wearing the same grubby clothes I'd been wearing all day. But I didn't feel like putting on any makeup or charm, or even changing into a more fetching outfit. I'd stick to my end of the bargain for Sam's sake, but only minimally.

Alex was waiting for me on the top steps of the museum, leaning back on his elbows, legs stretched out, eyes closed, face turned toward the surprisingly strong April sun. I sat down next to him, grudgingly admitting to myself that his body was impressive—muscular, but not with the dopey look of someone who spends hours in a gym staring at his pecs.

"Hello, I'm here," I said, parking my purse between us.

He opened his eyes and smiled. "Nice to see you, too."

"How was your trip?" I asked, tempering my voice so I didn't sound quite so cranky. Since I'd gone to the trouble of arranging this tête-à-tête, I might as well see it through.

"Interesting," he said, sitting up and stretching.

"Good or bad interesting?"

"That depends on how you view things. I learned a lot, but doing business with the Japanese can be torturous. They've got these Möbius-strip government regulations that make their bureaucracy so convoluted, it's almost self-contradictory. And basically, they don't like foreigners."

I studied his tanned face, wondering if the goggle marks around his eyes came from skiing or snorkeling, but I didn't ask. I didn't want to prolong the chitchat. "So," I said after a respectable pause, "what can I tell you about Sam?"

"Before we get to that, I want to explain why I reacted like I did when you told me about your mother—"

"Forget it. Neither of us was at our best that night," I said, trying to change the subject. If there was one thing I didn't feel like talking about with him just then, it was my mother.

He scrutinized my face. "Your left eye has a tic."

"Thank you for reminding me. I didn't think it was noticeable," I said, covering my eye with the heel of my hand. "Sam has degrees from Juilliard and Cooper Union. He's a percussionist and an electrical engineer—"

"It's so beautiful in the park with everything budding. Let's walk while we talk."

"Where to?" I asked suspiciously.

"Any suggestions?"

"How about the zoo?"

"I hate seeing anything caged. What about the stream in the center of the park?"

"You mean the lake?"

"Hey, my English isn't *that* bad," he said, standing up and pulling me to my feet. When we collided, I felt such a strong jolt, I nearly lost my balance. Rattled by my body's betrayal, I ran down the steps and started babbling about Stoddard, invoking his name as if it were a protective amulet.

"Stoddard sometimes bikes around the park on his way to work," I told him as we walked north. "If he's working on a mural uptown, that is. Otherwise, he stays home and paints at his—our loft," I added pointedly.

There was an awkward silence.

"Do you know how you can tell it's spring in New York?" I asked to fill the conversational gap as we headed into the park.

"When the cherry trees bloom?"

"Nope. It's when the local creeps crawl out of the woodwork to ogle bare skin," I said, pointing at a man hovering around a woman in shorts. "Of course, you uptowners only get perverts in good weather. We get four full seasons of lunatics downtown."

He laughed. "Well, as much as I miss the street theater in

the Village, I confess to a preference for grass and trees. It's really a pity New York doesn't have more parks. I was just reading a study that said out of twenty-one industrialized countries, the U.S. is last on measures like air and water quality and nature conservation."

"Who's first?" I asked, inwardly calculating how much time this little walk was going to take. I'd chat him up another couple of minutes, switch over to the subject of Sam, and *voilà!* I'd be done with him. Mission accomplished.

"Austria," he told me, sidestepping onto the grass to avoid tripping on a pair of ratlike dogs. "Japan was second even though their parks are much smaller than ours. They've got a real genius for maximizing resources over there. It's one of their most admirable traits. Not that it makes them less maddening to deal with, of course," he added.

"Because of the bureaucracy?"

"It's not only the laws, it's their social rigidity. Even now, people are locked into specific roles simply because of their backgrounds. At least in the States, your whole life isn't defined by who your parents are—" He stopped mid-sentence and gave me a small, half-apologetic smile. "Am I being tactless? I know you're rather sensitive about the subject of parents. Or is it just mothers you don't talk about?"

"Neither subject particularly interests me."

"No? Then what does interest you?"

"Your marriage to a society deb," I heard myself say, surprising both of us.

His smile shrank, I felt a shameful thrill. *You're not help-ing Sam*, a voice in my head warned. But now that I'd brought it up, I realized I genuinely was curious about how he'd snagged an heiress fresh off the boat. In my mind's eye, I saw him dressed in a chauffeur's uniform, driving a Rolls. Then I imagined him standing in front of a Chatterly-like cottage on a lush estate . . .

"It was a case of mistaken identity," he said after a long pause. I could see he was irked.

"Hers or yours?"

"Are you planning to publish this?" he asked, giving me a sidelong glance.

"This is a conversation, not an interview. I never confuse the two. I just wondered how you managed to cross paths with a debutante."

He bent down and picked up a handful of twigs, snap-ping them into little pieces before flinging them away. "She wasn't a debutante, and I'd rather not talk about it."

"Why not?"

"Probably for the same reasons you don't like discussing your ex-husband."

"Oh, I don't mind talking about Eric. He wasn't a bad person, just limited—sort of disabled by being too talented an actor."

"Why did you marry him?"

I was about to give him my usual answer—that I'd been too young to know better blah-blah-blah, but that's not what came out. "Because he asked me," I said honestly.

Alex laughed.

"I know it sounds ridiculous—I don't usually admit it—

but Eric was the big star in school, and I was so flattered, I couldn't think straight. The problem was, he couldn't stop acting. It was like a disease—a chronic condition. I think he did some of his best work offstage. Sometimes even he couldn't tell when he was being sincere. It took me a few years to figure out that he didn't want a wife, he wanted an audience. That's when I left."

Alex didn't say anything. I could see he was having trouble digesting what I'd told him, and I couldn't really blame him. When I looked back on my relationship with Eric, I could hardly believe it myself.

Alex slowed his pace, then stopped walking. From his faraway expression, I could see he was lost somewhere in the past, but I wasn't sure whose past he was thinking about.

"You know," he said, watching a father pitch a baseball to his son, "I can't remember ever playing sports with my father. He never had time for that kind of frivolity."

"What did he do for a living?"

"He was a doctor but couldn't practice because of his politics. He and my aunt managed a laundry together. They worked twelve, thirteen hours a day."

"Well, if it's any consolation, my father had the time but never played sports with me, either. He thought throwing a ball around was the height of stupidity—especially baseball."

"That doesn't sound very American."

"Oh, he didn't think of himself as American. He was born in England and came here as a child. . . . But weren't we talking about your former wife?"

"*You* were talking about her. I wasn't," he answered,

turning and striding away so abruptly, I was stunned. I stood there watching him get smaller and smaller in the distance, urging myself to go after him. But somehow, I couldn't galvanize into action. Wasn't this exactly why I'd been so flippant—to turn him off? *Fearful wish, wishful fear*, I mused, regretting now that I hadn't managed to keep my mouth shut long enough to arrange something for Sam.

I shrugged and started walking away. But by chance, I happened to take one last glance over my shoulder and spotted him still off in the distance, but heading toward me now.

"Lunch," he called out as he approached, tossing a bag of peanuts to me.

I laughed as I caught it, enormously relieved that I hadn't bungled Sam's chances after all.

"Have you ever heard the story about Helen Hayes and Charles MacArthur?" he asked.

"The actors?" I said, taking out a nut and crushing the shell as we began walking again.

He nodded. "On their first anniversary, he gave her a bag of peanuts with a card saying, 'I wish these were diamonds.' On their fortieth anniversary, he gave her a bag of diamonds with a card saying, 'I wish these were peanuts.'"

He said something else but I couldn't hear him clearly because we were walking single file across a narrow bridge that led into a wilder, less familiar section of the park. Huge boulders rose up on either side of us, casting deep shadows across the path and giving the landscape a spooky quality. When Alex veered onto a sharp uphill trail, and I lost sight of him, I glanced around uneasily. No one was in view but something was rustling in the dense brush. Suddenly, a blackbird exploded from the bushes, startling me so badly, I lost my footing and fell, skinning one knee. I quickly scrambled to my feet and hurried to the top of the hill, where Alex was standing, staring down at something. I followed his gaze into the ravine below, surprised to see a tremendous rush of water cascading over jagged rocks and crashing into a fast-moving stream.

"Are we still in Manhattan or did we just hike to Maine?" I asked in amazement.

"Great, isn't it? It's my favorite place in the park—especially in the early spring when there's lots of water. Let's go sit next to the falls."

Carefully, we picked our way down the hill. Alex sat on a large flat rock at the edge of the stream, and I sat down next to him.

"You've cut your knee," he commented, pointing to the thin trail of blood running down my shin and puddling at the edge of my shoe. He lightly splashed a handful of water on my scrape, letting his hand linger on my calf.

I suddenly felt self-conscious about the hair on my legs. I never shaved much in winter, partly because of my commitment to the feminist notion that leg shaving was dumb, and partly because of my cold-weather sloth. But why should I care if I turned him off? I said to myself. It wasn't as if we were about to stretch out and go for a pastoral quickie, realizing just then that that was exactly what I felt like doing. I was relieved when he removed his hand from my leg.

"Every time an article came out about us, Christie went wild," he said, startling me out of my reverie. "Reporters wrote so much garbage. Pauper Marries Princess, Janitor Weds Heiress—that sort of idiotic thing."

"Were you really a janitor when you married her?"

He nodded. "I lived in a basement apartment on Avenue B in exchange for being the super, while I went to school at night. That's how we met."

"She lived in a tenement?"

"She worked there part-time at a community center. It was a requirement for her social work degree. I watched her coming in and out of the building for months before I got up the nerve to talk to her. She had this blond braid down her back and big, perfectly shaped—"

"Let me give you some advice, Alex," I cut in. "Never talk about wonderful breasts to a flat-chested woman."

He laughed. "Not breasts, teeth. Wonderful American teeth, so perfect I didn't think they were real. In Romania, only Party members could afford good dental work, so most people's teeth were a mess. In fact, that was one of the first things I noticed about Americans—how often they smile."

"Did you know she was a society girl?"

He tossed a pebble into the water and watched it skim across the surface until it sank with a tiny kerplunk. "Yes and no," he said after a minute. "She was very out-front about her family's money, but said she hated her parents and wouldn't have anything to do with them. Not that what she said about being rich really registered on me. At that point, almost everyone in America seemed rich to me, and

Christie was very down-to-earth. No makeup, no fancy clothes or jewelry."

"Ah, the deb in disguise."

"She wasn't a deb. Not at all. She was genuinely committed to being a social worker." He paused. "I guess you could say I was her first case," he added with a bitter laugh. "Of course, I was so naive in those days, I had it all wrong. I thought if she ever saw how I lived in that basement—you know, furniture I'd picked up from the trash, a bathtub in the middle of the kitchen, cockroaches everywhere—she'd never talk to me again. So I didn't let her into my place for months."

"And then?"

"Then she got locked out of her office one night when it was pouring and I had to let her inside. To my amazement, she loved the place, stayed for days—"

"Really, I don't need the details of your sexual conquest."

"That wasn't my point, Sarah. It was the whole experience that amazed me. Her reaction, my reaction. It brought back something an old man had told me on the boat coming from Europe. He'd predicted I'd get the biggest hardon in my life when we sailed past the Statue of Liberty into New York Harbor. I hadn't paid any attention to him—I was too scared about surviving in New York alone. But when Christie lay down on my stained mattress that rainy night, I finally understood what he'd meant about coming into America, and it was one of the most erotic experiences in my—"

"Enough!" I protested.

"I'm just trying to even things out between us," he said earnestly.

"What things?"

"You told me a secret, so now I'm telling you one."

"You mean that you married your way out of the basement?"

"It wasn't the money. I didn't need Christie for that—I'd have gotten out of that basement myself even if it had killed me. Anyway, Christie had given her money away by the time I met her."

"Given it away? To whom?"

"She was part of a philanthropic group that thought it was immoral to inherit large fortunes. There were Pillsburys and Rockefellers and Vanderbilts who'd all given their money up to charity. When she first told me about it, I thought she was joking. But she was serious, so serious she wouldn't take any money back from the group even after her father cut her off for marrying me."

"What did you live on if you were both in school?"

"We worked part-time and didn't need a hell of a lot. Actually, money wasn't an issue until I started making it."

"Now you've lost me."

He smiled tightly. "I guess what it boiled down to was that I didn't think buying in meant selling out. To me, money's not good or bad, it's just an opportunity. But for Christie, poverty and virtue were practically synonymous. So, when the computer business took off in the late eighties and things started happening for me in a big way, Christie wasn't happy. We weren't leading the kind of life she'd envisioned for us. . . . Anyway, to make a long story short, she eventually moved back downtown and married a Jamaican guy, a community organizer—a radical activist."

"Are they still together?"

"Christie died of lung cancer seven years ago."

I winced. "I'm sorry."

"So am I. It wasn't a pretty ending."

I shivered and rubbed my goose-pimpled arms. The sun was fading, the air was growing cool, and Alex was growing increasingly gloomy, which wasn't good for Sam. I could have kicked myself for bringing up the subject of his marriage. But that's how my conversations with Alex always seemed to go. I'd start at point A intending to move on to B and C, but would somehow find myself at Q or X or R.

"Maybe we ought to head back to civilization," I suggested, buttoning my sweater.

"In a minute. I just want to explain. . . . You see, when my marriage ended, I accused Christie of having fallen in love with the idea of me, not who I really was. I felt like she'd needed a wedge against her parents, and I was it. They're terrible people—cold, controlling—particularly her father. But now that I'm older, I've begun to wonder which of us really did the using. I mean, I'd always told myself I'd have fallen in love with Christie no matter what kind of background she'd had. But on some level, I must have loved the fact that she was a golden girl even though she denigrated that part of herself. I just couldn't bear to admit it." He let out a complicated sigh. "I guess I'm telling you all this by way of an apology, Sarah. I had no right to accuse you of being a hypocrite because you buried that business about your mother—"

"There *is* no business about my mother," I said, jumping to my feet and brushing off my skirt. "Really, Alex, I think we'd better get out of here before we're mugged."

"But you haven't told me about your friend yet."

"We can talk about Sam on the way back."

Which is what we did. As we retraced our steps, I gave him a detailed description of Sam and the studio and Nina and the baby, explaining that Sam was long on talent but short on funds. "And just for the record," I told him as we emerged onto Central Park West and headed toward Broadway, "Sam thinks you're some sort of minor god."

"He'll be terribly disillusioned as soon as he talks to me. If you give me his home number, I'll call him tonight."

"So, I guess your driver wasn't lying about you after all."

"Who, Cornel?" he said in surprise. "What did he tell you?"

"That you like helping many peoples," I said, imitating the driver's accent.

"Cornel thinks anyone who pays him a decent wage is generous. It comes from living under Communism too long. What else did he say?"

"That many womens like for date."

"Not all women—you can attest to that." He leaned closer. "I have to confess something," he whispered. "I have an ulterior motive for helping your friend Sam."

"Not so ulterior," I whispered back.

"Then you realize I'd like to spend the evening with you, but I'm worried that asking you to dinner would be a social impropriety—if that's not too formal a phrase."

"The phrase is okay. It's the invitation that's the problem."

"Why? Are you teaching tonight?"

"No, but I have to get home."

"Early curfew?" he asked, raising an eyebrow. I knew he meant Stoddard.

I studied him for a moment. "Can I ask you something personal?"

"Go ahead."

"I don't mean to sound rude, but why do you keep flirting with me even though you know about Stoddard? Am I some kind of challenge because I'm not available, or is seduction a knee-jerk reaction to all females? I mean, you're smart, attractive, straight—almost a vanishing breed in this town. You're even rich, for God's sake. There must be at least twelve zillion women in New York who'd love to have dinner with you, not to mention the extra million who'd screw their brains out for a ride in your limo—" I caught myself and stopped. "Look, it's all very flattering, and you've been extremely nice about Sam, but Stoddard and I are—Oh damn, there's my bus. I'd better go before I blurt out something else I shouldn't say."

"Such as?"

"Who knows? I'm never sure what I'll hear myself tell you."

He smiled. "That's what I find so engaging about our conversations."

"And that's what I find so unnerving about them."

I ran for the bus and jumped on a split second before the driver closed the door. I could feel Alex's eyes on me, but I didn't look out the window or wave at him. I sat down with a preoccupied expression on my face, trying to look as if I'd already moved on mentally, but I breathed much more freely when the bus actually did move on and I was finally out of sight.

Chapter Eight

"What took you so long?" Al asked, punching his arm into his rumpled suit jacket as soon as I walked into his office.

"This was supposed to be my day off, remember?" I said through a yawn. I'd had a particularly bad night's sleep, and my nerves were taut, ready to snap.

"Here, drink some of my witches' brew and let's go," he said, shoving a cup of coffee into my hand and heading for the staircase.

"Where are we going?" I asked, racing after him. Al

could move pretty fast when he wanted to, and was graceful, too, which had come as something of a surprise the first time I'd seen him dancing with his wife at a NYAFS fund-raising gala. He knew all the breaks to dances I'd never even heard of.

"To see Doc Chin," he said, flagging down a cab as soon as we got outside.

"Oh no—not me, not today," I said so vehemently, I sloshed coffee all over my hand. "I'm not up for it."

"Gimme a break, Sarah. The kid's in jail for carving someone up, and he says you're the only one he'll talk to about it."

"Doc Chin attacked someone?"

"According to the cops, he cut someone up real bad with a big knife."

I got into the taxi. Al jumped in next to me and told the cabby where to go.

"What I'm hoping is you'll be able to sweet-talk the cops into letting us see him for a couple of minutes so we can hear his side of it," he said, unsnapping his briefcase. "And don't give me any of your feminist crap. Policemen love you because you stay cool. Me, I get pissed off and ruffle their little blue feathers. . . . So what's your take on this Chin guy, anyway?" he asked as he pulled out Doc's folder. "You think he's capable of attacking someone with a butcher's knife?"

I shook my head. "Doc wouldn't step on an ant if he didn't have to."

Al peered at me over his bifocals. "So how come you wanted me to kick him out of your class if he's such an angel?"

"Just because he unnerves me doesn't mean he's a killer."

"Well, he must have unnerved someone else pretty good, too, judging from all the blood on his clothes. What about drugs? Hey, don't look so shocked. Remember Hastelassie Testafaya a few years ago, how we thought he was the last guy who'd be dealing? I loved that kid like my own and he turned out to be a scuzzy sonofabitch. So who knows about Chin. Tell you the truth, Sarah, I didn't like his tagging after you any more than you did last term. Not that I can blame him for having a crush on you. You're a great girl—"

"*Woman*, Al. A female over eighteen is not a girl. And he doesn't have a crush on me."

"All your students have crushes on you."

"Stop trying to butter me up, or I'm getting out at the next light."

"Wow. You really are in a shitty mood," he said, looking at me funny.

"Sorry. It's just that I haven't been sleeping much for the past couple of weeks."

"Bad dreams, kiddo?"

"Something like that . . . So tell me more about Doc."

He shrugged. "I don't know much more. He showed up at my office covered with blood, babbling hysterically that he wanted to talk to you about a knife fight in his apartment—about a body in his apartment. I called the cops and—you know, if this makes it into the papers, we're fucked with the foundations."

"Is NYAFS money all you ever think about?"

"Yes, ma'am. Now take a quick peek at his file."

"I don't need a peek. I'm the one who wrote most of that after I interviewed him for my book, remember?"

"Speaking of which, how's it going? Any nibbles from publishers yet?"

I shifted uncomfortably in my seat. "I'm still working on it. . . ." My voice trailed off. In truth I hadn't done a thing with the manuscript—hadn't even looked at it—since the fiasco at Alex's. Somehow, the whole book had become tainted by thoughts about my mother, and I couldn't deal with it.

There was an awkward silence. Al seemed almost embarrassed, a rare occurrence. "Look, babes, I don't want to interfere in your private life, but what's going on with you lately?"

"Nothing."

"You look like shit. I'm worried about you."

"Don't be. I'm just tired."

"You've lost weight. Doesn't that boyfriend of yours feed you anything?"

"Thanks to your frequent and poorly timed phone calls, he's not going to be my boyfriend one of these days."

"Non vale la pena," he said with a shrug. "He ain't worth the aggravation. Believe me, Sarah. He's a cute kid and all, but in the long run, he's not for you."

"In the long run we're all dead. In the meantime, Stoddard and I have a good thing going."

"What would you know about a good thing, you have such lousy taste in men. Hey, we're here, let's go."

Inside the police station, we filled out a myriad of forms—pink, blue, green, the bureaucratic rainbow. Then I made nice to the sergeant, a man so soft-spoken and mild-mannered, I was sure he moonlighted as an ax murderer.

He consulted with about three hundred other cops and finally agreed to give us a few minutes with Doc. A police-woman escorted us down a long corridor to a windowless cubicle that was not exactly a triumph in design. I sat down beneath a blue-white fluorescent light and stared at the message etched into the wooden desktop: *Have a Nice Day!*

"I'll take a backseat, you run the show," Al said, cracking his knuckles ferociously.

"Cut it out!" I said, wincing at every crack.

"What's the matter, babes, nervous?"

Just then, Doc was led in wearing handcuffs. One eye was swollen shut, the lower half of his face was covered with dirt or dried blood, both hands were heavily band-aged. The moment he saw us, he began moaning.

"You're going to be okay, son," Al said, patting Doc's shoulder. "Yong Ouyang from the Asian-American Legal Defense Fund is looking into your situation, and Sarah's here to get everything straightened out." He gestured for me to get started and walked to the back of the room.

"What happened, Doc?" I prompted, searching his face.

His chin quivered, but he didn't say a word.

"Al says you've had some trouble."

Silence.

I fidgeted with my pencil. We were back to our standard routine: The more pathetic and helpless he acted, the less sympathetic I felt and the more I hated both of us. I stared into his inky eyes, trying to will him to respond. Instead, I felt myself being pulled into his loneliness, his sorrow. Down, down I fell, dropping into his nightmare. I pictured him as a baby being cradled at his mother's breast. Then somehow it was me as a baby I was seeing in my mind's eye, but my mother's face was blank . . .

"Maybe I should wait out in the hallway," Al offered, walking toward the door. "Call if you need anything, Sarah."

"Doc, why don't you take a few deep breaths and try to calm down."

He didn't move, nothing seemed to register. Was it shock? Drugs? I glanced at the policewoman, but she just gave me a withering look as if to say, Why bother with this hopeless mess? I turned back to Doc and saw that his bony chest was now rising and falling rhythmically as if he was trying to follow my instructions.

"Ashamed," he whispered. "FightLotusknifeSwoye-cousin . . ."

Shotgun bursts of words were coming at me so fast, I couldn't follow his story. I wasn't even sure I understood the theme. I wanted to tell him to be more consecutive but I knew he wouldn't understand. The room felt hot and airless. My stomach churned ominously.

"Excuse me, Officer, would you mind opening the door? There's no air in here, I'm getting dizzy."

"Door stays shut, that's the rule," she said impassively.

I glared at her and began fanning myself with my pad. Doc was muttering under his breath, shaking his head. I couldn't make out more than one of every three or four words, and none of it made sense.

"Slow down, Doc. I don't understand you, and they're not going to let me stay much longer."

He nodded and took another labored breath. "Room-mate Swoye having cousin visit," he said, speaking more slowly. "Doc not liking, but Swoye say Africa family important like Chinese. Too disgrace if send cousin away."

"You didn't like Swoye's cousin but you agreed to let him stay in your apartment," I said as I took notes.

"Having fight, and Doc stick cousin two times with big knife."

"What were you fighting about?"

He squeezed his eyes shut for a minute and then opened them, looking pained. "Swoye sexing with Lotus."

"Who's Lotus—your girlfriend?"

"No no, like little sister. Having only twelve years. Live next door. We very friend. Doc come home from work and hear scream. Open door, see Lotus cry. Every clothes on floor. Swoye cousin waving knife and laugh and say young girl best to sex. Lotus screaming so Doc try help. Cousin hit Lotus face, then attacking Doc with knife. So Doc grab meat knife from sink and stick cousin two time in belly. Very bad bloody."

I was writing all this as fast as I could, trying to get his whole story down on paper, when I suddenly had the odd sensation that my hand was a foreign object, attached to my body but disconnected from me. I stopped writing and stared at it in amazement. I spread my fingers wide and then closed them into a fist. It was my hand . . . and at the same time, it wasn't. Someone—some relative with a hand just like this—had sent its blueprint down through my genes. I'd been programmed. But by whom?

I gazed up at Doc. His mouth was moving. I could hear the sounds of the words but I couldn't process them. I broke into an icy sweat. My blouse clung to me like an extra layer of skin. The coffee I'd gulped during the cab ride rose from my stomach into my throat. I swallowed it back down but it left a bitter taste in my mouth.

"Al," I called out shakily.

He opened the door a crack. "All finished?"

I motioned for him to come inside. "You're going to have to take over."

Panic crossed Doc's face. His words started running together again. "Arrestdanganjobstarving!" he wailed.

"What's he saying?" Al whispered.

"He's worried his arrest will show up on his *dangan*—the personnel file Chinese employers keep on workers."

"Cannot going in jail!" Doc cried out, his eyes filling with tears.

I stood up. "I'm so sorry, Doc, but I can't stay. I'm not feeling well."

His face went white with fear.

"Don't worry, Al's going to help you," I said, edging toward the door.

"Teacher Sarah only one understanding alone," he whimpered.

"Sit down, Sarah," Al hissed. "You're making him nervous."

I ignored him and slipped out of the room. In the corridor, I leaned against the wall to steady myself, focusing on the huge poster overhead. *Lock it or lose it!* it screamed in Day-Glo colors.

"What the hell's going on with you?" Al said, storming out after me.

"I can't do this anymore, Al. I can't keep pretending."

"What are you talking about? Pretending what?"

"That I can fix up anyone else's life. I can't even fix up my own life."

Al pushed his glasses to the top of his head. "Bambina, you've handled some tough customers, and you've never let me down. You're not going to fall apart over this little guy, are you?"

"I'm not falling apart, I'm trying to put myself together."

His expression wavered between exasperation and bewilderment. He took off his glasses and polished them with his tie. "Look, Sarah, I wasn't planning on getting into this today, but I guess it's as bad a time as any. To be blunt, you've been off the wall lately. Missing meetings. Walking around the office like a zombie. Last week, you bollixed up that immigration hearing. And now this. If I didn't know you so well, I'd think maybe it was drugs." He threw a nervous look at the cops standing nearby and dropped his voice. "You're not on anything, are you? You know you can trust your old pal Al."

"It's not drugs."

"So what is it, the boyfriend?"

I shook my head.

"Maybe you've been putting in too many extra hours this term. Maybe you need a little break—you know, a couple of days off, a change of pace. Is that the problem? I mean, if that's what you want, you got it. Starting right now. I'll finish up with Doc and write out the report. You go home and catch up on things. I have the feeling you've got a lot of catching up to do."

I couldn't have said it better myself.

*　*

That night, while Stoddard was sleeping, I crept over to the storage closet where I'd stuffed the shopping bag of books Nina had loaned me and pulled them out. Crouching on the cold floor, I began reading about motherhood and uterine relationships, bonding and separation anxiety. An hour passed, then another. I was bleary-eyed and exhausted, but I couldn't put the books down.

At daybreak, I finally stood up and brewed myself a cup of tea, drinking it in front of the window as the sparrows began their day. Watching them, I envied the simplicity of their lives: They slept and ate, mated and raised their young, in the natural order of things. Now that I'd read Nina's books, it was clear to me that my mother had violated this natural order when she'd given me up, and had in effect turned me—turned both of us—into freaks.

Stoddard started moving around at the other end of the loft, so I quickly collected the books from the floor and stuffed them back into the closet behind some of his old canvases. Then I retreated into the bathroom and hung over the sink, staring at myself in the mirror for so long, my features began to blur and I could hardly recognize myself. Questions about my family swirled through my mind. Who was my mother? Why had she given me up? Why hadn't my father told me about her? Was she still alive? Had she ever tried to find me?

In a daze, I got dressed and left for work, hoping the early-morning air would clear my head. But once I was out on the street, I found myself scanning the faces of older women, listening to their voices, watching their gestures to see if there was anything recognizable about them. As I took my usual route through Washington Square Park, an eerie screeching noise pierced the air. I stopped and looked around, half expecting to see some exotic bird perched on a tree limb. Instead, my eyes fell on a set of rusty metal swings in a playground I'd looked at before but had never really seen. I stared at the babies squealing with delight as their mothers pushed them higher and higher into the air. I dropped onto a bench near the sandbox to study the scene, surprised at how often the babies replicated their mothers' features and body types.

"Gorgeous weather, isn't it?" the woman next to me said as she rocked a huge pram that seemed more limousine than carriage.

Her chubby baby was trying to stuff a reddened hand into his toothless mouth. Cracker crumbs littered his lap, drool covered his shirt, a gob of greenish mucous slid from his nose and hung suspended for a brief moment before continuing its journey—exactly the sort of mess that would have driven Ruth into one of her cleaning frenzies. As soon as visitors with infants or toddlers had said their last good-byes, she'd mobilize into action, wiping fingerprints, vacuuming stray cookie crumbs, hunting down moist lumps of bread as if they had posed some terrible threat.

"He's miserable when his nose is stuffed up," the woman confided as the baby's whimpers turned into a series of sharp wails. "Have any tissues? I've used mine up."

"Me? Oh, no. I don't carry them," I answered, hoping she wouldn't hear the relief in my voice. Unlike her, I didn't have to carry tissues because I wasn't saddled with a damp, drooling creature.

"Poor boy can't shake this cold," she said, wiping his goppy mucous with her hand and wiping her hand on her coat. When she leaned forward and covered his slimy cheek with kisses—an act that struck me as nothing less than heroic—I gazed at her as if she were an alien from another world. Or was I the alien for being unable to picture myself as a devoted mother? But how could I become a mother when I still wanted a mother? How could I possibly take care of a baby when I wanted to be the baby?

Freak.

I sprang to my feet and hurried out of the playground.

At work, I sat down at my desk but couldn't concentrate on the grant proposal I was supposed to be writing. Instead, I found myself spinning out endless fantasies about my mother. She was a lawyer, an actress, a professor, a physicist. She was single, married, widowed. Had no children, a huge family. On and on it went through the day, no matter where I was or what I was doing. That night, the fantasies turned morbid: Dark thoughts seized hold of my imagination and made me tremble. I pictured her a mental patient, a criminal, a shopping bag lady. She was the crazy old lady across the street who lived with seventeen stray cats.

It was then that I began following women who looked the slightest bit like me. The first one was the woman whose hand I noticed on the department-store escalator and who I followed into the medical laboratory. Then, a few days after that, I spotted a woman on line at the bank whose features were similar to mine. I shadowed her down the street to the bus stop, where I watched her board an express bus to Staten Island. The third time it happened, I saw a woman enter a small Italian restaurant and couldn't resist watching her through the window until the two men sitting at the window table finally rapped angrily on the glass and glared at me. I walked away, grateful I hadn't actually approached her.

In the meantime, I struggled through the motions of my daily life, trying to act as if nothing had changed. I let Stoddard attribute my mood swings and sleeplessness to the fact that I had turned thirty-five, and even encouraged him in this by sprinkling our conversations with references to my biological clock. But in truth, my emotions were rioting. And in sudden moments of panic and despair, I knew I had to do something soon or lose control completely.

Part Two

Chapter Nine

The luminous hands on the clock danced slowly through the night. At six, I threw on some clothes, tiptoed out of the loft without waking Stoddard, and hurried over to Rent-A-Wreck before I could talk myself out of the trip to Riverton.

"Hope you ain't goin' far," the garage attendant warned as he handed me the car keys. "Suppose to be a big thunderstorm comin'. Heavy rain like that, highway's gonna flood for sure."

I got into the car without answering and plunged into

early-morning traffic, gripping the steering wheel so hard my hands ached. The sky was a strange silvery gray. I suddenly regretted not having left a note for Stoddard. The way things stood now, if there was a storm and I skidded off the road and died in a crash, he'd spend the rest of his life wondering why I'd taken off in a fire-engine-red car at seven in the morning without saying good-bye or telling him where I was going. He'd rummage through my purse, find George Horton's name and address, and assume I was meeting a lover.

In spite of my nervousness, I smiled at the thought of Horton as my lover. He was around seventy-five by now, probably a shriveled version of his toadish, bulgy-eyed younger self. It had been years since I'd seen or spoken to him, and I hadn't called to make an appointment, knowing how easy it would be for him to say no to a disembodied voice on the phone. But I was sure he'd feel compelled to give me some simple facts about my mother once we were face-to-face. Would he even remember me after all these years? I wondered, as I turned onto the thruway. Of course he would. How could he have forgotten all those Sunday afternoons my family had spent sitting in his stuffy living room, listening to him drone on about his newest car? No, the real question was why my parents had spent time with a man they so clearly despised. . . .

A horn blasted. Startled, I glanced in my rearview mirror and saw a moving van bearing down on me full speed ahead. The driver shook his fist out the window and leaned on his horn again. I swerved sharply into the next lane to get out of his way, nearly sideswiping the limousine on my right. Brakes squealed, the chauffeur cursed soundlessly through the window. I slowed down and clicked on the radio to keep myself from daydreaming. Pounding rock music, idiotic commercials, news reports, interviews, country western ballads—nothing satisfied. I switched from station to station, remembering how my father had hated this habit, how he'd always said *Make a choice and stick with it!* as soon as I'd start to fiddle with the radio dials. But what about the choice he'd made? Why hadn't he ever told me about my mother?

Anger clawed at my heart; the lines on the road blurred. I swung the car onto the grassy shoulder of the highway and shut off the engine, leaning my head down on the steering wheel in an effort to get hold of myself.

"You feeling okay, miss?"

I flung my eyes open and saw a baby-faced policeman staring at me through the window, a tiny piece of tissue paper hanging from his chin where he'd cut himself shaving that morning.

"I'm . . . I'm fine," I said, wondering how long I'd been sitting there like that.

His eyes slid to the backseat as if he was looking for a clue, then returned to my face. I could see he didn't believe me.

"I felt a little drowsy so I thought I'd take a short nap," I explained, grinning madly to prove that I was now wide-awake.

"You sure you're all right?"

"Absolutely." I turned on the engine.

Still looking unconvinced, he saluted and stepped away from the car as I bumped gracelessly back onto the road.

At the next exit, I shot down the ramp and made a sharp U-turn. This trip was a terrible idea, a stupid mistake. I hated thinking about my claustrophobic childhood, had no desire whatsoever to see the repulsive Horton again. And I certainly didn't need another mother. Okay, so I'd gotten a little curious about what she looked like, where she'd come from, that sort of thing. It was only natural to have some questions about her after all these years, I should have expected it. But just because I'd lost a few nights of sleep was no reason to take this torturous trip down memory lane. Besides, even if Horton did give me her name, I wasn't about to spend the rest of my life searching for an old woman with whom I probably had nothing in common. Who cared what she looked like? I took after my father anyway, so what difference did it make? My parents were long gone, it was all behind me, and what I really wanted, I realized, was to go back home and forget the whole thing.

I zoomed south, tapping the steering wheel in time with a Beatles song, waving jauntily as I passed the baby cop who was now parked on the center island. The sun blazed through the clouds, the air turned hazy and warm. I pushed a damp strand of hair off my face, regretting my outfit—a stiff linen suit and high heels chosen to impress Horton. Well, if my luck held out and there wasn't much rush-hour traffic, I'd be back home in jeans and sandals in less than an hour.

What if your obsession gets worse? a voice in my head asked. *What if Horton dies?*

My smile sagged. Like it or not, Horton was my last link

to the past, my only source of information. Once he died, I'd be severed from my own history.

Forever.

I turned off at the next exit and got back on the highway heading north again. This time when I passed the policeman, I sank down in my seat and turned my head so he wouldn't recognize me. Too late. In my rearview mirror, I watched his patrol car crawl off the divider and onto the highway. He was coming after me to check my sanity and sobriety. He'd insist I follow him down to headquarters, wherever that was, and I'd end up losing the morning, maybe the whole day. . . .

I shot down the approaching exit ramp at a dizzying speed and drove onto a twisty country lane, hoping to lose him. After making a couple of fast turns, I found myself on a rutted dirt road in the middle of cow fields. The cop was nowhere in sight but neither was anyone else. I kept going, driving past one dilapidated farm after another. I was lost— yet I had the feeling the rocky landscape was familiar, almost as if I'd dreamed about it. Then I rounded a bend in the road and saw a lopsided sign advertising Capezio's Garage and I let out a victorious whoop. Somehow I'd managed to get myself onto the back road that led into town, the route all the locals used to avoid the highway—the route I'd always taken when I'd lived there.

Riverton, the armpit of New England.

No stately white homes or manicured town green, no greeting-card church with clock tower in this part of Connecticut. Riverton was the corpse of a town that had died in the thirties when its ball-bearing industry collapsed, leaving its inhabitants maimed, depressed, and embittered. *The only thing Riverton's good at producing is corrupt politicians*, Ruth always said when we went downtown on a shopping expedition. During my last visit home, the longtime mayor was arrested for extortion and loan-sharking.

The driveways were littered with the carcasses of abandoned pickup trucks and mowers, the yards were filled with pale, scrawny children toeing the dirt with scuffed brown shoes. At the railroad tracks, I turned onto Upper Main, expecting to see the row of pink buildings that had once been ball-bearing factories, but found myself in front of a huge shopping mall. Six-plex theater. McDonald's. T-N-T. Grand Union. Jeans by Gene. I turned into the parking lot and pulled up in front of something called Chew 'n Sip, hoping to grab a quick cup of coffee before visiting Horton.

When I spotted a group of sullen teenagers leaning against a store window, I was instantly transported back to my days at Riverton High, where I'd been something of an oddity because I hadn't worn black leather, smoked, or gotten drunk—and, most damaging of all, I'd been a serious student.

A blast of icy air engulfed me as I entered the Chew 'n Sip. I shivered and rubbed my arms as I looked around at the ceramic gnomes, cheap stuffed animals, plastic jewelry boxes, leftover Easter baskets—the same hideous junk Riverton had always specialized in. A hand-lettered sign at the soda fountain said: SNAK-BAR CLOSED TILL FARTHER NOTICE. I stepped over the mass of cardboard boxes on the floor, wondering if the owner had just moved in or was about to move out.

"Excuse me, do you have a bathroom?" I asked the clerk at the cash register. The enormity of her clublike arms made it impossible to guess whether she was fourteen or forty.

"Locked," she said, sucking on a pinkie.

"Could you open it for me?"

"Don't know where the manager keeps the key."

"Can you ask him?"

"Don't know where he is."

Again I was swept back to my childhood, when such mindless interchanges had been the norm. For the thousandth time, I wondered why my parents hadn't settled in one of the more civilized towns closer to the university, where my father's colleagues had lived. *Make a choice and stick with it*, I could almost hear my father say. And then it jumped out at me, what I should have seen years earlier.

My parents hadn't chosen to live in Riverton, they'd been exiled to it—maybe because of a scandal having to do with my mother.

Agitated, I hurried back to the car and drove out of the mall, but I didn't know where to go. It was still too early to drop in on Horton, and I had no friends left in town. I cruised around aimlessly and ended up in front of the Pleasant Valley Nursing Home, where Ruth had lived out her last years.

I watched a nurse wheel an elderly resident across the lawn in a wheelchair, suffering the pangs of an uneasy conscience. I hadn't wanted to move Ruth into the home, but her health had deteriorated so disastrously after my father's death that she'd suddenly needed full-time care. Round-the-clock nurses were prohibitively expensive, so the only alternative, short of moving back home and nursing her myself, had been to sell our house and use the money to move her to Pleasant Valley. It was clean and well run, and Ruth, herself, seemed entirely indifferent to the matter, as if the only thing that had kept her anchored to life had been my father, and after he was gone, it didn't matter where or how she lived.

The doctors had their pet theories about her, of course: manic depression, senile dementia, Alzheimer's disease, an undetected stroke. But no one had been able to reverse her decline, and in a matter of months, the brisk, efficient woman who had raised me was replaced by a confused stranger who rambled on and on about people I'd never heard of.

When she stopped being able to recognize me and started calling me by a variety of names, my visits became excruciatingly painful. Secretly, I believed she had me confused with her real daughter, the one she'd never given birth to, the petite, delicate girl who'd have looked just like her, and I began going up to Riverton less and less often.

By the time the director of the home called to say Ruth had "passed on" I'd long since mourned her loss, and was so devoid of feeling, I instantly thought of Camus's Meursault. I thought of him a second time at Ruth's funeral, where I sat dry-eyed and guilty for it until I heard Mrs. Horton, who was sitting behind me, whisper to her husband: "It always comes out at death when they're not the real child," and finally, tears had come.

I left the home and drove down South Main into the center of town. Stein's Department Store, the Cameo Movie House, and the News Hub hadn't changed much, but Ye Olde Treat Shoppe had been turned into a Pizza Hut, and all that was left of the Dew Drop Inn was charred wood on a weedy lot, giving Main Street the look of a mouth with a tooth missing. I turned left at the fire station and pulled up in front of my old house, a shingled Victorian that was mostly front porch. Even with its fresh coat of paint, it looked drab and sorrowful, as if my family's sadness had somehow seeped out and stained the exterior walls forever.

Not that any of my friends had known about the gloom. They'd considered my family "perfect" because my father was a professor, not a carpenter or plumber like their fathers, and because my only-child status afforded me my own bedroom. But secretly, I'd envied them their raucous kaleidoscopic families, yearning for the very things that embarrassed them—the cooking smells and family squabbles, the necessity of sharing rooms, clothes, toys with siblings in what seemed a great jumble of love and affection.

My eyes fell on the gnarled and twisted lilac tree in the front yard where I'd sat for hours and hours, telling myself stories and arranging elaborate tea parties. Every spring, when the fragrant lilacs had bloomed, I'd yearned to bring a bunch of blossoms into my room. But Ruth had remained fixed in her belief that cutting flowers was messy and wasteful. "To cut them is to kill them, just enjoy them on the tree," she'd said year after year. Would my real mother have understood me better? Would she have shared my passion for flowers?

I reminded myself that it was time to get some answers.

Chapter Ten

Horton lived in the so-called better part of town, which in Riverton meant shiny metal balls, ceramic deer, and gnomes on front lawns. Driving down the street, I puzzled over which of the look-alike houses was his until I spotted a gleaming antique sedan parked in one of the driveways, a machine that could only have belonged to Horton—a car fanatic who could wax poetic over engines, mufflers, and brakes.

I parked in front of the house and sat listening to my heart thump in my chest like a tom-tom. I was so terrified he wouldn't talk to me, so terrified he would, that I couldn't get myself to open the door. Then I noticed a lace curtain moving on an upstairs window and saw a wizened face peering out at me. Embarrassed, I hurried out of the car and walked up the front path, trying to look resolute.

No one answered the bell.

I stepped back and looked up at the window, but the face had vanished. Had Horton recognized me and retreated? Or hadn't he heard me ringing?

I walked around to the side entrance, remembering the Halloweens of my childhood when all the neighborhood kids had taken guilty pleasure in chalking up Horton's white picket fence and sprinkling homemade confetti on his lawn, tricks reserved for the most disliked families in town. I was about to step onto the cement stoop when I saw a dark shape out of the corner of my eye. I wheeled around just as a vicious-looking black mongrel hurtled out of the bushes and began barking furiously.

"Nice doggie, good boy," I yelped, clutching my purse to my chest, cursing at myself for not remembering that the Hortons always had some beastly creature patrolling the house. Rolf, the last one had been named. Or was it Wolf?

"Shut up, Phantom!" a voice commanded from above.

I shielded my eyes from the sun and gazed up at the second-story window. "Mr. Horton?"

"We don't want nothing!" the face yelled down at me.

The window slammed, the dog bared his pointy teeth and circled my legs as if deciding whether I was worth biting. When I took a step toward the house, his barking became frenzied again.

"Don't worry, he only attacks the parcel post man," Mrs. Horton explained, suddenly materializing in front of me on the stoop. She was wrinkled and bent, but blowzy as ever in a low-cut orange housecoat and white pumps that made me think of Minnie Mouse. I suddenly recalled that, as a child, I'd always thought her voice and shoes too high. "But that's his fault, not the dog's," she squeaked. "See, the garbage-man brings him a bone every Monday, the mailman throws him a tennis ball. But that parcel post man just drops off the package and takes off again and it hurts the dog's feelings— You the Avon lady or a Jehovah's Witness?"

"Neither. I'm here because—Is your husband home?"

"Who, George?"

"Yes," I said, recalling that even in her prime, she hadn't been too bright. Her role model had been Pat Nixon, whose picture she'd kept framed in the living room next to family portraits because, as she'd once confided, she'd read that Pat never got too uppity to iron Dick's trousers.

"I came for . . . some legal advice," I said, keeping an eye on the dog, who was now sniffing my crotch enthusiastically.

"Oh, he's retired. Can't hear so good. Keeps himself plenty busy working on that Buick, though," she added, nodding in the direction of the driveway. "Pretty snazzy, huh? Would you believe that car's twenty-five years old? Polishes it himself every single day, rain or shine. . . ." Her voice trailed off as she opened the door and stepped inside.

"I know you don't recognize me. I'm Sarah Bridges," I said quickly. "Maybe you remember my parents, Ruth and Phillip. Mr. Horton was my father's lawyer—"

"He was everyone's lawyer until he lost his hearing," she

said with a sniff. "Excuse me now. Can't miss any more Oprah."

As soon as she was out of sight, the dog began a rerun of his act. Growl, bark, charge, dash around, sniff. I inched my way over to the door and waited until he was distracted by a bird overhead, then scurried inside. The dog howled through the glass as if outraged he'd been tricked.

"Hello?" I called out tentatively.

A floorboard creaked overhead, but no one answered. The air in the kitchen had a stale mousy smell, the blinds were down. A picture of Ray, the Hortons' son, was taped to the refrigerator, the same furtive expression on his face that he'd worn as a child. One of his arms was thrown carelessly across the shoulders of a little boy with sad eyes. I still remembered Ray at that very age, skulking around school as if he'd just committed a crime or was about to. Hadn't there been a scandal in his senior year, something about stolen erasers, talk of expulsion?

"Hello?" I called out again, nearly tripping over a plant as I made my way down the hallway. Would they mistake me for a prowler and shoot me? Would Mrs. Horton call the police? Maybe I ought to call the police myself to say— what? That a dog had chased me into a stranger's house and I needed protection to get out?

"Don't need any more subscriptions!" a voice bellowed from the shadows, making me jump.

I peered into the living room and saw George Horton stretched out on the sofa reading a newspaper.

"Oh . . . sorry to disturb you, Mr. Horton. Your wife—"

"I'll turn on my hearing aid, but don't get any fancy ideas about me buying something," he said, sitting up slowly.

"I'm not selling anything," I said loudly.

"No need to shout. I hear you fine now."

"I'm Sarah Bridges—Phillip's daughter. I grew up a few streets away. . . ."

He gazed at me for a moment, then shook his head. The lines on both sides of his mouth deepened, giving him the look of a marionette, but I couldn't tell if he was scowling or smiling. "Of course I remember you," he said with a wave of his wrinkled hand. "My memory's good as ever, and don't let anyone tell you different. Spoke with you right after Ruth's funeral. Gave you some sound advice. I bet you haven't been up here since that time. Well, that's how it is with you youngsters. My own son out there in Los Angeles—you remember Ray, don't you? He doesn't get back here more than once every couple of years. What kind of car you driving?"

"Excuse me?"

"Your car, your car," he said, snapping his fingers impatiently.

"Oh, it's rented. A Ford, I think. Red."

"Buick's the best American car, and I should know because I always buy American. Bunch of nonsense what they're saying about our cars being junk. You can get fifteen, twenty years out of a Buick if you pay attention. That car out there in my driveway's solid proof. Take care of an auto and it'll take care of you, that's my motto. Of course, you have to follow the manual and then some, the way I do.

Most people, they're excited about a new car maybe a month or two, then soon as that new-car smell wears off the upholstery, they forget everything except the oil change. Your daddy was a perfect example of that mind-set. To him, an automobile was a hunk of metal took him from one place to another and that's that. Smart as he was, he never got more than seven, eight years out of any machine."

"Actually, it's my father I'd like to talk to you about—"

"Of course, of course. Uncle George knows exactly why you're here. Sit down, make yourself comfortable. Always expected you'd turn up someday."

"You do? You did?" I said, sinking onto the puffy sofa, feeling the pillow deflate beneath me as if it were letting out its breath.

"When you've lived long as I have, you learn a few things, and one thing I've learned is that adoptees—particularly females—show up sooner or later."

My face flamed. I began playing with the crocheted antimacassar on the arm of the couch exactly as I had during childhood. "Uh . . . actually, that is what I came to . . . ask about—" I swallowed hard, feeling like I was about ten years old. "It's kind of hard to get the words out. I haven't had much practice talking about this," I added with a nervous laugh.

"Don't you worry about a thing," he said, patting my hand. "This peculiar weather is making everyone feel funny. Can't remember such seesawing temperatures in the spring before. Freezing one day, boiling the next. Must be that greenhouse effect they keep talking about, whatever that is. Want some fresh lemonade?"

"Oh, no thank you. I'm fine. I'm just so . . . pleased you're not upset to see me. I was a little concerned you might not want to talk to me."

"I know how it is, honey," he said, an avuncular smile on his face. "Adoptions are sticky business. That's why I never liked handling them. When George Horton did a job, he liked knowing it was done forever. To be honest, I'd never have gotten involved in your situation if your daddy hadn't been such an old friend. We went a long ways back—all the way to junior high school down there in New York. That's how he hooked me, you see. George, he said, you're the only person in the world I can trust with all this. Oh, he was in quite a state that day," he said, shaking his head sadly. Then he caught himself and smiled. "So tell me, Sarah, you still teaching those foreigners? I wish to heck Ray'd take up a nice profession like teaching and settle down. He's been married twice already, you know. Doesn't seem to have the patience for long commitments . . ."

He nattered on about Ray, but I was still thinking about what he'd said about my father needing someone he could trust. As far as I knew, my father hadn't trusted him at all. In fact, I'd often heard him say Horton was a fifth-rate lawyer with first-rate fees and fewer scruples than a rat.

"What exactly did my father hire you to do?" I asked when there was a break in his monologue.

"Now before you ask me a single question, I want to give you some good advice." He leaned so close, I could feel his warm breath on my neck. "Don't open Pandora's box."

I forced myself to smile. "That's what you told me after

Ruth's funeral. And that's what I've been doing—pretending none of it happened."

"Good," he said, nodding with approval. "Always told your daddy you were a smart little girl."

"But lately I've been thinking things over and, well, actually I've been—You see, it's as if—my engine's stalled," I said, trying to come up with words he could relate to. "So I thought maybe if I got a few facts, I'd be able to—jump-start my life."

"Honey, if you'd taken Uncle George's advice ten years ago, you'd have saved yourself tolls, gas, and all those jolts in that Ford. No shocks in Fords. They're real flivvers."

"Excuse me?"

"Lemons. Heaps of junk, as far as I'm concerned . . . Now here's a mind-puzzler for you: Why is it Americans park in the driveway and drive on the parkway?"

"I don't really know—"

"That's my point. Sometimes there aren't any good answers to questions."

"Don't misunderstand, Mr. Horton—"

"Uncle George," he corrected, clicking his false teeth for emphasis.

"Uncle George . . . I don't expect you to give me a lot of information about my mother—"

"I've always said your mother was a wonderful woman. No one could have been better to you than Ruth, and that's why you turned out respectable like you did. Not like some of these wild-type girls around here, the quiffs Ray always dated—smoking, drinking."

"Ruth was a wonderful mother, but she really doesn't

have anything to do with this," I persisted. "I was talking about my biological mother."

He pulled back and stared at me for a moment. "Don't you know there are laws about these matters to protect all concerned? As I always say, live according to the law and you'll live happily ever after. That's what I told Ray after he . . . um . . . did a little time. Just a childish prank borrowing that car, but like I told him, at thirty-plus years of age, it's time to abide by the rules or you'll come to some real harm. . . . Now, you and I both know your parents wanted nothing but the very best for their little girl, so I'm saying this purely with your interest in mind. Disturb the sleep of the dead and you'll never have any peace yourself. Be sensible, Sarah. Go on back home and get this foolishness out of your mind once and for all."

He paused for a moment as if the matter were finished and then smiled. "So, you still living down there in Greenwich Village?"

"Mr. Horton—I mean, Uncle George—I know you mean well, but I'm too old to pretend none of this happened. It did happen, and there's a hole in my life I've got to fill—" I stopped, too choked up to continue.

"Now, getting yourself all worked up about this isn't going to do either of us a bit of good. Believe me, there's not a darn thing more I can do for you except offer you a cool drink before you're on your way."

"Can't you just tell me her name? You don't have to say anything else about her if it makes you uncomfortable."

"It's not my comfort I'm thinking about," he said indignantly. "And as you recall, I gave you all relevant documents—including your birth certificate—upon Ruth's demise."

"Yes, but my birth certificate has Ruth's name on it, not my real mother's name."

He clucked his tongue. "Hurts me to hear you say that, Sarah. As far as I'm concerned, Ruth was and always will be your real mother." His voice was still sugary, but his eyes had hardened.

I bit my lip, trying to think of a way to convince him without alienating him. I looked down and saw I was still clutching the antimacassar, twisting it all out of shape. "But what if . . . if I need the information in the future and you're not . . . available?" I stammered.

"You mean if you're having some kind of medical problem?"

"Yes, that's right," I said, seizing his cue. "My doctor's been asking about my . . . uh . . . family medical history because he's worried my biological mother might have had some condition he ought to know about."

"Hmm," he said, rubbing his silvery stubble. "That does cast a different light on the matter, seeing as it's a medical question and not just idle curiosity. . . . All right," he said, nodding his head. "I can tell you Gina was a healthy specimen."

"Gina," I repeated dumbly. "You knew her?"

"Of course I knew her. Who do you think made all the arrangements? Your father was so discombobulated, he couldn't think straight. Practically got down on his knees and begged me to help him. Like I said, I normally wouldn't have touched a messy case like this with a ten-foot pole, but Phil and I—well, I just couldn't say no. A ticklish situation like that needed special handling. Sealed records are one thing, sealed lips quite another. And believe me, it wasn't easy sweet-talking Ruth into taking you, and hunting up a house in Riverton for them, and finding a home for Gina to wait out her time. Fact is, it was me and the wife who picked you up soon as you were born. Carried you home in one of the wife's hatboxes—a shiny black box, brand-new."

He cocked his head to the side and studied my face. "Don't see much of Gina in you except maybe around the eyes. She was a cute-looking gal. Small and shapely with nice features and jet-black hair. I used to call her Betty Boop, but she didn't cotton to that nickname and always gave me a dressing down for it with that sharp tongue of hers. Not much polish but lots of spunk, that girl. A real little spitfire. Intelligent, too, I believe. Like I told your father, I couldn't really blame him for going after her. Your father always did have a way with the ladies, even when we were youngsters. To be honest, I never understood how he ended up with a woman like Ruth when he could have—Now don't get me wrong. Ruth may not have been much to look at, but she was a good woman. Otherwise, she'd never have consented to moving here and raising you up the way she did. Even adopted you, made you legally hers and all. Did it for Phillip because she felt so bad about not being able to have a child of her own. . . . Now, let's see, you must be in your thirties."

"I'm—"

"No, don't tell me, I can figure it out myself. You were

born the year I got the four-door Fury model, so that would make you just about thirty-five years old. . . . Seems like it happened last week. Oh, you were a noisy little thing at first. Kicked up quite a squall the whole way home as if you knew what was happening to you," he said, chuckling. "To be honest, we were a bit worried at first, but you turned out okay. A quiet little girl, well behaved. Ruth gave you a first-rate upbringing. As I say, she wasn't my type of woman, Ruth, but you had to respect her. If that happened to some wives, they'd apt to be hostile to the child. Not Ruth, she was a fine lady, through and through. Of course, no one else in town knew the real story. Thought you belonged to Ruth natural-like."

"Th-they never told me any of this," I said, struggling to keep my smile going so he wouldn't see how shocked I was.

"I know that, honey. I was the one who advised them to keep silent about it. See, I was afraid you might harbor resentment or act difficult if you found out the truth. . . . Well, I'd say it's all worked out for the best, wouldn't you?" he said, reaching over and squeezing my shoulder.

I tried not to recoil under his clammy touch. "And my mother—I mean Gina," I said, feeling the muscles around my mouth ache from my mad grin. "Do you know where she is now?"

"Don't know a thing about her. She left the university and never went back, and none of us ever heard a word from her. Probably found herself a nice husband and had a couple more kids. That's the way it usually is in these cases. See, it's in the girl's best interest to keep silent what happened and just get on with her life. And that's what I advise you to do, young lady," he said with a wink. "Go back home and tell that doctor of yours Gina was a healthy specimen, and then put all this unpleasantness out of your mind."

"I'm . . . I'm not sure I can do that. It's very disturbing."

"Precisely why we never told you about it. Wanted to protect you from upset."

"But I'm not a child anymore. I don't need that kind of protection. In fact, I think I'd feel much better if I knew more about her."

"Well, that's out of the question. Completely out of the question."

"I'd be happy to pay you for your time—"

"Money's not the issue. Your daddy wanted me to keep mum, and I've got to respect his wishes."

"But why respect the dead at the expense of the living?"

He sat up straighter in his seat. "Young lady, I cannot and will not violate your father's trust in me."

"But it doesn't make sense—"

"I knew it!" he said, frowning. "The same thing always happens when one of you adoptees walks in here. I give you an inch, you want the whole mile and then some. Today you're after her name, tomorrow it'll be a copy of your original birth certificate from my files—"

"You still have it?" I said in surprise.

"Of course I do. All my records are upstairs in my office in perfect order."

"Well, what harm would it do anyone if I took a quick peek at it?"

"For one thing, I don't believe you're entitled to that information."

"Not entitled to know who my mother was? But even the most primitive animal knows its own moth—"

"Hope you didn't let her talk you into buying anything, George," Mrs. Horton squeaked from the doorway.

"Please, Mr. Horton—Uncle George. Just let me see my birth certificate, and I promise I'll never bother you again." I opened my purse and took out my car keys, dangling them in front of him to prove my point. "I swear, I'll drive away and never come back."

He got to his feet slowly. "Young lady, it's not going to do either one of us any good to get all emotional about this."

I stood up, towering over him. He was such a tiny man, I could easily sweep him aside, run upstairs, and lock myself in his office. By the time the police got there, I'd have searched through his files and gotten her name.

"At least say you'll think about it," I pleaded.

"I'm warning you not to press me on this matter," he said, his mouth contracting to a thin line. "You'd better be on your way now. I've had enough of you."

I was so taken aback by his hostility, I dropped my car keys. By the time I picked them up, he was standing at the front door, holding it wide open.

"But I—I don't have anyone else to ask," I sputtered, trying to blink back my tears.

"That's something you should be grateful for. This information is none of your damned business!"

I looked at him in disbelief. "My father always said you were unscrupulous, but he never said you were cruel."

Horton's eyes narrowed to malevolent slits. "You know, maybe you did inherit something from Gina after all—that wicked tongue of hers!"

I charged down the driveway, too distraught to worry about the snarling dog at my heels. When I passed the antique car, I had the urge to dig my car keys into the glossy paint and scratch it from one end to the other. I could almost hear the scream of metal against metal. But I kept going, still too much the good girl to damage Horton's precious sedan.

I got into my car and sped away so fast, I skidded and swerved onto the curb and nearly hit a tree. When I'd left the neighborhood, I pulled into a parking lot, too shaken to get onto the highway. Endless questions echoed through my mind. Had my father been in love with Gina or had it been a casual affair? Had there been other affairs? Had Ruth known about his extracurricular activities? Had Gina wanted an abortion?

An icy hand wrapped itself around my heart and squeezed.

I saw myself as a tiny infant in a coffinlike hatbox in the back of Horton's car, screaming for my mother.... How did he expect me to forget all that? Why should I forget it? It was my life—it belonged to me. And now that I'd heard part of my story, I needed to find out the rest of it. Horton couldn't stop me from finding her. No one could. I'd write to local hospitals. I'd hire a lawyer and take him to court. I'd steal my birth certificate if I had to. One way or another, I'd get my mother's full name. . . .

Something nagged at a corner of my mind just out of reach, something important Horton had said about her.

She left the university and never went back.

I started the engine and drove back to the highway, certain that I'd have my mother's name in a couple of hours.

Chapter Eleven

As soon as I started wandering around the university, my confidence evaporated. The sedate, ivy-covered grounds I remembered from childhood had been invaded by glitsy high-rises, a futuristic dome, a hulking marble library, stark dormitories. The campus now looked more like an outpost of Disneyland than a dignified university. Confused and disoriented, I wondered if anyone would even remember my father after all these years. Or was it just the opposite? Had his affair created such a scandal, he'd never been forgotten?

I climbed Heartbreak Hill and headed over to the history building, girding myself for the sight of yet another modern monstrosity. But miraculously, the castlelike Sloan Hall still stood proud with all its stained-glass windows and gargoyles intact. I tugged on the heavy oak door and ran up the stone steps, remembering how amazed I'd been as a child when my father had explained that even something as solid as rock could be worn away over time.

The only sign of life in the history office was a cigarette stub smoldering on the secretary's desk, but the chairperson's office door was open a crack, and I caught a glimpse of an owlish man sucking on an unlit pipe as he read at his desk. When I knocked on the door, his hand reflexively rose to the top of his head to make sure the long strands of hair combed across his bald spot were doing their job.

"Excuse me, Dr.—" I glanced at the door for his name. "Dr. Skog. Can I talk to you for a minute?"

He took the pipe out of his mouth and gave me a smile that was cautious but not unfriendly. "Come in, have a seat, such as it is," he said, pointing with the pipe stem to a sagging chair.

"Looks like the same furniture that was here twenty-five years ago," I remarked as I tried to fit myself between the protruding springs.

"Ah, an alum," he said, looking perplexed. "What class?"

"I didn't actually go to school here, I just used to visit the campus with my father sometimes. He taught history. Perhaps you've heard of him—Phillip Bridges?"

His eyebrows shot up in surprise. "You're Phillip Bridges's daughter? Well, well, well, delighted to meet you," he exclaimed, reaching across his desk to pump my hand. "We're still using his course outlines, you know. I'm not ashamed to tell you he's one of my heroes. In fact, I've always regretted that I didn't get here until after he'd retired. You in history also?"

"No, I teach English in New York."

"Columbia or NYU?"

"English as a second language."

"Interesting," he said, his smile almost imperceptibly narrowing.

"I hardly recognize the campus, it's changed so much," I began, wondering how much to tell him. He seemed friendly enough, but then, so had Horton at the beginning of our conversation.

"Yes, we've won all sorts of architectural awards, especially for the library. But frankly, I miss the old place—the creaky floors, windows you can open and shut yourself, that sort of thing. Thank goodness the trustees ran out of money before they got to Sloan Hall. I suppose we'll elude the wrecking ball for another decade. And at least we haven't lost our view of the Connecticut hills yet."

I followed his gaze out the window, but it wasn't the view I was thinking about. I was remembering how much my father had loved this building, how animated he'd been whenever he was on campus, almost as if he'd saved the best of himself for his students.

"So, what can I do you for?" he quipped, adjusting the angle of the picture frame on his desk. The photo was of twin babies, his children no doubt, probably saddled with historical names. Lincoln and Grant, I guessed.

I took a deep breath. "Well, actually, I'm trying to trace . . . do some research on an . . . associate of my father's who . . . collaborated with him on a major project." I smiled inwardly at my little joke.

"So, the apple didn't fall far from the tree after all. Which journal is it for?"

"It's not exactly an article, it's more a . . . biography of my father. I'm trying to fill in some details because he . . . kept his professional life quite separate from his private life and I want to locate this . . . friend of his."

"Was the fellow in this department?"

"It's a woman, and unfortunately, I don't know much about her. That's why I've stopped in here before heading over to the administration building. I was wondering if any of my father's colleagues were still around."

He closed one eye and looked up at the ceiling. "Let me think. . . . Most of the old-timers retired in the late eighties. Did you say it's a woman you're trying to find?"

I nodded. "All I have to go on is that her name was Gina and she left in sixty-five."

"Well, she shouldn't be hard to track down. Weren't too many women here in the sixties, this place was a bastion of conservatism back then. It's all changed now, of course. We've got a tenured African American and two female lecturers in the department. . . . I suppose your best bet would be to go over to the records office in the administration building and ask for Ed Carnabatti. Make sure to tell him Frank Skog sent you. With all those newfangled computers, he should be able to run her down in no time."

"Terrific," I said, propelling myself out of the caved-in chair. "I really appreciate your help."

"Oh, it's my pleasure, Ms. Bridges. Your father was—still *is*—something of a myth around here, so keep me posted. We'll have to get an autographed copy of your book for the library."

"My book? Oh, on my father. Yes, of course."

"As I say, one of my biggest regrets was that I never had a chance to meet him. There are so many questions I'd have loved to ask."

"Yes, me too," I said from the doorway.

I hurried toward Larson Hall, wondering how much time it would take the computer office to pull up my mother's name and address. She wouldn't still be living there, of course, not after all these years, but at least I'd have a starting point. And my grandparents might still be there. Grandparents! I thought with a thrill. I'd been so focused on my mother, I'd almost forgotten I had a whole family I knew nothing about. I was still thinking about this as I followed the walkway past a row of cinder-block dormitories and around the math and science buildings. But when Larson Hall came into view, I stopped short. Even from the distance I could see something was terribly wrong. Waist-high weeds blocked the entrance. Windows were smashed. A chain hung from the front door.

"What happened to the administration building?" I asked a student just as he tossed a red Frisbee to his friend. The three of us watched the disc arc high into the sky and drop into a clump of bushes.

"They're tearing it down to build a new technology center," he explained. "All the deans have moved to the north side of campus, over there," he said, pointing toward a high-rise glittering on the horizon like a mirage.

I glanced at my watch. If I didn't catch Ed Carnabatti before he left for lunch, I'd end up having to wait around for hours until he showed up again. And if it got too late in the afternoon, he'd probably tell me to come back another day. I broke into a nervous trot, wishing I'd worn sneakers instead of foot-crimping high heels. Of course, when I'd gotten dressed that morning, I'd hardly expected to be dashing around all day. . . .

Sweaty and disheveled by the time I crossed the campus, I entered the lobby and ducked under a ladder. Despite its flashy facade, the building was still under construction, and the floor was a tangle of electrical cables. I hunted for a wall directory, then gave up and asked the guard stationed in front of the elevator where I could find Ed Carnabatti.

"Tough to say, darlin'," he told me in a heavy Irish brogue. "Everyone's playin' leapfrog while they rip up defective floor tiles in some of the offices." He took off his hat for a minute as if to give his head a rest and then plopped it back on. "That Carnabatti fella's got so much equipment, he's spread out between the fourth floor and the basement. Best use the stairs if you're goin' anywhere. The elevators have been gettin' stuck today, and there ain't no electricians around, don't you know, they're like doctors, never there when you need 'em. . . ."

I walked up to the fourth floor. The only people in sight were the workmen eating lunch and drinking beer. No one was smoking, but the air was fragrant with grass. One of the men belched and offered me a sip of his beer. I declined his offer and asked about the computer office.

"They're down in their other office today 'cause we're up here tearin' up the friggin' floor. But don't get on any elevators, 'cause they're out of friggin' order."

I ran back down the staircase to the basement and found a door marked RECORDS—PRIVATE.

"Gee, what a pity—you just missed Ed by two minutes," the secretary told me. "He went for allergy shots and won't be back until tomorrow morning."

I cursed under my breath and collapsed onto a plastic chair, wondering what to do next. Go back to Skog's office? Talk to a different dean? Give up for the moment and come back another day? While debating with myself, I prised off my left shoe and studied the angry blister on the back of my heel.

"Ick! Wouldn't want to be in your shoes," the secretary said sympathetically, leaning across her desk to study my foot. "Maybe I can help you."

I looked up hopefully.

"It's eency, but it's all I've got," she said, taking a small Band-Aid out of her drawer and offering it to me.

"Oh, thanks. But it's an employee list I really need," I told her as I taped the Band-Aid onto my heel. It was so tiny, it covered less than half the blister.

"No problemo," she said, reaching for a thick booklet on her desk and tossing it to me.

I shook my head after glancing at it. "Not for the current year. I'm talking about 1965."

"Sixty-five?" she said, her eyes widening in surprise. "That's ancient history. I don't even know where they keep stuff that old."

"Aren't your records computerized?"

"Not that far back they aren't."

"Is there anyone around who might know where to look?"

"Dean Fields probably. She's been here forever and kind of runs the place when the president's gone, which is like all the time. The problem is, you'll have to get past the bulldog. But you can give it a try. Her office is on the eighth floor. Don't take the elevators—they're a mess."

I limped up the staircase, trying to lean forward so my weight wasn't on my left heel.

"What time is your appointment?" Dean Fields's secretary asked brusquely without looking up from her computer.

"I don't have an appointment," I said, still panting from the climb. "I just want to ask the dean a quick question."

"She's not here. Can I help you?" When she thrust out her jaw, I understood the other secretary's reference to the bulldog.

"It's about a rather . . . um, personal matter."

"I'm her personal secretary."

I hesitated. "Well, I'm trying to trace a former faculty member because . . . her family needs to locate her."

"If you're a detective, I must see your credentials."

"I'm not a detective. This is biological—I mean biographical research. I was told the dean might be helpful."

Her eyes dropped to the calendar on her desk. "There's an appointment slot after classes end on the tenth of next month."

"Actually, all I need is a quick peek at some old records."

"University records are closed to the public," she said so sharply, I felt like she'd slammed a door in my face. I stared at her for a moment, then put my hands on the desk and leaned down close to her. "This is important to me—very important," I said in an unfamiliarly menacing voice. "I'm not leaving without some information—"

"What's up, Millie?"

I turned around and saw an androgynous-looking woman sweep into the room and pick up a bundle of mail from the desk. With her short gray hair, wide pink face, and rimless glasses, she looked exactly like a Norman Rockwell nun. Discussing my father's campus sex life with her was going to be like going to confession.

"Excuse me, Dean Fields, may I talk to you for a minute about a personal matter?"

"Sure, shoot," she said absently as she shuffled through her mail. "If it's about a sabbatical, you'll have to talk to Dean Ganz." She headed toward her office.

"I'm not on the faculty, my father was Phillip Bridges," I said quickly, throwing his name out like bait.

"The historian?" she said, looking up in surprise.

"You have an appointment with Dean Furth in five minutes," the secretary warned.

"Watch the clock for me, Millie. Come in, Ms. Bridges."

I followed her into the office. Leather-and-metal furniture, glass coffee table, aluminum ashtrays. Ruth would have loved the operating-room decor. Easy to clean.

"I feel like you've just rescued me from a dragon—Millie, I mean," I said, smiling nervously. The dean did not smile back. I cleared my throat and looked down at my hands on my lap, lacing my fingers together as if in prayer. *First comes love, then comes marriage, then comes baby in a brand-new carriage.*

"How can I help you, Ms. Bridges?"

"Well, you see, I'm doing some research on my father and—"

"Ah, well, then, I'm afraid I'm not going to be of any use. Never knew him—not personally, that is. Knew of him, of course. Everyone did. He had quite the reputation in his day."

My gut tightened. "Really?"

"Oh yes, his popularity was legendary. He was known as the most passionate of teachers."

I searched her face for signs of irony but found none. My foot was shaking so wildly, the tiny Band-Aid on the back of my heel came loose and flapped in the breeze. I recrossed my legs and shifted in the chair. "Well, actually, to be more specific, I'm trying to find someone my father worked with—had a relationship with on campus. Dr. Skog suggested I inquire at the records office, but the secretary there doesn't know where the information is stored, and unfortunately, all I have to go on is the fact that she left the faculty around 1965—" I stopped mid-sentence. Why had I automatically assumed she was a professor? Horton said she was at the school but he hadn't said what she was doing there. Maybe she'd been a dean or a secretary or a student. Maybe she'd been a cleaning lady. My father had been an intellectual snob but even *his* cock couldn't read.

The door opened, Millie peered in. "You're going to be late, Dean Fields."

"Yes, yes. We're all finished," she said, grasping the handle of her briefcase and standing up. "I suggest you walk over to the rabbit hutch, Ms. Bridges—the computer research center. Or send a written request to the records office. Once the dust settles around here and the semester ends, I'm sure they'll be able to do some checking for you."

She waited for me to stand up, but I didn't move. I was lost in a vision of future conversations I'd have with other Hortons and Skogs and Millies and deans. Everyone would be polite. No one would help.

"Dean Fields, tracing this woman is extremely important to me because—" I glanced over at Millie and dropped my voice. "Because this woman and my father were—you see . . . well, actually, she was my . . . biological mother."

Distaste spread across the dean's face. She let go of her briefcase and dropped heavily onto her chair. "Shut the door, Millie," she said, taking off her rimless glasses. Without them, her face looked disconcertingly naked. I could almost hear what she was thinking: The famous Phillip Bridges and a colleague. Illicit sex. Pregnancy. Scandal . . . She spun around in her chair and gazed out the window without saying anything.

Rage caught at the back of my throat. How could my father—a brilliant historian—have left me so little of my own history that I had to beg strangers to help me reconstruct my life? How could he have written whole books on the Civil War without writing me a single letter explaining his own civil war?

The dean spun around again. From her set expression, I could see she'd made a decision. When she picked up the phone, I half expected her to be calling the campus police to tell them to eject me.

"Dr. Geoffries?" she said, keeping her eyes fixed on me. "This is Marlene Fields. Fine, fine. Yes, the president's still in Poland. I'll tell him as soon as he gets back. Listen, I'm sending over a young woman who needs to look at the—" She stopped and covered the mouthpiece. "What year did you say?"

"Sixty-five."

"The sixty-five faculty records."

"The entire staff list," I interjected. "I'm not actually sure she was on the faculty."

"She needs a list of everyone who was on campus that year," she said, nodding at me. She listened for another moment and then hung up. "Geoffries is pulling up the list at the computer center. It'll be ready by the time you get there."

"The form please," Geoffries said, extending his hand. He was a small, thin man who smelled vaguely like Vicks VapoRub.

"Excuse me?" I said, looking at him blankly.

"Can't give you the list without a signed form from the dean." He pulled out a handkerchief and blew his nose forcefully.

"Dean Fields didn't mention any form. Maybe it's not necessary."

"It may not be necessary for her, but I have to protect

myself. Administrators have this nasty habit of only remembering the rules *they* make up. . . . Hey, don't look so crushed," he said, stuffing his handkerchief into his pocket. "Just run back and pick it up. I'll be here another fifteen, twenty minutes."

"But she was on her way out to a meeting—and I'm just up here for the day. I live in New York."

He thought for a moment and then shrugged. "Well, I'll probably get my ass handed to me, but if I can't make some judgment calls, I'm no different than my computers, right?"

He darted out of the cubicle and returned a few moments later, staggering under the weight of a huge sheaf of papers. "So what's this all about, anyway?" he asked, handing it to me.

"I'm trying to find a woman named Gina who left here in nineteen sixty-five," I answered, setting the papers down on his desk.

"Gina what?"

"That's the problem—I don't know."

He laughed. "Well, I sure hope they're paying you by the hour. It's going to take years to get through that list. And that's only full-time people. Students and part-timers have their own lists."

"Well, there can't be that many Ginas."

"Records this old, we only list people by first initial and last name. How are you spelling *Gina,* anyway?"

"G-I-N-A, I guess. Isn't that how it's always spelled?"

"My girlfriend's little sister spells her name J-E-A-N-A, so I guess you'd better check the J's, too."

I scanned the first page: G. Abbot, G. Adams, J. Andlis, G. Arlington, J. Axel . . . No phone numbers, just addresses. He was right. It would take years to find her this way.

"Don't you have a master list with first names?"

"Yep, but I could get fired for giving it to you without proper authorization. It's got all sorts of personal information—salary, marital status, mental and physical disabilities."

"Is Dean Fields the only one who can okay it?"

"Any dean or department chairman can do it."

"So a letter from Dr. Skog would be okay?"

"Forget Skog. He's such a tight-ass, he never signs anything."

"No, I'm sure he'll do it for me."

"Well, better hurry. I'm closing up in a couple of minutes."

I rushed back across the campus to Sloan Hall and took the steps two at a time, so intent on my mission that I nearly crashed into a group of professors exiting from the history office.

"Ah, Ms. Bridges, how propitious that you've returned," Dr. Skog said, looking up from his paperwork and smiling ambiguously. "I was just telling some of the men about your exciting project."

"That's great. The thing is, I've run into a bit of a problem. Dr. Carnabatti's gone for the day and Dean Fields suggested I speak to Dr. Geoffries—"

"You told Fields and Geoffries about this?"

"Yes, but it turns out I only need a short letter of authorization from you and then I'll be able to check the master list—"

"Why don't you sit down for a moment. I'd like to ask

you a few more questions." He reached for his pipe and tamped down the tobacco for what felt like an hour.

"Excuse me, I don't mean to hurry you, but Dr. Geoffries is waiting and I—"

"In my experience," he said, striking a match and lighting the pipe, "researching someone you admire—particularly a close relative—can be a complicated matter. Sometimes you find out more than you wish to know. An occupational hazard, as it were."

"Thank you for the advice. I'll consider myself warned," I answered, wondering if one of the other professors had just tipped him off about my father's campus love life. Obviously, something had happened. His whole demeanor had changed.

"In fact—taking it one step further—I'd venture to say biographical research can even be irksome . . . not only for the biographer, but for others as well. Of course, I'm confident you'll do an A-1 research job. But before I attach my name to your project, I really ought to know a bit more about it. Unfortunately, so many contemporary biographers seem to go for the sensational. You see, we had a bit of a problem here a few years ago with some fellow who was researching Bill Whaley, our nineteenth-century man. He ended up writing a piece for *Modern History* about Bill's so-called drinking problem, and naturally, the alums were up in arms about it. As you can imagine, I was hard-pressed to explain how it had happened."

"I assure you, Dr. Skog, this department has nothing to worry about. I'm going to be very protective of my father's reputation."

"Yes, of course. Nevertheless, it would be irresponsible of me as chairperson to write a letter on your behalf before seeing a detailed outline of your project. Perhaps even a résumé wouldn't hurt as well, if you don't mind. After all, I will be held accountable."

"Well, actually, Dr. Skog, this project is of a . . . more personal nature than perhaps I've led you to believe. I'm not actually planning to publish anything about my father. I'm just trying to get this woman's name because she was . . . involved with him. Intimately involved," I added, meeting his gaze.

His face darkened. "I'm not sure what you're insinuating, Ms. Bridges, but I warn you, I have a real bugaboo about rumormongering."

"This isn't a rumor, it's a fact. I found out from a lawyer who was professionally involved that this woman was my mother. My father kept it a secret during his lifetime, and now I'm trying to put the story together." The words rolled out of my mouth easily this time. No stuttering, no blushing, no shame. Just the not-so-simple facts of my life.

His face darkened. "You have no right to slander your father's reputation with such a vicious story."

"I'm sorry if it offends you, Dr. Skog, but it happens to be the truth. It's my life we're talking about, not a research paper. I certainly have the right to find out who my own mother was, whatever the effect on your department."

"Be that as it may," he said through clenched teeth, "you'll have to work out your personal problems elsewhere. I'm calling Geoffries right now to instruct him to refrain from any further intercourse with you. Now if you'll excuse me."

I tore out of his office, getting angrier at every step. When I saw the elderly secretary at her desk, I stopped short and did a double take.

"Sophie?"

"That's the name."

"You're still here after all this time?"

"Please, miss, don't remind me of my age," she said sourly.

Her hair had turned completely white, and a wattle of flesh now hung beneath her chin, but when she looked me over I saw that her black eyes were as penetrating as ever.

"You don't recognize me, do you? I'm Sarah Bridges—Professor Bridges's daughter. When I was little girl, you used to give me color pencils to draw with while my father was in meetings. And candy canes. You always had candy canes in your top drawer."

"Still do," she said without smiling. She opened her drawer and took out one of the striped candies. "I'll give you a candy cane and some advice to chew on. If you're here for a job interview, you'd better quit arguing with Skog. He's the touchiest person I've ever worked for—a real stickler for rules."

"My father used to say you were the real chairman of this department. He was convinced the place would fall apart without you."

Her hand fluttered into the air like a bird and alighted on the cameo brooch at her neck. "Your father always was big on flattery," she said, her expression softening slightly.

"Sophie," I whispered, glancing over my shoulder to make sure Skog's door was still closed, "my father practically lived in this office. You knew him for years and years, maybe better than anyone else here. I've been running around all morning trying to find out about my mother, but no one'll tell me anything."

"Hardly knew Mrs. Bridges—Ruth," she added after a slight pause.

"Ruth was my adoptive mother. I just found out today that my biological mother was here at the university. Did you know anything about her?"

She sat up straighter in her chair. "Your father was a brilliant man, universally admired by faculty and students. I enjoyed working for him, but our relationship was strictly professional. That's why I've lasted here forty-three years. I've always minded my own business."

"But did you know he was . . . involved with someone? Emotionally, I mean. Was there a Gina in this department? That's all I know about her."

"Thousands of people have passed through this office since I arrived. If I'd been interested in gossip, I'd have stayed home and watched soap operas. Plenty of that sort of thing on television."

"But did he—was he especially close to anyone?"

"I really couldn't say. . . . Now if you'll excuse me, I've got to finish this report or you-know-who will have my head."

Slowly I limped out of the office. My mother had probably spent a lot of time in this building. What had she been thinking about when she'd walked down the staircase for the last time? How pregnant had she been at that point? Where had she gone? Where was she now?

"Miss Bridges—wait!"

I turned and saw Sophie coming down the staircase after me on her spindly legs, waving a piece of paper in the air. When she reached me she stopped and leaned against the banister for support.

"Her name was Jeanne, not Gina," she said in a tremulous voice. "It was short for Eugenia. In those days, I knew every student by name."

"She was a *student*?" I gasped.

She nodded. "A senior. I swore to your father I'd never tell a soul and I've stuck to my word. Never even told my own husband about it. But I kept this all these years." She thrust the yellowed piece of paper into my hand and started slowly up the staircase, taking one step at a time like a little child.

I looked down at the spidery script and felt a chill run down my spine: *Eugenia Lydia Forrest, 36-10 110th Street. Ozone Park, New York.*

"Thank you!" I called up to her as she reached the top step. "I can't tell you how much this means to me."

"You don't have to," she said without turning around. "I was an adopted child myself, Miss Bridges. Never had the courage to look for my own parents, and now, of course, it's impossible. Good luck to you. I believe you'll need it."

Chapter Twelve

I sped home in a fever of excitement, so lost in fantasies about my mother that the highway dropped away and I almost forgot I was driving. I pictured her as a college student—petite, dark-haired, vivacious. My father had been at least twenty years her senior but still handsome with that patrician face and thick shock of wavy hair. Sex must have been what he'd been researching in his office all those evenings when he'd been working late. Maybe Ruth had even known about their affair. She'd clearly disliked sex

("Men are only interested in one thing—and they never grow out of it!" she'd often said). She might even have been relieved he'd had other women. Or had his infidelity been the price she'd paid for staying married to him?

My eyes dropped to the speedometer, startled to see that the needle had climbed past seventy. I let up on the gas pedal and slowed down, inwardly calculating my mother's age. . . . If she was a senior in college when she got pregnant, she'd have been around twenty-one. That meant she'd be in her mid-fifties now—a far cry from the elderly woman I'd been imagining these past weeks . . . I started fantasizing about her again, imagining all sorts of dramatic reunions. Scene after scene played in my mind, all of them joyful, all ending with tears of happiness, embraces . . .

I'd start the search immediately—on my way home—I decided, patting the slip of paper in my pocket. I'd drive straight to Ozone Park and see if my grandparents were still living at this address. I'd talk to them but wouldn't introduce myself—not until I'd contacted my mother. And then the two of us would visit them together.

The sun compressed itself into a strip of orange on the horizon, traffic increased as I approached the city. I began worrying about my plan. I didn't have a clue how to get to Ozone Park or whether it was a safe neighborhood to drive through at night. And wouldn't my grandparents wonder why I hadn't simply phoned them for Eugenia's address? And how long would my manic energy last? I'd been operating on coffee and a rush of adrenaline all day, but at some point I was bound to crash. I was overwrought, I needed a break, I told myself as I passed the turnoff for Queens. I'd go home, tell Stoddard everything, and get a good night's sleep. Then, in the morning, I'd start the search.

I threw down my purse and hurried toward the back of the loft, practically exploding with emotion. Stoddard was hunched over his workbench, knocking together a frame he'd been working on for the past couple of days. He looked up at me with a terrible expression on his face.

"Where the hell have you been all day? I was about to call the police."

"I know I should have called, but I—"

"First you sneak out of here at the crack of dawn. Then some guy calls from Rent-A-Wreck to say you dropped your change purse when you rented the car. So I figure you're off somewheres with Al, but then Al calls to see how you're doin' and all sorts of strange ideas start floatin' into my head."

I looked askance at him. "You're not actually jealous, are you?" I teased, trying to wrap my arms around him. His body was stiff and unyielding, he pulled away. When he bent over his frame and started slamming it again, I saw this was more serious than I'd realized.

"I'm sorry I didn't call, Stoddard, but I couldn't talk about this on the phone—"

Suddenly, he let out a howl and dropped his hammer, doubling over in pain, cradling his smashed fingers to his chest. He hobbled into the kitchen and stuck his hand under the faucet. I rummaged around the medicine cabinet for a Band-Aid, but when I offered it to him, he snatched it out of my hand and wound it around his thumb himself as if he didn't want me to touch him.

"What am I to you, some dumb hick you use for sex?" he said in a burst of anger. "I been sittin' here all day tryin' to see this thing from your point of view 'cause I know how twitchy and depressed you always get around your birthday, and the number thirty-five seems to have blown you out. Then I started thinkin' about how you've been cryin' over nothing lately, not sleepin' or eatin' much—and it hit me like a ton of bricks. . . . Why didn't you tell me?"

"You mean you figured it out?" I said in surprise.

"It took me long enough, didn't it? You should have told me right away, goddammit."

"I *tried* telling you, but you didn't seem to want to hear about it. I knew I had to do something one way or another, so I decided to handle it myself."

Blood drained from his face. "You went ahead and had an abortion without telling me?"

"An abortion? What are you talking about?"

"These," he said, opening the storage closet and pulling out Nina's two bags of mother/baby books. "Since I couldn't work today, I figured I'd organize my old canvases, and look what I found. *Nurture versus Nature*," he said, reading the title out loud, "*The Mother Knot, The Early Bond, The Reproduction of Mothering*. This one's my real favorite— *Secret Mothers*."

"Stoddard, those are Nina's books. She's using them for

her new course and wanted me to read them. I'm not pregnant."

He blinked a few times. "You mean it?"

"Of course I mean it!"

"Whoa, mama, I need a drink." He grabbed a bottle of scotch from the cabinet and took a long swig. "Good ol' Dr. John always fixes what ails," he said, patting the bottle. "Damn, I nearly went crazy today thinkin' how it'd be having a baby. You know, fixin' up this place, gettin' a straight job and all. And let me tell you, I was scared shitless. I'm not ready for all that domestic stuff. Marriage I could maybe deal with, but a baby's a life sentence."

"Not always," I said, leaning my back against the refrigerator. The cold metal bit into the bare skin on my neck, but somehow the pain felt good.

"So where'd you go today?"

"I drove up to Riverton."

"Riverton? Why?"

"To ask my parents' lawyer some questions. About my mother—my birth mother."

"Your *what*?"

"I never told you, but Ruth wasn't my biological mother. She adopted me. I was my father's child, but something happened to my mother."

"You mean she died?"

"I don't know. My parents never talked about her, and I was afraid to ask questions. It was a taboo subject. I don't even remember thinking about it. I have a kind of amnesia about my childhood. But lately—I don't know why—I can't get it off my mind. So I thought maybe if I got a few facts about my mother from George Horton—their lawyer—I'd be able to let it all go."

"So what'd he say?"

"Not much. At first he treated me like I was five years old and said I should forget the whole thing because it would just upset me. When I persisted, he told me her name—except he got it wrong. Then he basically threw me out of his house. The one useful thing he said was that my mother had been at the university with my father. So I drove over to the school, ran all over the campus, and finally got her real name and address from the secretary in the history department."

"Amazing!"

"What's amazing is that as recently as this morning, I was apologizing to people for asking about my own mother! Horton actually said I wasn't entitled to the information. And the creepy chairman of the history department was worried about damaging my father's reputation. It was infuriating."

"I guess they were just being protective," Stoddard said, lacing his fingers with mine and pulling me closer.

"Who were they trying to protect? Me from the fact that my father slept with one of his students?"

"She was his student?"

I nodded. "She never graduated—just drifted off and disappeared. But I'm going to find her."

Stoddard looked at me thoughtfully, then picked up the bottle of scotch and took another swig. "I don't know, Sar.

What's the point of digging up all this stuff. It's not going to change who you are, and it might cause a lot of grief—for you and her."

"Hey, come on. You're beginning to sound like Horton."

"I'm just bein' realistic. What if she turns out to be a fruitcake or junkie. It could be a horror show for you."

"Well, at least I'll know the truth."

He let go of me and banged his fist against the wall. "Shit, here we go again! Now that your book's done, you're looking for another fucking crusade. Isn't taking care of the Third World enough for you anymore?"

"What's my job got to do with this?"

"Okay, fine. Go ahead and start lookin' for your mother. Join one of those adoptee groups. Hire a lawyer. Pretend you're Sherlock Holmes. Do anything the hell you want. But don't expect any sympathy from me when you screw up your life."

"Thanks, Stoddard. It's great to know I can count on you through thick and thin."

"Now that really chaps my ass. I've put up with a lot of crap since we've been together. Your weird hours, students bugging you all the time, those nightmares you've been having. I've been biding my time 'cause I thought things'd ease up once your damned book was finished. But now you're startin' in on this crazy roots jag."

"It's not crazy, and it's not a jag. Like it or not, family happens to be important. The past is important. You can't have any kind of authentic future if you don't understand the past, and first you have to get all the facts right," I said, echoing Alex's words.

"There are no facts!" he yelled. "The past is whatever people imagine happened. It's all fiction."

"Well, my family's not fiction, and neither is yours. And it probably would do you some good to think about your own family."

"I don't give a damn about those people. I learned a long time ago suckin' on a wooden tit just gets you splinters."

"Come on, Stoddard, you're still carrying around a ton of adolescent anger. Maybe that's why your paintings are so—" I stopped mid-sentence. Stoddard had never been good at taking criticism about his work, and this wasn't the moment to start.

"My paintings are so what?" he said, the vein on his forehead pulsing wildly.

"Nothing. Forget it."

"Go ahead, say it. I want to hear."

"I was just going to say what you're always saying—that your paintings never seem finished to you. I've been thinking lately that maybe it's because you spend so much of your energy deadening your anger at your parents—"

"You think my work's adolescent?"

I closed my eyes and pressed the heels of my hands against my lids, suddenly dizzy with exhaustion. "That's not what I meant, and you know it. I'm so tired right now, I don't know what I'm talking about. I need some sleep. We can talk later."

"No, goddammit, finish what you started! I want a few things clarified right now before Al calls and you go waltzing out of here for a couple of days. Like who's this Alex person who keeps leaving messages on your answering machine?"

"Since when did you start checking my answering machine?"

"Since I went over to your place today to see if you'd left word about where you'd gone. I wasn't sure how to work the damned thing and it played back a bunch of old messages."

"You know perfectly well who Alex is. He's Ann's friend—the guy in the music business who's going to help Sam."

"So how come he only calls your place, never here?"

"You think I'm seeing him behind your back?"

"You certainly aren't seein' much of *me*. I'm lucky if I run into you every couple of days."

"This is pretty bizarre in light of the fact that you're the one who's always saying no commitments, no ties—let's not fall in love and mess up our sex life. Five minutes ago, when you thought I was pregnant, you acted like an animal caught in a trap."

"That was about my freedom—my work. Not about us."

"Isn't freedom what you're always saying we're about?"

"Hey, Sar, I don't know what we're about anymore," he said, his voice cracking with emotion. He sank onto a chair. "Lately, even when you're here, you're not really here."

"It's because I've been preoccupied by my mother. It's been driving me crazy. Al's been complaining about the same thing—"

"Hey, speaking of Al, I've got a great idea," he cut in. "I've been thinking that since you're spendin' so much time in your office, you ought to stick a futon next to your desk and start calling *that* home."

"Are you serious? You really want me to move out of here?"

"You may not have noticed it, Sarah, but you already have."

Chapter Thirteen

I dropped my clothes in a soggy heap and started wandering around my living room, reacquainting myself with my things. It had been years since I'd lived there full-time, the place was dusty and neglected. I knocked a spiderweb from the corner of the bookcase and trailed my fingers across my desk, letting them linger on the carved jade bottle my former boyfriend Raj had given me. The bottle was a bittersweet reminder of the summer we'd lived together when he'd named my apartment Little India because of the way the sun poured in all day. Thinking this, the apartment suddenly felt stifling. I went into the bedroom, opened all the windows, set my small fan on the trunk I used as a night table, and flopped onto the bed. As soon as I shut my eyes, the air smelled like someone was baking a cake, but I was probably half-asleep and dreaming about living with Stoddard over the bakery because when I woke up the next morning, the cake smell was gone and I was lying naked and listless in the heat, feeling as disoriented as a traveler who falls asleep in one continent and wakes up in another.

Eugenia Lydia Forrest.

I sat up with a start, suddenly remembering my plan to take the subway out to Ozone Park so I could check out my grandparents. The thought overwhelmed me. I sank back onto the mattress, too exhausted to get out of bed, much less make an expedition to Queens. I lay there for a while, then reached for the phone intending to call information to see if my mother was listed in any of the boroughs. When the dial tone buzzed in my ear, I decided it was a waste of time to look for her this way. Even if she happened to live in New York, she'd be listed under her married name. And anyway, I had to settle things with Stoddard, stabilize my life before I could involve myself in a complicated search. I put the receiver down and fell back to sleep.

The next time I woke up, I was light-headed and dizzy. I hadn't eaten much in the past day or two, so I forced myself out of bed and into the kitchen and ate some tuna straight from the can, vaguely wondering if its strange bitter taste meant it was contaminated with botulism. I began contemplating my death with surprising calm. Stoddard would feel guilty, of course: My death would rest heavily on his conscience.

Somewhat cheered by this thought, I went in for a shower. But when I came out of the bathroom and found a terse message from him on my machine asking when (not if) I was coming over to pick up my stuff, my mood darkened again. Was he in such a hurry to get me out of his life that he couldn't spare a few minutes for a single powwow?

I didn't call him back.

I dragged myself to class. When I returned home, I was surprised and pleased to see Stoddard slumped over my dining table looking ragged around the edges. I brewed a pot of Red Zinger to pep us up and silently congratulated myself for having had the foresight to change the sheets on my bed. Or would we end up at his place?

As things turned out, I needn't have worried about the setting for our reconciliation. Three sentences into our tea party and we were back to arguing about my search. Some ugly things were said, charges were leveled. In a heated exchange, I accused him of being childish and insensitive, he called me a masochistic workaholic and then left. The fight escalated on the phone the next day and by the time I hung up, I knew we weren't going to patch things together this time. I waited until I was sure he'd left for work and then slipped over to his place and packed as much of my stuff as I could fit into a suitcase and three giant shopping bags. When I finished, I took a last survey of the place and my eyes fell on his red suspenders hanging from the back of a chair. I faltered. Why was I giving up on him so quickly? Surely he'd cool down in a day or two and we'd be able to talk things over calmly, rationally. But then I remembered a few of the uncharitable remarks he'd made the night before and I sat down on my overflowing suitcase to snap it shut.

I was out of there for good.

By the time I settled into my place, summer had begun in earnest, and with the warm weather came an unexpected tidal wave of new students, most of them Russian, all of them ambitious. My already-crowded classes nearly doubled in size and I was besieged by people who needed private tutoring, which solved my budget problem (I'd almost forgotten how much more expensive it was to live singly than à deux), but which created a time squeeze. My life took on a triangular shape: I ran from the classroom to my office to my apartment and back again, too busy and frazzled to brood much about Stoddard or my mother.

And oddly enough, now that I possessed my mother's name, my mania to find her weakened. Not that it disappeared entirely, of course. Late at night, I'd sometimes take out the piece of paper Sophie had given me and study it as if it were the Rosetta stone of my life, silently vowing to renew the search as soon as my workload eased up. But what was the hurry? I'd made it through thirty-five years without her; I could certainly wait another few weeks to introduce myself.

At the end of August, Sam threw a party in his studio to celebrate his third year in business, an event I'd been dreading since Nina first mentioned it to me. Making cocktail chitchat at big noisy parties was my least favorite activity, and I always felt particularly dull and dowdy around Sam's hipper-than-thou rock and roll crowd.

To make matters worse, Nina had let fly that Alex was going to show up (albeit late in the evening after attending some black-tie business dinner) and my feelings about him were very murky. I couldn't deny that I found the man attractive—he'd been barging into my sex fantasies with an alarming frequency of late—but he made me extremely nervous. From our past encounters, I knew I couldn't trust myself around him, and I was too fatigued from having left Stoddard to add any extra agitation to my already flying-apart life. So my game plan for the evening was to show up early, congratulate Sam and Nina, mingle with the hordes for a bit, and slip out before Alex arrived.

I milled around the steamy studio checking out weird hairstyles and body jewelry, creative tattooing and imaginative makeup. The sound system was committing ear-rape, but the marijuana smoke was so dense I was enjoying a contact high, which sort of evened things up. Out of the corner of my eye, I caught sight of a tall, slender man in evening clothes standing with his back to me. His hair was much longer than I remembered Alex's being, but I didn't want to take any chances so I crossed to the other side of the room and burrowed into a cluster of people, realizing too late that the small group included Stoddard.

"Hey, Sar," he said, grinning broadly when he saw me.

I quickly took in the fact that his arm was casually draped around the shoulders of a woman who looked vaguely familiar. From the way he was stroking her long pumpkin-colored hair, I guessed they were sleeping together and was shot through with a surprising pang of jealousy.

"You remember Miriam, don't you?" Stoddard drawled. "You all met at her show last year at Mack's gallery—the wall hangings, remember?"

I did remember. I recalled, too, that during my short conversation with Miriam she had referred to herself as a fiber artist, not a weaver, and that Stoddard and I had agreed afterward that she was extremely pretentious.

"So, how're things goin'?" he asked, giving me a sly, seductive little smile. I could see he was thinking sex, but with which one of us?

"I'm fine," I said airily.

"You're lookin' good. That shirt's a real eye popper."

I laughed at his Texas-ism, trying to discern whether his voice registered any genuine regret or he was just signaling that he wanted a truce. He hadn't called me since we'd split up. But then, of course, I hadn't called him, either. And now there was Miriam.

"As you know, this shirt's a versatile piece of clothing," I answered, sure from his expression that he, too, was thinking back to the time we'd used it as a blanket in the woods. I'd had my period then, and blood and semen had added to its decorative embroidery.

"Nice seeing you again, Sarah," Miriam said, giving Stoddard's arm a not-so-subtle tug.

"Just a sec," Stoddard said, his eyes glinting. "I want to know if Sarah's still runnin' after her mother."

"And I want to know if Stoddard is still running away from his," I answered, smiling sweetly as I strode off.

I joined a group of Nina's academic colleagues, trying not to notice that my short interchange with Stoddard had left me feeling thoroughly depressed. Not that I wanted him back in my life again in a serious way. We didn't fit together the way we once had, and there wasn't anything either of us could do about it. Nevertheless, the image of Stoddard and Miriam meshed like two pieces of a jigsaw puzzle remained in my mind's eye like a tiny piece of grit that was more irritating than it should have been.

"Aha! Found you at last," Sam said, suddenly appearing at my side with a fancy camera slung around his neck. "Come on," he said, seizing my elbow and whisking me toward the door, "I want to take a snapshot of you for posterity. You've been so reclusive this summer, Nina and I are worried we're going to forget what you look like," he added with a mad cackle.

"What are you high on, Sam?" I asked as he led me through a maze of corridors and down a deserted hallway into his office.

"Success!" he roared, sitting down behind a slick black Formica desk. "Check out the thickness of the carpet."

I kicked off my shoes and walked across the plush broadloom to the oversize sofa. "Is this your casting couch?" I asked, sinking onto the cushions. It was only then that I realized that I was more stoned than I'd noticed.

"Maybe it'll be my casting couch in my next life. In this life, I just sleep on it—alone—when we're having an all-nighter. You know, this place used to be a real shithole, but thanks to your friend Alex, I'm starting to upgrade. Seriously, Sar, he's been fantastic. He knows everyone in the biz."

"So, are you going to take my picture?" I asked, studiously ignoring his reference to Alex.

"Okay. Fluff up your hair and smile pretty for the snapshot," he said, positioning the camera in front of his face. "Oh damn," he said after a minute.

"What's the matter?"

"I'm out of film. Look, just stay where you are. Promise you won't leave?"

"Gladly. I could use a little break from the noise pollution."

"I'll be back in a jiffy," he called out over his shoulder.

I thumbed absently through a trade magazine inexplicably named *Destination: Destiny*, trying to make sense out of articles on woofers and tweeters and digital sound systems. When I heard footsteps in the hallway, I tossed the magazine back onto the table, but it wasn't Sam who came through the doorway, it was Alex. I threw a sharp look in the direction Sam had fled, but by then, of course, he was nowhere in sight. Obviously, I'd been set up.

"Don't look at *me* like that," Alex said with an apologetic laugh. "This was Sam's idea."

Feeling like a cornered animal, I greeted him with a limp smile, meant to discourage. "Actually, I've been meaning to call you—to thank you for helping Sam," I said feebly. In fact, I'd been feeling guilty as hell for *not* calling him, but hadn't wanted to provoke any interaction between us.

He responded with a modest wave of his hand. "I didn't do much for him."

"That's not what he says."

"Sam exaggerates. All I did was put him in touch with a

couple of people I know, and he did the rest. He has a good product."

I watched him undo his bow tie and open the top button of his dress shirt. A few dark hairs escaped and curled over the edge of his collar. I'd forgotten how attractive he was, and how libidinous I became around him.

"Actually, if anyone should be grateful for the introduction, it's me," he said. "You were right about Sam being talented. I've learned a lot from him. In fact, we've decided to work on a project together." He walked over to the sofa and stood in front of me.

"So Nina tells me," I said, gazing up at him uneasily.

"And Nina tells me you're not living with Studly anymore," he said, shifting his tone.

As a response, I jumped to my feet, expecting him to step out of the way. But he held his ground so that we were now standing only inches apart. "You know, speaking of Nina, I really should find her and say hello. . . ."

"It's too noisy in there. Why don't we go someplace quiet for a drink."

"You know I don't drink."

A shadow of impatience crossed his face. "Lemonade, if you prefer. Or you could come back to my apartment."

"I appreciate the invitation, but I don't want to insult Sam by leaving so early."

"I wouldn't worry about Sam. It was his idea. . . . Look, Sarah, I know you're a very skittish woman, but before you run off, I want to tell you something."

He gently took hold of my shoulders and pushed me

back onto the sofa. Then he sat down next to me, so close I could smell his lemony aftershave lotion.

"Despite what you may think, I'm not in the habit of chasing around after women trying to seduce them. My behavior with you has been entirely out of character. But I—well, I don't fall in love often or easily, but it happens fast."

"Love?" I said in surprise. "You barely know me."

"It's not anything rational, it's a feeling from the gut."

"It's sex, Alex, and it originates in a different part of your anatomy—and mine."

"Yes, exactly."

He leaned over and kissed me, gently at first and then more insistently. I fully intended to push him away but found myself kissing him back. Very enthusiastically. He was talented, inventive. We became a tangle of arms and legs, and slowly sank back onto the cushions. I was melting, spreading out toward him . . .

"Come home with me. We'll have more privacy," he whispered as he slid his hand beneath my skirt and up my thigh.

"I don't think so," I said huskily. But I didn't pull away. It was as if there were two of me—one person participating, the other observing us with detachment while running a commentary: Now you're kissing him. Now you're biting his lips. His right hand is making a foray into your panties . . .

"What if someone walks in here?" I asked, suddenly picturing Stoddard standing in the doorway watching us.

"I locked the door," he murmured, sliding his other hand under my blouse and caressing my breasts. Then somehow my bra and blouse were off, and he was slipping out of his shirt. His chest hair felt feather-soft against my breasts as he lay down again, a new sensation after Stoddard's hairlessness. There was a pantherlike languorousness, a smoothness to his movements that I found irresistible. I struggled to remember whether I had any condoms in my purse. I knew I had to make a decision. But my body had already made a decision on its own and was spinning completely out of control even as my head desperately tried to jam on the brakes. *Okay, so the sex is going to be great*, the voice in my head warned. *But then what? Sex with this man is just the beginning of a trip, and you're not in the mood to travel. . . .*

I grabbed his wrist and pulled his hand away from my body. His skin felt hot to the touch. I glanced at his watch, surprised to see how long we'd been at it.

"Do you want to continue this at my house or yours?" he panted.

I shook my head. "That's not it."

"I have condoms—"

"No."

"What, then?"

I let go of his hand. "I don't think this . . . unseemly grappling is a good idea," I answered in an absurdly schoolmarmish voice.

"This what?"

I slid my body out from under his and sat up. "I mean having sex. I don't think it's a good idea."

"Which one of us are you trying to convince?"

"You. I'm already convinced."

"You sure had me fooled," he said, in a voice tinged with anger.

"I'm sorry." I shivered and reached for my blouse, buttoning it slowly. "I didn't mean for this to happen. I shouldn't have kissed you like that. I'm very . . . vulnerable to kissing. And also you seem to have this peculiar effect on me. Every time I'm with you, I feel like I'm getting ahead of myself, and I panic. Maybe it's pheromones or something, but I act crazy around you. I'm not usually like this."

He gave me a hard look. "You send me very mixed signals. I find it confusing."

"Actually, it's simple. My body says yes and my head says no. I've decided to vote with my head."

"Is this because you're still involved with Stoddard?"

"No. Stoddard and I are just friends—nothing more."

"What, then? Do you find me repellent?"

"How can you ask me that?" I said, giving him a slanted look.

"Because I'm partial to the truth. It saves time."

I stared down at the floor as if it had the answer. "No. Yes. I mean, obviously, I don't find you physically repellent. Quite the opposite. That's sort of the problem. You're too intense for me. Or rather, I'm too intense around you. That's why having sex tonight wouldn't be a good idea. I mean, it would have been fine if I thought we were going to be casual about it. But I don't think it would turn out like that and I can't handle any serious involvements right now. Is this making any sense?"

"Are you sure it's not Stoddard?"

"It doesn't have anything to do with Stoddard. I just need to be on my own for a while. It was happening before I moved out of his place—it's *why* I left . . . I can't really explain it except to say that my edges feel blurry."

He pulled on his shirt without saying anything. "Sam's worried," he said after a long pause.

"I thought the studio's on its feet now—"

"No, I mean he's worried about you. He says you've been so depressed, you've cut yourself off from everyone."

"Sam exaggerates. You said it yourself. I'm just busy with my students. Distracted by . . . other things."

"Such as?"

I took a deep breath. "Sam and Nina don't know any of this, but I've been thinking a lot about my family, and I've decided to do some research."

"Really?" he said, looking surprised. "How far have you gotten?"

"I have my mother's name and address. Or rather, her former address—you know, where she grew up. The thing is, I haven't had time to follow up on it."

"Why don't you hire a professional to help you?"

I shook my head. "Too expensive."

"Not necessarily. I know a retired detective who loves this kind of work and doesn't charge much. I could give you his number."

"No thanks. I'd rather take care of it myself."

"How long have you had her name?"

"Three, maybe four months."

"But you're afraid to meet her?"

"No, of course not. I've been incredibly busy at work this summer and just haven't had time to get to it."

He continued to study me for a moment, an odd smile playing across his lips. "I understand perfectly. . . . Well, I guess you want to get back to the party now," he said briskly as he got to his feet.

I felt like we'd been playing tug-of-war and he'd suddenly let go of his end of the rope. I knew I should have felt victorious, but I was left feeling completely off balance instead.

"I don't blame you for being angry," I said miserably.

"I think *disappointed* would be a better word."

"You're disappointed in me?"

"It's not you, it's the situation. You see, I'm quite willing to compete with Stoddard or some other man, but I won't compete with your ghosts. In my experience, ghosts always win, hands down. It's never even a contest."

With that, he grabbed his jacket and walked out, leaving me in the room all alone, listening to the distant throbbing of the party's hip-hop music.

Part Three

Chapter Fourteen

The winter day was peculiarly bright; the sun cast a harsh and unforgiving light on the row of shabby attached two-story houses. I stood in front of my mother's childhood home suffering a dark and terrible longing for everything I hadn't had and would never have.

It was the moment I'd been putting off for months.

I kicked at a pile of dead leaves and tried to picture my mother as a little girl jumping rope and roller-skating on this very sidewalk, but the only child I could conjure up was myself—a shy skinny girl, self-protective and obedient to a fault.

I forced myself up the front walk.

"Wha' you wan'?" a man with a heavy Spanish accent asked, opening the door a crack.

"Do the Forrests still live here?" I asked, peering over his shoulder into the living room. All I could make out was the bluish glow of a television screen.

"No more here."

"Do you know where they've moved to?"

"You ask the lady across street, maybe she know."

Slam.

I clenched my fists into two tight balls and jammed them into my coat pockets as I crossed the slushy street, thinking that my grandparents had probably moved away years before any of these neighbors moved in.

"I'm looking for the Forrests," I told the eye staring at me through the peephole.

The door was flung open by an old woman whose sharp look made it obvious that her business was knowing everyone else's. "They're up there," she said, pointing to her ceiling.

For a split second, I thought she meant my grandparents were boarders in her house, then with a pang realized what she was telling me.

"Happened after they sold to them Spanish across the street and moved to Miami. The way I heard it, Ellie went first in a car accident, Martin soon after from a stroke. Now it's cuchifrita music playing day and night, driving the whole neighborhood crazy."

"Wh-what about Eugenia?"

"Who?"

"Their daughter. Did she move to Miami with them?"

"Oh, no. She stayed behind and took over their jewelry store." She compressed her lips and shook her head as if thinking about some tragedy. I steeled myself for the story: a fatal car accident, a brain tumor, cancer.

"Still burns me up the way she don't bother with them for years, then somehow finagles the shop out of 'em when they retire. And believe me, the place is a gold mine."

"Do you have any idea where it is?"

"I know exactly where it is. It's over in New York, on Broadway, maybe Ninety-eighth, Ninety-ninth Street. I used to take the bus in all the time before the legs went on me. If you see her, don't forget to tell her Doris Petchky's coming in one of these days for a new watch."

I took the subway back to Manhattan and ran the two blocks up to Ninety-eighth street. At the corner, I stopped to scan the row of stores and catch my breath. The only jewelry shop in sight was the run-down place across the street with a ripped and saggy awning, a sign with missing letters (GO D JEW RY), and filthy windows. My spirit sank. What sort of shopkeeper would arrange a broken clock next to a WE REPAIR WATCHES sign? Was my mother stupid? Incompetent? Lazy?

With a sinking sensation in the pit of my stomach, I crossed Broadway and approached the window. Cheap jewelry sat on a dusty blue velvet cloth; the display signs were faded and speckled with dirt. I shaded my eyes and looked through the glass. A woman was sitting behind the counter reading a magazine.

My mother!

My heart slammed in my chest, my left leg started twitching in an uncharacteristically violent way. I craned my neck to see more of her, but a coatrack blocked my full view. Frantic to get a better look, I ignored my resolve to take things slowly and rang the bell. She looked up as if astonished to have a customer and buzzed me in. I took a deep breath and opened the door, then stood there gaping at her. Black eyes. Ski-jump nose. A broad overlipsticked mouth. Blue-black hair teased into a puff on her head. Crimson Fu Manchu nails. My heart shriveled with disappointment. We looked nothing alike.

"Can I help you, hon?" she asked, closing her magazine and smiling vacuously. Her yellowish teeth pointed inward as if pigeon-toed.

"I'm . . . just looking," I answered in a whispery voice. I could barely breathe.

"Well, I hate to rush you, but Artie—my hubby—he's pickin' me up soon, and he's very impatient," she said, punctuating her sentence with a giggle. "Need an idea for a gift, or is it something for yourself?"

"It's a . . . gift," I managed to answer, feeling as if I were dreaming. I couldn't believe I was actually talking to my mother. My mother! I squinched my eyes and tried to picture her as a college student. She must have been pretty in a kittenish sort of way, with a hint of wild sex behind that ridiculous giggle. She'd been Ruth's opposite, and my father hadn't been able to resist. So what if she pronounced *idea* as if it had an *r* at the end? Sex wasn't a spelling bee.

"How about a pair of earrings?" she suggested, motioning for me to join her at the counter.

Slowly, I walked over to her. She was so heavily made-up, she looked like she was wearing a mask.

"We'll start with the cut glass and work our way up expense-wise," she told me as she took out what looked like two pieces of rock candy from the showcase. "I know they're a little young-looking, but girls'll always be girls." She giggled again.

Who would I have turned out to be if she'd raised me? I wondered, pretending to inspect the earrings. My clothes, my room, my mind would have been pink and frilly. I'd have grown up obsessed with fashion and jewelry and hairstyles. I'd probably have married my goonish high-school boyfriend instead of going to college . . .

"What type's this friend of yours, glamorous or brainy?" she asked, shaking her arm to untangle the mass of gold bracelets on her wrist. "Bet she's something like you," she said, giving me an appraising look.

I stiffened under her scrutiny. I knew how she'd see me: a pale plain woman, not particularly young and doing nothing to hide it. *Don't you recognize me?* I wanted to cry out. *Don't you recognize my father in my face? Are you blind? Stupid? Have you completely forgotten me?*

"You're the natural type—a teacher or psychologist, right?"

"A teacher."

"I thought so. I got a fifth sense about this kind of thing. . . . So what do you think of these for your friend?" she asked, pointing to a pair of double-hoop earrings the size of Christmas tree ornaments.

"They're not . . . what I had in mind," I stammered.

You're not what I had in mind, either, I thought. *Well, who'd you expect to find in a tacky jewelry store—Susan Sontag?* a voice in my head mocked.

"Ah, you girls with your no makeup and straight hair, you need a little pizzazz. Come on, try 'em on. I swear I won't report you to the department of serious."

Before I could protest, she leaned toward me and hooked the hoops onto my ears. She was so close, I could smell her sickeningly sweet perfume, see the line where her makeup ended on her neck. A smudge of mascara ran beneath her eye.

She stepped back and studied me critically. "You look like a different person."

I gazed at myself in the mirror. She was right. I did look different—a cross between a gypsy fortune-teller and a call girl. Just like her.

"Nah, they're not for you," she said after a minute.

"Oh, but I want them," I told her, still studying my reflection. I knew the earrings looked ridiculous. They even sounded ridiculous, tinkling loudly each time I moved my head. But the idea of buying something completely unsuitable from my mother gave me a perverse and inexplicable satisfaction. It was like seeing my double—the person I'd have been if she'd been my mother.

"We got plenty other earrings. You could do much better—"

"No, really, these are perfect," I insisted.

She opened the cash register to ring up the sale. I gazed at
the picture of a baby taped to the wall over her head.

"My son's kid," she explained. "Only nine months old,
but already he's a little pistol."

Would I ever get to meet my half brother? He probably
didn't know I existed. My sudden appearance would set a
bomb off in my mother's life. And in my life, too. Was it
worth it? Did I really want to saddle myself with this
clown, this fool—a woman I'd be embarrassed to introduce
to friends? Meet my mother, the aging sex kitten. Then I bit
the inside of my cheek so hard I tasted blood as shame
washed over me for being such a snob.

"Here, I'll show you another picture of the baby—"

"The customer came in for jewelry, not to hear your life
story," a woman's voice boomed from the back of the store.

"My boss don't like I should get too friendly with the customers," she whispered, handing me my change.

"Y-your boss? Aren't you Eugenia?"

"Who?"

"Eugenia Forrest—the owner."

"Nah, I'm Arlene Martino. Jeanne's back there. See, people come in, they want a little glamour, that's me. They got
a gripe, that's her."

I seized the glass countertop and slumped onto the
leather stool, dizzy with relief.

"Something wrong, hon?"

"No, nothing," I murmured, staring into the office. The door was partially shut; all I could make out was the silhouette of a woman sitting in a haze of smoke.

"Do you—could I use your bathroom?" I asked shakily.

"Jeanne don't like no strangers going near the vault."

I'm not a stranger—I'm her daughter!

"I think I'm going to be sick. . . ."

"Okay, okay, I'll give it a whirl." She hurried to the rear of the store and wedged into the office sideways as if afraid of opening the door any wider.

"Something wrong, miss?" the gravelly voice called out a moment later.

I walked toward her, squinting against the glare of the overhead lights. My knees felt like they might buckle under me. When I reached the office, I leaned against the door frame for support as I stared at the small, heavyset woman with pixieish dark hair, badly pitted skin, and a deeply lined face. I was crushed. I didn't look anything like her, either! But then she twisted around in her chair to look me over and I saw her eyes—pale green eyes exactly like mine—and my heart turned over.

"Bathroom's over there," she said, gesturing to the other side of the room. "Listen, Harry," she barked into the phone, "I've had it with your crappy sob stories. No tickee, no shirtee."

The bathroom stank of soggy paper towels and cigarettes. An overflowing ashtray sat beneath a yellowed sign.

DOG AND HUSBAND MISSING

$.25 REWARD FOR RETURN OF DOG

I bent over the chipped enamel sink and splashed water on my face to cool down.

When I emerged, she was hunched over a ledger, scowling at the figures. I stood so close to her, I could have reached out and touched her shoulder, but she pretended not to notice me. Her foot was jiggling beneath the desk the way mine did when I was impatient or angry.

"Feeling better, hon?" Mrs. Martino asked from the doorway.

Her genuine warmth was such a contrast to Jeanne's gruff manner, I almost wished she *had* turned out to be my mother after all. Okay, so she wore a few pounds of eye makeup and an ankle bracelet. At least she was kind. But, of course, being who she was, she'd never have given up her baby in the first place.

"Want to see some more earrings?" she asked, escorting me out of the office.

"Maybe another time—when I'm feeling better," I told her. My eyes strayed toward the back of the store. To my surprise, Jeanne was watching me. Our eyes locked for a moment, and then, as if worried I might disturb her again, she extended her leg and kicked the office door shut.

Chapter Fifteen

Still reeling from the shock of seeing Jeanne, I made my way downtown and somehow managed to make it through class without breaking down, but by the time I got home, I was a wreck. Anger, disappointment, bitterness, curiosity—an overwhelming tangle of feelings roiled inside me as I crumpled onto my rocking chair and began sorting it all out.

At least she wasn't a junkie or a shopping bag lady, I told myself. At least she was sane, stable. . . . But now that my fantasies had fallen in on themselves, I had to face facts: She was an awful little woman—nasty, hostile, angry—exactly the sort of person I always steered clear of, and I knew instinctively that trying to connect with her would be like slamming my head against a brick wall.

Now what? Should I write to her? Call her? Go back to her store? But did I even *want* to claim this woman as my mother? Maybe Horton had been right when he'd told me to forget all about her and get on with my normal life. But what was so normal about a life based on a lie? And where had it led me? Here I was on the brink of middle age and all I'd accomplished so far was one minimarriage, a series of halfhearted relationships, a job that left me broke and exhausted at the end of each semester, and an almost-book no one wanted to publish.

I started pacing around my living room, trying to calm myself. Why was I judging her so quickly? Maybe she wasn't as horrid as she seemed. Maybe I'd just caught her at a bad moment on a bad day. It was stupid to make a decision until I found out more about her. But how could I do that without revealing my identity?

I stayed up half the night wracking my brains to develop a sensible plan, but by morning, the only thing I'd come up with was making a second trip to her store so I could watch her in action.

Mrs. Martino's smile wasn't quite as friendly this time, and Jeanne was nowhere to be seen. I browsed through the jewelry cases, lingering over a pearl necklace in the hopes that Jeanne would appear.

She never showed up.

I returned the following afternoon, trying not to show

my excitement when I spotted Jeanne sitting in the office talking to someone—or rather, shouting at him. I couldn't hear what they were arguing about, but I caught the word *lease* twice and guessed the visitor was her landlord. I asked Mrs. Martino to show me some rings, all the while keeping an eye on Jeanne, who never budged from her desk. Her visitor left and she shut the door. When I asked Mrs. Martino if Jeanne ever waited on customers herself, she gave me such an odd look, I knew she suspected me of being a shoplifter. At that point, I admitted to myself that my plan wasn't going to work. Frequent appearances in the shop would make both women suspicious of me, and in any case, shopping was no guarantee that I'd have further contact with Jeanne.

Then I remembered Alex's offer to put me in touch with his detective friend, and I began fumbling with the idea of hiring him to tail her. It was the logical thing to do—to let a professional find out who she was and report back to me— but it seemed so weirdly cold-blooded, I couldn't quite stomach it. And also, it meant calling Alex to get the detective's phone number, which presented a whole other set of complications I wasn't up for at the moment.

By the time the weekend rolled around, I was in a quasi-crazed state. On Saturday morning, I forced myself to follow my usual ritual of doing errands before going over to my office to tutor several students. By late afternoon, I was in the grips of such intense curiosity, I canceled my last appointment and took the subway uptown even though I knew the store would be closing any minute.

A major snowstorm had begun during my train ride, but

it was one of those show-off snowfalls with huge flakes that never add up to much. Even so, I was soaking wet inside and out by the time I stationed myself in the grimy alcove next to her doorway, holding a newspaper in front of my face and pretending to read while waiting to catch a glimpse of her. It wasn't much of a plan, but it was better than spending another evening moping around my apartment daydreaming about our possible reunion. Nancy Drew at work, I thought, tucking my hair under my knit hat and nervously fingering the hoop earrings that jangled in my ears like tiny warning bells.

The weak winter sun faded and disappeared, the temperature plummeted. My breath made fuzzy balloons in the air as I watched clerks at surrounding stores roll up awnings and lock up for the night.

No Jeanne.

I stomped my feet to keep warm and cursed inwardly for not having checked to see if she was inside before subjecting myself to frostbite. She might have gone home earlier in the day; she might not even work on Saturdays. I eyed the phone booth on the corner and was still debating with myself about making a dash for it when the door opened. In a panic, I sucked in my breath and flattened myself against the wall as Mrs. Martino emerged in a fake leopard-skin coat and trotted over to a double-parked car, driven, no doubt, by her impatient husband, Artie.

Before I'd fully recovered—I was practically hyperventilating by then—the store lights went out and it was Jeanne who was standing next to me on the sidewalk, standing so close that her cigarette smoke wafted past my face. Terrified she'd see me lurking in the shadows, I pulled farther back into the alcove and waited a few moments before peering out to see if she'd left yet. She was still there, standing on her tiptoes, straining to grasp the just-out-of-reach handle of the overhead security gate. I imagined stepping out of my hiding spot, offering my assistance. She'd be grateful. I'd lead us into a casual conversation . . . Then I remembered that she'd barely been civil when she'd thought I was a customer; she'd never strike up a conversation with a total stranger.

She tossed away her cigarette as if she really meant business now and jumped into the air with surprising agility, this time managing to grab the handle. The gate came barreling down onto the pavement and landed with a horrible crash. Oblivious to the glares of startled passersby, she fastened the rusty lock, brushed off her hands, lit another cigarette, and took off down Broadway.

I plunged after her. When she stopped at a newsstand to buy a paper, I hung back, pretending to window-shop at a bagel bakery. At the corner bus stop, I hovered at the edge of the crowd, watching her skim the *New York Review of Books*. Inwardly I tallied her score: minus three for being curt and impatient and having a messy store; plus one for being literate. Mrs. Martino probably would have scored much higher.

I waited at the end of the line and boarded the bus, wedging into the aisle so I was only one row behind her seat. With some relief I noted that she wasn't as homely as I'd first thought. In fact, her features weren't unattractive at all. It was her taciturn expression that was so off-putting—the annoyance etched on her forehead, the angry mouth . . . I inched closer to get a better look at her, taking in the gold tassel earrings (classier than anything I'd seen in her store), suede shoes, perfectly groomed and polished nails. Obviously, her vanity resided in her extremities—hands, feet, ears—but she'd given up on her body entirely. Maybe because she'd never forgiven it for getting pregnant with me. Suddenly, I felt the urge to tap her on the shoulder and whisper my name in her ear. *I'm your daughter*, I imagined saying. She'd stare at me in shock, then would throw her arms around me and weep . . .

At Eighty-sixth Street she stood up and shoved her way to the front exit. I hurried to the rear of the bus and hopped off exactly when she did, but somehow lost sight of her on the crowded sidewalk. I ran halfway up the block and back down again but she seemed to have vanished. On a hunch, I ducked into the A&P, grabbed an empty cart, and began cruising up and down the aisles at high speed, finally spotting her in the fruit section. I came to a screeching halt and swung my cart around so fast, I left rubber marks on the linoleum. Grabbing a jar of pickles from the shelf, I pretended to read the label as I surreptitiously watched her toss apples and pears into her wagon without so much as a glance at their condition. I thought back to Ruth's grocery store expeditions, her merciless scrutiny of fresh fruit, her rejection of anything with even a microscopic blemish. She'd have deemed Jeanne careless and wasteful. A lazy homemaker, she'd have said disdainfully—the most damning thing she could say about any woman. My own slapdash style had puzzled and frustrated her and had provoked an endless stream of criticism that still resonated in my mind: Why don't you keep your books lined up on a shelf instead of scattering them around your room? Why can't you fold up your clothes instead of shoving them into drawers haphazardly? Why can't you close cabinet drawers, stack up newspapers neatly, shut off lights. And now, as I watched Jeanne, I wondered if I'd inherited my casual style from her. Could a trait like that travel through genes?

She moved on; I traipsed after her, analyzing her food selections as if they might reveal her darkest secrets. The steak told me she was no vegetarian. The ham said she wasn't an orthodox Jew. White bread and diet soda showed an indifference to nutrition. Ritz Crackers, doughnuts, and Sara Lee cakes meant she was either planning a party or was a junkaholic. Again I thought of Ruth, whose painstakingly planned meals had been so wholesome and attractive, so nutritionally balanced. But what good had all her perfectionism in the kitchen been when I'd been too nervous to eat?

I followed Jeanne out of the supermarket and around the corner to a seedy apartment building at Eighty-fifth and Amsterdam. When she disappeared inside, I paced the sidewalk like an animal who's lost its prey, consoling myself with the thought that at least I'd found out where she lived. Or had I? Maybe this wasn't her apartment at all, maybe she was visiting someone.

The lobby reeked of thousands of dinners cooked and eaten over the years. Two Spanish-style chairs were chained to the wall like prisoners of the Inquisition. An ominous black-rubber mat led to the tenant directory. *Forrest J.—5B*.

I held my trembling finger over her buzzer, struggling against the urge to crash into her life. Why shouldn't she know I existed? Why shouldn't she know what I'd suffered because of her—what I was *still* suffering?

"Can I help you, miss?"

I whirled around and saw a man in a disheveled uniform staring at me curiously.

"Oh, I . . . I was just—a woman who lives here left something in the supermarket," I stammered.

"Oh, yeah? What she look like?"

"She's short, heavyset. Wearing a brown coat." *Abandoned a baby thirty-five years ago*, I added silently.

"Sounds like it could be a lot of the ladies in here," he said doubtfully.

"She's kind of somber. You know, doesn't smile much."

"Maybe it's Miss Forrest up on five. She never joke around. She been here longer than me and that's more than fourteen," he said, hitching up his trousers. "All the ladies, they call me Handy Andy. Always axing me to walk the dogs, water the plants when they go on vacation. But Miss Forrest, she got the only balcony on the fifth, but she don't got no pets. Just a bunch of cactus don't need no water. You want I should give the package to her?" he asked with a tip-me glint in his eye.

"No, no. I'll take care of it myself."

"Okay, baby, anything you want."

Outside, I counted up to the fifth floor and saw the narrow balcony—a ledge, really—wide enough for plants but not humans. Her place was probably a mess, just like her store. There'd be a rug dotted with cigarette burns. Lumpy uncomfortable furniture. Lamps with yellowed shades. A television on a metal stand. A stack of old *TV Guide*s piled next to a donkey-shaped ceramic planter . . . She was probably sitting in front of the TV at this very moment, chain-smoking and eating Ritz Crackers—suffering a bleak and lonely existence. I could change all that by ringing her doorbell and introducing myself . . . I closed my eyes and imagined her shocked expression when I said my name. She'd tell me she'd been searching for me for years and years. . . .

I opened my eyes, startled to see the real Jeanne coming out of her building with a tall man whose overcoat flapped around his bony frame like misshapen wings. I hurried after them, straining to hear snatches of their conversation. The man was saying something about Germany and France, Jeanne was nodding vigorously. Were they talking politics or planning a trip? Jealousy ate away at me like acid as I watched the dorky-looking man smile at her. How could this stranger have entrance into Jeanne's life when her own flesh-and-blood daughter didn't even exist for her?

At the corner, I watched them climb into a taxi and drive off. Suddenly, my arm was waving in the air and I was hailing my own taxi.

"Follow that car," I told the driver as I got in.

"Which one we after, lady?" he asked, shooting me a nervous glance in his rearview mirror.

"It's the cab behind the red truck, the one weaving through traffic. Over there in the right lane. Please hurry—I don't want to lose them!"

As we approached Forty-second Street, I took out my wallet and checked my supply of cash. Eleven dollars, not nearly enough if I had to follow them into a theater, not even enough for entry into a movie after I'd paid the cab fare. Maybe there was a cash machine nearby.... Brakes squealed, the cab shuddered to a sudden stop that sent me flying into the plastic barrier. I winced and rubbed my forehead as I watched their cab cut through the red light, careen around the corner, and disappear down the block.

I paid the driver and got out, barely aware of the icy wind lashing at my cheeks. By the time I trudged home, my toes and fingers were half-frozen, and the bump on my forehead had grown to the size of an egg. I scarfed down some scalding tea, wrapped myself in a blanket, and huddled on the radiator to warm up but couldn't stop shivering. I was chilled to my center, not just from the cold, but from a deep, aching loneliness, the kind of loneliness I'd never experienced before. I felt totally insignificant. Invisible. A microscopic piece of dust on the planet, drifting aimlessly, meaninglessly. No one felt deeply about me, no one cared. My own mother didn't even know I was alive.

I threw off the blanket and stalked into the kitchen to unearth the half-empty bottle of wine Stoddard had left months before. When I found it, I hugged it to my chest and carried it into bed with me. And then, without a moment's pleasure, I glugged it all down and passed into a deep dreamless sleep.

Chapter Sixteen

Civil war raged in my classroom.

Students shouted at me in a babble of twenty different languages as I peeled off my coat and shook snow out of my hair. I waited for the excitement to die down, but the noise only grew worse. Finally, I held up my hand for quiet.

"Okay, what's going on?" I demanded, directing an icy stare at Boris Rabitsky, the focal point of the storm.

"I make suggestion we discuss future plans tonight and they get upset," he explained with an innocent shrug that I suspected wasn't so innocent. Boris's frequent requests for fewer language lessons and more time spent on assimilation skills had engendered fierce, sometimes acrimonious debates in class.

"Better now learn correct read and write, worry for plans after educated!" Filossaint Terlegran yelled angrily from his perch on the windowsill.

"But is good practice speaking while discuss future job," Mina Sattee called out, siding with Boris.

"Excuse please, what matter dream for future?" Mgwabe Ursa asked in his musical Ghanaian voice. "Today, I empty bedpans at hospital, maybe I be fired tomorrow. What good is dream to become doctor, for people like me?"

"Why you come to U.S. of A. if you have no dream?" Boris asked, looking exasperated. "You *must* have plan or spend whole life pushing broom. Might as well never left home!"

He bent down and pulled something out of the red-and-gold Bloomingdale's shopping bag he'd been carrying around as a briefcase since Christmas. He sat up again and waved a copy of a newspaper in the air. "My personal plan is become journalist," he announced, rolling *journalist* off his tongue slowly as if savoring it. "Already, I become reporter for *West Sider* newspaper."

"Sounds impressing but how accomplish?" Korn Wangserochin asked with the same fury that characterized all his comments. A bitter man from Thailand, he'd spent his first year in New York plagued by bad luck.

Boris turned to me. "You want I explain, Sarah?"

I stared at him without answering. What I *wanted* at that moment was to cancel class so I could go home and crawl into bed. My nerves were shot, I was totally spent from following Jeanne around town, which was what I'd been doing for the past week. The worst of it was that despite all my effort, I'd only managed to find out the most mundane facts about her—where she shopped for food, took her clothes to be dry-cleaned, et cetera—none of which had illuminated her soul. Whereas gleaning this meaningless information had all but wrecked mine. I no longer made dates with students or friends since I never knew where and when my surveillance operation would end, could barely even get to class on time, which was driving me crazy. At odd moments, I wondered if I already *was* crazy. Maybe I was in the middle of a nervous breakdown without noticing it.

I pulled my scattered thoughts together and nodded yes to Boris, not wanting to squelch his boundless enthusiasm. "But please make it short," I begged. "We have to go over last week's test papers tonight. And we also have to spend time planning our food-from-around-the-world dinner party."

"Okay, sure," he said, rubbing his hands together. "So, first step is continue live on uncle's sofa while save money from work at dry-cleaning store. Same time, keep volunteer at small newspaper to get experience. Already, I been interview many people in neighborhood, including owner of dry-cleaning store. When save enough money in few years, now to enroll in journalism school for degree. After finish, then starts job-hunting. Is plan possible or no, Sarah?" he asked, turning toward me again.

The class waited anxiously for my reaction but I was still having trouble focusing. The word *journalism* had triggered another reunion fantasy: I'd publish my book, Jeanne would see my photograph on the back cover and immediately recognize me. . . .

"Becoming journalist is impossibility!" Korn called out sharply.

"Not necessarily," I countered. "Journalism's a tough field to break in to, but I don't think it's impossible, especially for someone with a lot of energy and determination. . . . Boris, what kind of work did you do in Russia?"

"Work?" he answered with a derisive laugh. "In Russia we had big saying: They pretend to pay us, we pretend to work. That's reason whole country is in mess. Very bad place, especially for Jewish." He turned his head and spat lightly over his shoulder three times. "Tell you honest," he continued, "always from student days, I been interested in political aspects, especially of America. Of course, in Russia, I have no chance for self-expressing, because number one, I have Jewish problem, and number two, no newspaper interested in hiring me."

"But liking work no guarantee you be that job," Tika Ram cried out from the back row.

The argument heated up again, several people gave impassioned speeches, but only part of me was listening. Jeanne's dark face remained fixed in my mind's eye, her husky voice reverberated through my head, drowning out my students' voices. I stared at the newspaper Boris was still waving in the air as the glimmer of an idea began to take shape.

"Why the hell would you want to interview *me*?" Jeanne snorted when I showed up at her store the next day. "What is this, some real-estate scam?"

I forced my lips into what I hoped would pass for a smile and handed her the copy of the *West Sider* I'd borrowed from Boris. "We're interviewing local shopkeepers about the . . . changes in the neighborhood." My voice sounded brittle and false to my ears, the stage voice of a terrible actress.

As I sat down at her cluttered desk, I tried to appear casual and relaxed. How would a normal person behave in this situation? I asked myself as I took a deep breath. A normal person wouldn't be in this situation, I reminded myself.

She studied the newspaper, I studied her: scarred skin, fleshy jowls, cropped hair. She'd obviously had a hard life, and it showed in her face, but there was a sharp intelligence burning from her eyes and a feistiness in her manner that said she'd been through a lot but was still alive and kicking. Two points for Jeanne.

"Well, if it's gentrification you're talking about, I'm an expert. Hippies, yippies, yuppies, nimbys—I've seen 'em all come and go. Now we're getting the inchies." Ashes dropped onto her black tent dress but she didn't seem to notice. Nor did she notice I'd been waving smoke out of my eyes for the past few minutes. I added insensitive and inconsiderate to my list of indictments against her.

"Who are the inchies?" I asked, resting my briefcase on her desk next to the remnants of a McDonald's lunch. How could she work with so much garbage piled up around her? the Ruth part of me wondered.

"Made up the acronym myself. Interested in nature, children, health, Indians, and ecology—inchies." She laughed and then stopped abruptly, tilting her head back and staring at me intently. "You know, you look familiar. You live around here?"

Blood pounded in my ears. "No, but I'm . . . I'm a customer. I bought these earrings from you—well, actually, from Mrs. Martino—a few weeks ago."

"You sure Columbia's not trying to squeeze us out so they can gobble up the whole block?" she asked, fishing a piece of tobacco off her tongue and studying it for a minute before flicking it away.

"Oh no, really, this has nothing to do with Columbia or real estate. It's just a . . . an attempt to—" I paused. "To get to know you better."

"Been a reporter long?"

"I'm not really a reporter. I just work at the paper part-time . . . as a sort-of volunteer. I'm actually an English teacher."

"Well, don't get too comfortable," she warned as she stuffed a pile of invoices into a drawer. "Store's closing in four minutes. I never stay past six."

"Are you going to be here tomorrow?"

"Nope. I'll be at a trade show the rest of the week."

"But . . . an article like this would be such great publicity for you—and it won't cost you a dime."

Interest flickered on her face. She took a long drag on her cigarette, mulling over my offer. I stared at the tiny scar cutting across one of her eyebrows. The product of a childhood accident—maybe a fall from a bike—or from something that had happened to her as an adult? I suddenly felt the hopelessness of the situation. We were two lifetimes apart. There was no way I could cover the distance between us.

"Anyone actually read this paper?"

"A few thousand people see it. It's distributed free to all the local buildings."

"Yeah, maybe I should give you a couple of minutes. Free publicity's an offer I can't afford to refuse. . . . What'd you say your name is?"

"Sarah," I answered in a whispery voice, praying she wouldn't ask for my last name. I wanted to stick as close to the truth as possible so if I decided to tell her who I was, she wouldn't think I was a liar.

"I guess you want a little background material on me. . . . Okay, I grew up in Ozone Park, Queens—real glamorous," she said with a grimace. "Why don't you just say I'm a New Yorker through and through, that's why I know the right jewelry for sophisticated clientele—" She stopped talking and frowned. "Aren't you taking any notes?"

"Right," I said, opening my briefcase and pulling out my notebook and pen. My hands were shaking so hard, I looked palsied, but she didn't seem to notice. Or maybe she did notice but chalked it up to my being a novice. I hunched over my notebook and pretended to jot down a few sentences, keeping the pad close to my chest so she wouldn't see my illegible scribble. I wasn't interested in facts at the moment; I just wanted to watch her facial expression when she talked about the past.

"—was a mixed bag," she was saying. "I guess you could say I'm a hundred percent mutt. My father was Swiss, my mother was half-French, half-Italian."

"Sounds very international," I murmured, picturing my

grandfather in lederhosen, my grandmother stirring a huge pot of pasta.

"Hardly," she snorted. "When my parents eloped to America, both families wrote 'em off and wouldn't have anything to do with them. Since I was their only kid, it wasn't much of a family."

It was more of a family than you gave me! I accused silently, as she reached for a half-empty pack of cigarettes.

"What else you want to know?" she asked, lighting up and inhaling deeply. She didn't seem to be able to last for more than a few minutes without a cigarette.

"Have you always lived in New York?"

"Yeah, pretty much. Years ago, I moved out to Southern California, but I couldn't stomach those phonies—always guzzling imported water, smiling each other to death. Blech. It was the pits. New York ain't beautiful, but at least it's real. Know what I mean?"

I gave her a weak smile, wondering what she'd think of me if she found out *I* was a phony. "Uh . . . so, how'd you get started in the jewelry business?"

She blew two perfect smoke rings and watched them drift away before answering. "This was my parents' store originally, and when they retired, I took over. It wasn't what I'd planned to do with my life, but it's what *they'd* always planned for me."

"What had you wanted to do?"

"The store's small, but I've got a tremendous inventory," she said, ignoring my question. "Plus, I can order anything on a week's notice."

"Was there one particular subject you wanted to—"

"We also do beautiful custom work in gold and silver. Engraving's free on orders over twenty-five bucks."

I hesitated. Her tone wasn't exactly hostile, but an edge had crept into her voice, and I knew if I pushed too hard, she'd push back—maybe even end the interview.

"What about your education?" I asked cautiously.

"What about it?"

"Did you go to college?"

"CUNY. The best bargain in town in those days."

Liar! I thought, leaning over my notebook so she couldn't see my expression.

"Never got to grad school, but I've kept at it on my own," she explained, reaching behind her and unlocking a floor-to-ceiling metal cabinet. The doors swung open to reveal shelves crammed with textbooks, magazines, journals.

Just like in my apartment!

"Surprised, huh?" she said, her angry expression softening for the first time. She looked almost pretty now that she was smiling. I could even see a glimmer of the dimpled girl she must have been. Betty Boop, Horton had called her.

"I'll tell you something funny. I read so much as a kid, my parents hid books from me, if you can believe it. I spent most of my allowance on flashlight batteries so I could read in bed after they'd shut my light. Not exactly the most progressive people, my parents, especially when it came to educating girls. . . . Maybe you should play this up in the article—not the part about my parents, but that I'm a big reader. You know, you could say something like my shop's well suited to intellectuals and that's why I give a ten percent discount to students and professors from City or Columbia. . . . Here, I'll show you a brochure."

While she searched through her drawers, I scanned the titles in the cabinet and felt a jolt of recognition. The books were mostly history texts—American history. Nineteenth century. Civil War. My father's century—my father's passion! Now I was getting somewhere.

"So . . . you must have been a history major in college."

"Here, you can keep this," she said, handing me a dog-eared brochure announcing a Christmas sale. She shut the cabinet doors and locked them again. "You might want to mention that we have seasonal sales going most of the year. I'll be doing a spring promotional around Passover and Easter."

Her foot was jiggling beneath the desk. I could see she wasn't going to last much longer, and I still hadn't made a decision about her.

"I just have a couple more quick questions," I said, feeling desperate. "Are you married?"

"Divorced."

I kept my eyes riveted on her face. "Any children?"

"Nope," she said without missing a beat.

Her answer was like a physical blow—a punch in the gut. If she'd blinked or hesitated even for a microsecond, I'd have felt better. But that she'd killed me off so completely sent a chill down my spine. My teeth started chattering like a pair of those plastic windup teeth in party stores.

Tell her who you are! a voice in my head screamed.

Don't get involved! a second voice warned.

"So I guess that's about it, Susan," she said, stubbing out her cigarette.

"Sarah," I corrected under my breath.

"When's this article going to appear, anyway?"

"I—I'm not sure."

"Don't forget to mention the fact that I do custom ordering."

I stood up slowly and put on my coat, fumbling with the buttons. My heart was beating so hard, I could feel it all over my body—in my hands, my legs, my chest. I took a final look at her and walked stiffly to the door.

My decision was made.

"Night, Susan," she called out.

I spun around to face her. "My name is *Sarah*. . . . And I'm . . ." I paused, then swallowed hard. My mouth had gone completely dry. "I'm not a reporter for the *West Sider*."

Her eyes grew round with incomprehension. "What is this, some kind of joke?"

My mouth opened and shut, but no sound came out. I could hear my voice in my head, but I didn't seem to have enough oxygen in my lungs to power the words. "I'm . . . I didn't plan to—there's no newspaper article, but everything else I told you is true. I guess I was hoping you'd recognize me."

No reaction.

"I was born in 1966."

Silence.

"My father was Phillip Bridges."

Her face was completely blank.

My mind raced back over the fragments of information

I'd learned from Horton and Sophie: My mother was Eugenia Forrest from Ozone Park, Queens. She was in her fifties. Her nickname was Jeanne. She was dark and petite. She had green eyes. Eyes that were exactly like mine.

"I wasn't planning to tell you tonight—wasn't sure I'd ever tell you. I've had your name for months, but I—I probably should have written or called first. . . ." My voice trailed off.

Her eyes remained fixed on me. I knew she had to be seeing my father's features—her own eyes reproduced on my face—but her expression was stony.

I burned with shame and confusion. It was like one of those terrifying nightmares when you're in danger but can't scream or run or grab on to anything solid. I don't know how long I stood there staring at her, but I finally gathered my wits and fished out a piece of scrap paper from my purse. Shakily, I wrote my address and held it out to her.

She didn't move.

I ripped the paper into tiny shreds and let them flutter to the floor. Then I left without saying another word.

Outside, I leaned over a garbage pail and was sick, heaving until there wasn't anything left in my stomach except bitter-tasting bile.

I didn't cry until I got home, but once I started, I couldn't stop. I wept as I got undressed and continued weeping as I sat in a hot bath. By the time I stopped, my tears had washed away all my feelings and I was numb. I stepped out of the water and stared at the shriveled skin on my hands and feet. I looked like I'd aged a hundred years.

Chapter Seventeen

A horrible buzzing noise cut into my peace. Without opening my eyes, I groped in semidarkness for the alarm clock and heaved it across the room with all my might, listening with satisfaction as it crashed against the bureau.

The buzzing continued.

I kicked through a tangle of sheets and cursed loudly, wide-awake now and aware that the sound was coming from my intercom. Thief, kook, or Al? I wondered, staggering out of bed.

"Who's there?" I yelled into the speaker.

"Jeanne," a voice yelled back.

I leaned my forehead against the wall without answering. My face felt raw and swollen, my throat hurt. Even my neck hurt from crying. The buzzer started up again a few seconds later, and with it came another sound I couldn't identify right away, a strange creaking noise. Then I realized it was coming from my own throat and I understood that something had snapped in me the night before. I no longer wanted to see or talk to her. I'd even lost my curiosity about her. I was worn-out, filled with regret that I'd turned myself inside out for such a bitter, cold, unspeakably cruel woman. Maybe she was crazy, too. Who but a crazy person would abandon her child twice in one lifetime?

The buzzing stopped, she'd finally given up. My body went limp with relief. She was probably relieved, too. Now she could go home with a clear conscience and tell herself that I'd rejected her. Which was fine with me: I'd had enough.

I'd almost made it back to bed when I heard a rapping noise.

"Sarah?" she called from the hallway. "It's me—Jeanne."

I continued tiptoeing toward the bedroom, inching my way along so the floorboards wouldn't creak.

"No use pretending you're not in there! I know you're home," she shouted as she pounded heavily on the door.

I heard another door open. Footsteps resounded in the corridor, there was a murmur of voices.

"You okay, Sarah?"

It was Archie Dugan, my overprotective next-door neighbor. I cursed under my breath and leaned against the wall, trying to decide what to do. Archie was a prosecutor in the sex crimes division of the D.A.'s office and saw potential danger lurking everywhere. Once, when Stoddard and I were rearranging my furniture late at night, we'd sent a large vase crashing onto the floor and Archie had thought we were having a violent argument and had called the police. I knew if he got nervous enough, he'd have twenty cops and a mob of firemen climbing in through the windows to rescue me.

"What's up, Sar?" he called again. "Anything wrong?"

"No, I'm perfectly fine, Arch," I answered, trying to sound perfectly fine. "You can get back on your treadmill now."

"Your mother wants to talk to you."

"Yes, I know, but I'd prefer not to talk to her right now."

"Why don't you open up and tell her yourself so she'll know you're okay?"

"Because I'd prefer not to," I answered. I was beginning to sound like Bartleby.

"I'm not leaving until I see her," Jeanne insisted.

Another door opened. "What's wrong with Sarah?" It was Mrs. Guggenheim, my elderly neighbor across the hall.

"She won't let her mother in," Archie explained in a hushed voice.

"Really? That doesn't sound like Sarah. She's always so friendly. Maybe we should call the police."

"That's what I'm thinking. . . . Sarah, just give us a hint about *why* you can't open up," he said in the careful voice people use on three-year-olds and lunatics.

"Because six in the morning is not an attractive time of the day for a fucking visit!" I shouted.

"She definitely sounds weird," he said to them. "I'm worried some perp's in there with her, maybe holding a gun to her head."

I gave up and yanked the door open, startling all three of them. Jeanne's face was puffy and gray. Pouches hung beneath her eyes. Her clothing was disheveled, her hair a mess.

"This is grotesque," I said to her.

"See, she's fine," Archie said, patting Jeanne's shoulder reassuringly.

"You inviting me in or are we going to have to settle things out here?" she asked with raised eyebrows.

"Not to worry, your audience is leaving." Archie tactfully took Mrs. Guggenheim's arm and escorted her across the hall before scooting into his own apartment.

"No wonder you're such a beanpole. It's from walking up all these stairs every day," Jeanne said as she gazed around at my apartment with undisguised curiosity.

I'd never felt such hatred for anyone in my life.

"See, I taped up all the ripped pieces," she said, taking a patched-up piece of paper out of her purse and waving it in the air like a white flag.

When I didn't say anything, she put the paper away and began fooling with the magnetic sculpture on my hall table, moving the tiny metal acrobats into a variety of positions.

"About last night," she began, glancing up at me almost shyly. "What I want you to know—the thing is, I've always been terrible with surprises. I freeze up when I'm shocked, sort of like a deer caught in a headlight. Sometimes I run in the wrong direction."

"I'd have thought thirty-five years was enough time to get used to having a daughter."

"I never had a daughter, I had a pregnancy. Last night was the first time I've ever laid eyes on you, and that's the God's honest truth!"

I released the door. It shut with a nasty bang.

"I couldn't sleep all night," she said, rubbing her eyes. "I was worried you'd take my reaction personally."

"Personally," I repeated, totally dumbfounded. This woman didn't have a clue about what the evening had cost me. If I hadn't been so heartsick just then, I'd have laughed in her face.

"Like I said, it was the suddenness of it all. I wasn't thinking straight. . . . I guess both of us are going to have to make the best of a crummy situation."

"Well, thank you very much for your concern," I said, almost panting with rage, "but I'm not feeling very well, so you'll have to excuse me now."

"You don't want to talk?"

"Last night I wanted to talk. Now I want to be left alone."

"Look, last night was last night, this is today. I know I made a big mistake, but I can't keep apologizing or I'll sound like a broken record. Anyway, what you did—you know, lying about being a reporter and then springing it on me—that wasn't so great, either."

I didn't respond. I turned around and went into my bedroom, shut the door, and sat down on my bed, staring at Stoddard's painted garden on my wall to calm myself. This was the perfect ending to a sadistic fairy tale. Now that I'd decided I didn't want anything to do with her, she appears on my doorstep waving a white flag. The end. Except my life was a total shambles and she was sitting in the living room, waiting for me to playact at being her daughter.

I got up and threw on an old pair of sweats. A white waxy face stared back at me from the mirror, so I dabbed on some rouge. Then I wiped it all off. Who cared what I looked like?

"Hope this thing's an ashtray," she said, when I came back into the living room. She was sitting on the edge of the couch holding up the conch shell Stoddard had given me as a present. She was still wearing her coat.

"I guess it's one now," I answered, sitting across from her on my rocking chair.

She studied the lengthening ash on her cigarette for a long minute. "You know, I almost looked you up when I read Phillip's obit in the *Times*. But I—well, I didn't know how you'd take it—my appearing all of a sudden. And I thought Ruth might get on her high horse and come after me with a lawyer. I'd just had surgery on my ulcer and I wasn't in the greatest shape just then and . . . well, anyway, like I said, I wasn't sure it would be a good idea to show up out of nowhere and pull the rug out from under you." She cocked her head and studied my face. "I don't know why I didn't recognize you right off the bat. You look just like Phillip—an improved version, of course. His features were craggier. You've got my mother's eyes, though. Green eyes run in her family. I'll have to show you some pictures."

I shivered and stood up. "Would you like something to

eat or drink?" I asked formally, still trying to catch up to the fact that this stranger was my mother.

"A double shot of whiskey— Hey, don't look so shocked, I'm just kidding. Never touch a drink before 9 A.M. That was another joke, by the way. Better get used to my perverted sense of humor. . . . Forget the hostess bit and tell me how you found me. You hire a detective?"

I stared at the cigarette dangling from the corner of her mouth, half expecting it to fall any minute and set her coat on fire. "I got your name through George Horton. Indirectly, that is. He wasn't very helpful."

"How much did you have to pay him?"

"He wouldn't take money. He said he wanted to protect your privacy."

"Oh, sure," she scoffed. "Protect his own ass he meant, the slimy bastard . . . So how'd you find me?"

"He mentioned in passing that you'd been to the university, so I drove over there and got your name from Sophie."

"Who?"

"Sophie Woodhouse—the secretary in the history department."

"Jesus!" she exclaimed. "You mean she's still *there*? She must be a hundred years old by now. . . ." She lapsed into silence for a minute, chewing on her bottom lip. "So what's Ruth up to? She still playing house up in Connecticut?"

The tiny hairs on the back of my neck prickled with the thought that she'd known where I was all those years. "Ruth died a decade ago."

She exhaled loudly. "I guess I should say I'm sorry, but

tact isn't one of my strong points and Ruth wasn't one of my favorite people. . . . What'd she die of?"

I frowned. "It wasn't clear. She had all sorts of problems after my fath—after Phillip died. Her life pretty much revolved around him, I guess."

"Ah, yes, the model wife."

"Ruth had high standards," I defended.

She made a sour face. "That's what Phillip used to say. He claimed only a strong man could live with a woman like her, but I never bought it. No offense intended, but Ruth locked up his balls the day they were married and threw away the key. Know what I used to call her? The iron butterfly. She flitted around with her gossamer wings until you got in her way, and then *bam!* she mowed you down before you even knew you were hit."

Out of loyalty to Ruth, I stared at the floor so Jeanne wouldn't read agreement in my eyes, wouldn't know I'd spent my whole childhood waiting—hoping—my father would stand up to Ruth's household tyranny. Jeanne was right, but I didn't want to give her any ammunition.

"So what'd they tell you about me?"

"Nothing."

"You thought Ruth was your real mother?"

"Ruth *was* my real mother."

She blinked as if I'd flung something at her. "I meant your biological mother, as you put it last night."

"They never told me much about you—at least, not that I can remember. It's all very vague in my mind. I just knew I had another mother somewhere. I knew I was adopted."

She started to say something, but her words turned into a deep cough. When her face turned purple, I hurried into the kitchen to get her a glass of water. I had a fleeting vision of her keeling over and dying at my feet. I wasn't sure I'd feel anything.

She took a few swallows, then put her glass down with a bang. "Okay, I guess you want the story, so here goes," she said in a matter-of-fact voice that caught me off guard. "I was twenty-three when I met Phillip. It was the end of my senior year. I was young but I'd been knocking around on my own a long time by then. Like I told you last night, my parents weren't big on education, especially for girls. Expected me to work in the store right after high school, wouldn't give me a nickel for college. I wasn't even eighteen when I moved out. I was just a kid, really, but I got a job, saved up for a few years, and went off to the university on a work-study program. It wasn't easy, believe me, but it was better than working for my parents. With them it was either do it their way, or get out of their way. . . . Well, I guess the joke's on me. If I hadn't inherited their store, maybe I'd have become a teacher or lawyer—something worthwhile. But there was the store, all set up. Not much of a profit, but a steady income. I'd been on my own so many years, I figured I'd take a little breather before selling the business and going back to school—"

She paused as if she'd just thought of something. "You have a husband stashed away back there in your bedroom? He can join us if he wants."

"No husband."

"You're not married?"

"I was married right after college, but it didn't work out."

"That was a long time ago, college. No one's come along since then?"

"I've been living with someone for a couple of years. You're sitting under one of his paintings."

She twisted around in her seat and studied Stoddard's canvas briefly before turning back to me, clearly unimpressed. "So where is he, this painter?"

"We're not together anymore. It wasn't a permanent arrangement."

I got up and opened the shades. Sunlight flooded into the room but did nothing to lighten my mood. I glanced out the window at the throngs of people hurrying to work, remembering how hopeful I'd been as I'd scanned strangers' faces, fully expecting to recognize her. I'd also expected to feel undiluted elation if I found her. Yet here she was, sitting a few feet away from me, and all I could feel was anger. It was as if a black hole of rage had swallowed up all my other feelings, leaving me as cold and hard as stone.

I turned around and leaned against the windowsill, crossing my arms on my chest. "What about you? Who's the man I saw you with a couple of times—the skinny guy with the bow tie?"

"Oh, that's just Frank."

"What's so 'just Frank' about him? You two looked pretty chummy to me."

"He's my ex-husband," she said with a chuckle. "His wife doesn't play bridge and he's a fanatic, so we still play together once a week at a bridge club. Now that he's learned what I call second-marriage etiquette, we get along pretty well. He doesn't even yell at me when I make a bidding mistake."

"You didn't have any children? With him, I mean."

She blew two streams of smoke out of her nose like a dragon. "Frank traveled a lot for his work and somehow we never got around to kids. I guess there was more to it than that, but we didn't look at it too closely. Maybe that was our problem."

"Does he know about me?"

She was gazing past me now, staring out the window. "No one knows about you except for a shrink I saw a couple of times. Not that I believe in that Freudian crap about being able to talk problems away. But after I got this ulcer, Frank bullied me into seeing someone at a clinic. I didn't keep it up—quit after four, five sessions. I hated having my psyche turned into some graduate student's classroom, you know?" She paused and then shifted her gaze to my face. "So, things with this painter fellow are kaput, huh? A pretty girl like you, you must have lots of men chasing you."

"Oh, sure. Didn't you see them all lined up in the hall-way?"

"That Archie fellow seemed awful concerned."

"Archie's gay."

"There's no one else?"

"I don't know. Maybe," I said, thinking of Alex. "My life's been on hold since I started looking for you. I haven't had time for much else."

"Well, now you've found me, the Queen of Sheba. Some disappointment, huh?"

"Not at all," I lied, forcing myself to smile back at her.

She was working so hard at being friendly now, I wished I could sound more convincing.

"I know you want to hear about me and Phillip," she said, leaning back against the sofa cushions and staring up at the ceiling, her face clouding over. "It all started when I sat in on one of his lectures. I was bowled over, not just by his looks, but by the way he made history come alive, his excitement. And that voice, smooth as smoke ... So, I talked my way into his honors course and ended up doing some research for him. We spent a lot of time together and ... well, eventually the sex just happened. Not that we were casual about it," she added, pointing her cigarette at me. "It was the sixties but it was still a big deal."

"You mean sleeping with a professor?" I said coolly.

"I mean we were serious about each other. Even before you got started. At least *I* thought so."

"Are you saying he lied to you?"

"I don't know. Maybe he was lying to himself. The problem was, I was too young to understand how scared he was."

"Of what?"

She pursed her lips. "Ruth."

"Ruth? What could she have done to him?"

"Are you kidding? Back then, if a professor got involved with a student—got her pregnant—he was in deep shit. Phillip was terrified of a scandal. When he told Ruth he wanted a divorce, she drummed it into his head that if word spread he'd gotten a student pregnant, he'd be blackballed in every school in America. Of course, what she failed to point out was that there didn't have be a scandal unless she created one. ... Oh, sure there'd have been plenty of flak if he'd left her and married me, but he could have weathered it. After all, it wasn't the fifties. But that's not how he saw it, not after Ruth got hold of him. The way she worked it, he ended up thinking she was a goddamned saint for adopting you."

"I guess I'd have to agree with him," I said quietly.

"Yeah, well, Ruth's sainthood is up for question in my book," she said, her eyes flashing with anger. "She'd had a couple of miscarriages and couldn't get pregnant again, and Phillip desperately wanted a kid. In fact, they'd been talking about adopting for years. Then you happened and—" She stopped talking and gave me a hard look. "You don't believe a word I'm saying, do you?"

"I believe you slept with your professor and got pregnant and talked him into—"

"Stop right there," she said, holding up her hand. "Let's get one thing straight. I didn't talk your father into anything. He held all the cards—all of them. You girls today can't imagine what it was like for an unmarried mother in those days. I knew damned well I'd have a tough time if I raised you alone, but I figured I'd manage somehow. Then Phillip started chipping away at me, saying I was being selfish, saying you needed a normal home with two parents, financial security. He was so goddamned sure he was right, I started believing him and I—Oh Christ," she said, squeezing her eyes shut, "in my wildest dreams, I never figured it'd end like it did."

The only sound in the room came from the ticking of my wall clock. I sat there trying to dredge up some sympathy for her, but the problem was I didn't believe her story. Her recitation had been so neat, so pat, I was sure she'd stayed up all night rehearsing her lines to make the truth more palatable to me. Because the whole time she was talking, a single question kept echoing through my mind.

Why didn't you ever try to meet me?

She flung her eyes open as if she'd read my mind. "There's a whole lot you don't understand—especially about your father. . . . What did he tell you about his family?"

"Not much. I know his father was killed during the war and his mother got too sick to take care of him, so she sent him to relatives in New York when he was around twelve. I've met a few of his distant cousins—"

"So he did a number on you, too," she said with a triumphant laugh. "Well, let me tell you something. Phillip's parents were English all right, but his father wasn't any war hero, he drank himself to death. When the mother wanted to run off with her boyfriend, she shipped Phillip to New York to live with her down-and-out cousins in Hell's Kitchen."

"Who told you all this?"

"Phillip. But he didn't have to tell me. I saw through his royalty act from day one. That's why he was so comfortable around me. Never had to pump himself up with liquor when we were together. I don't really know how he pulled it off—smoothing out his rough edges—but he had everyone believing he came from old British money. But actually Ruth was the one with the money and the pedigree. That's why he couldn't leave her."

"You're wrong about Phillip—he wasn't the least bit materialistic."

"Correct. *Things* didn't matter to him. But money didn't mean things to Phillip, it meant security, respectability. Oh, he gave me all sorts of high-minded crap about why he couldn't leave Ruth, and I was so young, I believed him. I even thought he was being noble, for God's sake. It took me years to understand what had really happened. See, your father loved me, but not enough to risk his cushy life or his career," she said, her voice vibrating with emotion. "He was so scared people would find out about us, he paid Horton a small fortune to make all the arrangements for me. It was Horton—not your father—who found me a place to live. A dump up in New Hampshire run by nuns. Horton must have pocketed most of the dough Phillip gave him because he certainly didn't use it for *my* comfort—"

She stopped talking and took a labored breath. "I worked so hard to forget that place, to forget the time I spent there, but there's one thing I've never been able to forget—the expression on the nun's face when I said I didn't want to see you. She looked at me like I was . . . I don't know . . . some kind of monster." Her chest heaved, tears rolled down her cheeks. She fumbled around in her coat pocket for a tissue and blew her nose. "Too bad there's no statute of limitations on memories," she said, sniffing loudly. "Well, who the hell knows. Maybe Phillip was right after all. I'd probably have been a lousy mother. I'm very quirky and I've never been the domestic type. That was one of his big arguments—that Ruth was so great at that housewifely crap. Cooking, sewing. He even claimed she loved to clean, but that I never believed."

"It's true," I said. "Ruth did love to clean—it was her hobby."

"Oh, yeah?" she said, crumpling up her tissue and tossing it into the ashtray.

"I guess she was sort of a cleanaholic," I admitted with a twinge of guilt. "I mean, she had a permanent campaign going on in our house against dirt—had about a thousand different rules about where we could eat, what we could touch. My friends loved imitating the way she'd vacuum right around our feet and wander around the house picking up lint from the rugs. She was fanatical about lint."

"Why didn't she get a maid?"

"She hired people all the time, but they never lasted more than a few days. Either they'd miss a dust ball when they were vacuuming or they'd leave streaks on a waxed floor. Fingerprints on mirrors sent her over the edge."

Jeanne let out a barking laugh. "You've got to be kidding."

"No, I swear," I said, unable to restrain my own bitter laughter. I went on with a series of Ruth stories, the anecdotes spewing out of me with almost volcanic force. I told her about Ruth's affection for disinfectants and air fresheners, her need for furniture to be lined up symmetrically, her nervousness when little kids visited, her hatred of pets.

"She didn't even want me to get a pet rock when they were the fad because she thought it would be a dust collector. And she was even more of a perfectionist in the kitchen. Everything had to be made from scratch—no shortcuts. She spent days preparing for holidays. People always told me I was lucky to have a mother who cooked like that, but I never had any appetite. I used to throw up every morning before going to elementary school. Nerves, I guess."

"You must have inherited my touchy stomach," Jeanne said, her laughter dying.

"Maybe I did," I said, wiping my eyes with a tissue.

"Well, she must have done something right, judging by how great you turned—holy cow, is that the right time? That dingbat Arlene's on jury duty all week and the accountant's coming in early to do the bank rec. I'm supposed to be there now to let him into the store." She scrambled to her feet. "Hate to rush off like this, but I got to get up there."

"It's okay. I'm supposed to show up for a meeting at my office in a couple of minutes anyway."

"Let's have dinner one night," she said briskly as she picked up her pack of cigarettes and stuffed them into her purse.

"Great. We can plan it on the phone."

There was an awkward moment at the door. I couldn't decide whether to shake her hand or kiss her. Both gestures seemed wrong somehow, so I did neither.

"Oh, by the way," I called to her as I leaned over the railing and watched her run down the staircase. "I forgot to ask you something."

"Sure, shoot," she said, looking up at me from the next landing.

"Do you like flowers? I mean cut flowers, in vases," I

added, thinking back to Ruth's prohibition against bringing flowers into the house.

"Yeah, I'm crazy for them. Can't keep them around, though. They make me sneeze from here to eternity. Why? You inherit my allergies?"

"No, nothing like that. It was just a silly question."

Chapter Eighteen

I was so giddy, I practically floated out of my apartment and down to work. Every time I passed someone on the street, I felt like shouting: *I have a mother!*

"I've got some great news," I announced as I barged into Al's office.

"Bambina!" he said, looking up from his paperwork and gesturing for me to come inside. "You're just the person I've been looking for. I've got news for you, too."

I sat on the edge of his desk, alarmed by his Cheshire cat grin. He hadn't greeted me this effusively in months. If anything, he'd taken to grumbling when he saw me, which wasn't often since I'd been staying out of his way as much as possible. A dark thought passed through my mind. Maybe he was softening me up before giving me the ax.

"What's up?" I asked lightly.

"Hold on to your seat—you're going to be shocked."

"Listen, Al, I know I've been screwing up lately, but before you do anything drastic, I want to explain—"

"Thanks to you, kid, we're in the money," he said, leaning back in his chair and putting his hands behind his head.

"We are?"

"Yes, ma'am. Remember all those SOS letters you sent out, the ones I thought were too soppy?"

"How could I forget them? They were written in blood."

"Yeah, well, corny or not, they did the job."

"Who came through—the feds or a private group?"

"VIP."

"The little foundation that does ten a year?"

"That's the one. They've added a zero to the annual gift."

"VIP's doing a hundred next year?"

"And for the next five after that. It ain't the Diamond grant, but a hundred grand ain't bad. And let me tell you, it's going to make a hell of a difference around here. . . . So now I've shown you mine, you show me yours. And you'd better not be quitting."

"Just the opposite, Alberto," I said, reaching over to straighten his lopsided tie. "I came to tell you I'm in great shape."

"What happened? You move back in with Tex or are you listening to Prozac?"

"Very funny. It's because I've just found my mother."

"I didn't know you'd lost her," he said, looking puzzled.

"It's a long story. I'll tell you about it when we have time. All you need to know right now is that I'm back on track."

"Well, this is good news. I've missed your smiling face around here. You know, if I weren't married to Suzanne—"

"You'd be married to someone else just like her who knows all the breaks to the rhumba, so would you please take your hand off my thigh, thanks very much." I picked up his chunky hand and dropped it onto his own knee.

"How come when a skinny man gets sexy, it's called flirting. When the guy's bald and a little stocky, suddenly it's sleaze."

"Because sex is the reward people get for not eating Italian pastries like the ones you buy at Carmine's bakery every day," I said, elbowing his soft gut and standing up. "Now if you'll excuse me, my boss is a slave driver and I've got some catching up to do."

I started to leave, then hesitated at the door. "By the way, how's Doc doing? When he stopped coming to class, I sent him a note, but I never heard back from him."

He frowned. "I don't know what's with him. His phone's been disconnected, and he hasn't answered any of my letters, either. I even sent someone downtown to knock on his door a few times and ask around about him, but Chinatown's still a pretty closed place and nothing turned up. Short of tracking him down and dragging him back to class, I don't see what we can do."

"I feel so guilty about him."

"We can't save 'em all, Sarah."

I stopped by the conference room for a staff meeting and hung out afterward to gossip with people about our grant increase. Then I went into the metal cubicle that served as my office and looked around as if I hadn't been there in months. The place was scruffy and depressing. A crippled umbrella sat in the corner, a student's ripped sweatshirt dangled from a hook behind the door, the travel posters I'd Scotch-taped to the walls years before were faded, their edges curling like elves' shoes. In a single swift motion, I ripped the posters down and stuffed them into the garbage pail, vowing to buy replacements the next time I hit a museum.

I sat down at my desk and began riffling through my mail: a letter from a former student with a picture of her new baby, an ad for a new basic English workbook, an announcement of a conference at SUNY Purchase, an invitation to a publication party for a colleague's book . . . I studied the announcement with a curdling mixture of envy and shame. My own book was languishing in the bottom drawer of my file cabinet, unfinished, unwanted . . . I wrinkled up the card and made a hook shot into the garbage, refusing to let it tarnish my mood. I was flying high. I wanted to see friends—celebrate. Get my life going again. I'd been living in a vacuum too long.

I looked through my wheeldex. I felt like talking to Ann, but she and her husband had finally sold their store and moved back to San Francisco, and it was too early in the morning to call California. I started to look for Nina's office number but found myself thinking about Alex. In truth, I'd been thinking about Alex a lot lately—holding long interior conversations with him about all sorts of things—and right then, I had a particularly intense desire to talk to him. He was the only person who could appreciate the monumental nature of what I'd accomplished, the only one who understood what it had cost me to confront my mother. I smiled as I imagined how I'd gloat when I gave him my news. He'd been so sure I'd never have the courage to find her, so smug in his assessment of my cowardice that I was dying to prove him wrong.

But—and it was a big enough but to give me pause—a phone call to Alex could not be a cavalier gesture, not after my cock-teasing nuttiness at Sam's party. No, I decided as my thoughts accelerated, if I ever called him, I really had to mean it, and I was much too emotionally disorganized to commit to anything at the moment.

I glanced at the pile of papers on my desk. I'd spent enough time daydreaming. I put away my phone book and got down to work.

"Danger zone," Sam announced, striding into my living room and looking around critically. While he unplugged lamps and moved low-lying objects out of reach, Nina unzippered Jesse's plaid jacket. I stared at the baby, surprised by how much she'd grown. Had it really been that long since I'd seen the three of them?

"Okay, you can let her loose," Sam called out as he headed into the kitchen to check the contents of my refrigerator, a vestigial habit from his bachelor days.

Nina and I half sat, half reclined on my Tibetan floor pillows, watching Jesse crawl toward my bookcase.

"What's the big mystery?" Nina asked, munching on one of the carrot sticks I'd cut up. "Sam says you're going to make some sort of announcement tonight."

I pretended to be preoccupied by the baby's efforts to stand up and didn't answer, but I was actually trying to figure out what to say. I'd been practicing how to break the news about my mother to Sam and Nina ever since I'd issued my dinner invitation. But now that I was with them, I was tongue-tied, not just because old habits die hard, but because I hadn't heard a word from Jeanne since she'd descended on me. I'd been hanging around my phone, checking my answering machine ten times a day, practically accosting the mailman each morning, but so far, nothing. My euphoria had grown thin, then evaporated entirely, and I no longer felt like talking about her. So I hemmed and hawed, and ended up telling Nina about Thongchai Kedjumnong, one of my more complex students, inwardly deciding that I'd wait for the perfect moment to bring up the subject of my mother.

Thanks to Sam, I didn't have to wait long.

"So what's this Alex tells me about your parental problems," he said, stretching out next to us on the floor.

"Sam and Alex hang out a lot together these days," Nina explained with a wry look on her face. "They spend hours talking about tweeters and digital filters and digital-to-analog converters. And you should hear them talk about musicians. . . . You dig early or late Ravel?" she said, imitating Sam. "Oh, I much prefer the early work," she said, exaggerating Alex's slightly formal tone. "Except, perhaps, for the Trio in A major. Ravel's music became so acerbic after his mother's death, don't you think?" Then she switched back to Sam's gruffness. "Yeah, his later stuff's a bitch."

"Laugh if you want, the man happens to be a walking encyclopedia. Did Nina tell you we're all going to Chicago next weekend for a big electronics show?"

"Alex wants us to bring Jesse along," Nina added, tucking a loose strand of red hair behind the baby's ear. "He's terrific with her."

"Yeah, the kid's bonkers over him."

"And, by the way, he's a fabulous Chinese cook."

"What is this, a public-service commercial? Try our wonderful new product—Alex!"

"We don't think you've given him enough of a chance," Nina said, glancing at Sam conspiratorially.

"Yeah, what do you have against the guy?"

"Nothing."

"But?"

"But nothing. We just haven't . . . meshed . . . Yet."

"Maybe the timing's been off," Nina offered.

"Well, it's a moot point, ladies. He's hooked up with another woman."

"If you're referring to Kasey, that's essentially a business relationship," Nina explained. "She does some photography work for him."

"Yeah, well, he must be taking a hell of a lot of pictures, because they're together all the time."

"But he still asks me about Sarah."

"If I were you, Nina, I'd take his interest in Sarah with a grain of salt. In fact, I'd take it with the whole saltshaker. Alex is no masochist and it seems your friend, here, gave him the shaft. Anyway, Kasey's perfect for him. She's smart, talented, attractive—But I want to backtrack a minute. What did Alex mean by your parental problems, Sar? I thought your parents were dead, if you pardon the expression."

"Not all of them."

"What's that supposed to mean?"

"Ruth and Phillip are dead but my biological mother's still alive. In fact, I just found her."

"You were *adopted*?" they said simultaneously.

"How come you never told us?" Sam asked.

"Because I never told anyone."

"Except Alex, apparently," he said with a snort.

"That wasn't intentional. It just sort of . . . came out when I was interviewing him. I got very flustered and made a real fool of myself."

"So *that's* what you have against him," Sam said, slapping his thigh. "See, Nina, I told you it was some cockamamie reason like that."

"Sarah, if I'd known you were adopted, I'd never have gone on and on about Jesse's birth the way I did," Nina said, looking pained.

"It's okay, Nina. It was good for me. It made me realize how jealous I am of babies."

"Everyone's jealous of babies," Sam said. "They've got the world by the balls. They get unconditional love. Complete acceptance. Total security—everything we spend the rest of our adult lives looking for . . . Listen, Sar, if you'd told me you wanted a mother, I'd have gladly given you mine."

"Don't mind Sam," Nina cautioned. "In his crude way, he's trying to cheer you up."

"In my crude way, why should she need cheering up? Her story's got a happy ending."

"What's the happy ending?" I snapped.

"You just said you found your mother—"

"This isn't a fairy tale, Sam. It's complicated."

"Yeah, like every other parent-child relationship. Welcome to the club."

"No. You don't understand. You're not an adoptee. This is very different."

I got up and went into the kitchen, rattling pots and pans to make it sound like I was cooking even though I'd already finished preparing everything. In truth, it was me who was rattled.

"So what's she like?" Nina asked when I joined them again.

"I'm not sure. She seems pretty tough and has this street-wise way of talking, but I think it's an affectation."

"So what's the story?" Sam asked.

"If you don't mind talking about it," Nina added delicately.

"She was one of my father's students and they had an affair and she got pregnant. He wouldn't get a divorce, but he talked her into giving me up so he and his wife—Ruth—could raise me."

"That's wild!" Sam exclaimed.

"Well, it's her version, anyway," I said, frowning. "I'm not sure how much to believe. I mean, the whole thing's so weird, I can't really connect with the fact that she's my mother. We don't look anything alike, and basically, the only thing we have in common is the fact that she hatched me thirty-five years ago."

"But that's a biggie," Nina said.

"So when are we going to meet her?" Sam asked, reaching for the baby as she crawled by. She snuggled up to him and put her head down on his chest. A moment later, her eyes fluttered shut, and she was fast asleep.

"I don't know. Maybe never," I said, ripping a paper napkin into tiny strips and lining them up on the coffee table like soldiers. "I'm not even sure I'm going to see her again."

"Why not?"

"Because I haven't heard from her since we got together last week."

"Have you called her?" Nina asked.

"No. I'm not going to foist myself on her. I made the first move, now it's Jeanne's turn to keep things going—if she's interested."

"Hey, come on, she's got to be interested," Sam said.

"Not necessarily. She didn't contact me in thirty-five years even though she knew how to find me. Maybe she doesn't want to be anyone's mother. Maybe she thinks I'm a creep."

"That's ridiculous," Sam said.

"What's ridiculous is that I never asked my parents about her. I knew I had another mother somewhere, but I went along with their little game and pretended she didn't exist. It's probably why I was addicted to those stupid Nancy Drew books. I read them over and over again. And the whole time, I was living out my own mystery—*The Case of the Missing Mother*."

"Well," Sam said, squeezing my shoulder, "it's all over now. You've finally exorcised your djinn, pun pun."

"Very funny, Sam," I said sourly. "I think we'd better change the subject. This conversation is depressing me. And would you mind not mentioning this to anyone?"

"Our lips are sealed," Nina said, throwing Sam a you'd-better-back-off look.

Sam immediately switched gears and started telling funny stories about the studio. Nina described her department's despotic new chairperson. Jesse woke up from her mininap and we marveled at her antics. But I was dejected, and they knew it. After we finished eating dinner, Sam yawned a couple of times and announced that he had to get up early in the morning for a meeting. He gathered Jesse into his arms, kissed me good night, and started down the stairs. Nina lingered in the doorway looking worried.

"Listen, Sarah, I know Sam's your bosom buddy and all, but he doesn't have bosoms. Want me to stay for a while so we can talk?"

I made light of her concern and shooed her out with the promise that I'd speak to her in the morning, but after she left, I felt gloomy and restless. I washed and dried the dishes and opened the cupboard to put them away, noting that a thick layer of dust covered the top shelf. Without thinking, I wiped up the grime with a wet sponge, then moved down to the next shelf and the one after that, continuing on until

I'd washed out the whole cabinet. Then I started going through my overstuffed drawers, tossing out all the useless objects I'd been saving for years—splintered chopsticks, a rusty egg timer, unused Baggies ties, a ladle with no handle. By the time I was finished, my clothes were as damp as my spirit. On an impulse, I reached for my phone book and dialed Alex's number. I didn't know what I wanted or expected from him, but I was tired of holding myself back, tired of being so frightened.

The phone rang a couple of times before someone picked it up, a woman with a musical voice. I hung up without saying a word. Out of desperation, I dialed Stoddard.

"Hey! I was just thinkin' about you," he said as a greeting. "Miriam and I are finished."

"Oh? What happened?" I asked, feeling a shameful rush of pleasure. The last time Stoddard had called me he'd been surprisingly friendly, but he'd extolled his girlfriend's virtues ad nauseam.

"Well, you'd never guess it to look at her, but I finally figured out that she's so mean, she wouldn't spit in your ear if your brain was on fire. And she's got these two angora cats she won't leave alone overnight, so we always had to stay at her place. With all that cat fur flyin' around, and the wool from her weaving, my asthma came back and I nearly suffocated the other night. That's when I decided I'd had enough. . . . So, how've you been? Who are you gettin' it on with these days?"

"My right hand, but it's a terrible conversationalist. That's why I wanted to talk to you."

"Why don't you come right over. You know my bed's bigger than yours."

"I said talk, not fuck, Stoddard. There must be angora stuck in your ears."

"You can check my hearing when you get here. And maybe," he added softly, "we can chat about startin' things over again."

Chapter Nineteen

I was cooking breakfast the next morning, beating eggs in time with a moronic rap song on the radio, feeling somewhat cheered by the fact that I'd survived my evening with Stoddard without falling—or rather backsliding—into his bed, which, I confess, had been more than a little tempting after my months of celibacy. I'd just started pouring the eggs onto a sizzling pan when the phone rang. Sure the caller was Nina, I picked up the receiver and sang out a cheery hello. When I heard Jeanne's husky voice on the line, my heart and breakfast both crashed to my feet.

"What's doing?" she asked, intoning my least favorite phone greeting, the one I could never think up a snappy enough answer for.

"Oh, nothing much," I said, kneeling to scoop up the oozing eggs. "I'm kind of busy—"

"If this isn't a good time, I'll call back."

"No, I meant busy at work," I said quickly. "We had a real money crunch at NYAFS. In fact, I thought I might be out of a teaching job."

"Public assistance," she said darkly.

I struggled to interpret her words. Did she think I was about to hit her up for a loan? Was she suggesting I get unemployment insurance? Was she referring to NYAFS?

"Well, anyway, we got a new grant, so I'm okay now."

"Want to have dinner one night?" she said so abruptly, it came out like an accusation.

"Sure, that'd be great," I answered, my thoughts continuing to rave out of control.

Yippee! Your mother wants to see you again!

Oh yeah? So how come it took her this long to call?

"How's tomorrow night?" she asked, still sounding annoyed.

"No good. I'm teaching or tutoring every night this week. How about lunch on Saturday?"

"Saturday's my biggest day at the store."

We finally settled on Sunday. She suggested a restaurant I'd never heard of on the Upper West Side, we agreed on the hour and said good-bye.

I turned up the music and danced around the apartment, then collapsed on the sofa in a sweaty heap. I felt like a teenager who'd just been asked to the big prom—no, who'd been crowned prom queen. In my mind's eye, I pictured the two of us laughing and gossiping over lunch like all those sympatico mother-daughter combos I'd envied my whole life. . . . Then reality came crashing down on my fantasies, and I started thinking about some of the things she'd said to me. True, she was more open about her feelings than the buttoned-up Ruth had been, but her honesty sometimes bordered on cruelty. And her bitterness about my father colored every remark, every joke.

By Sunday, I'd whipped myself into such a lather that when it was time to get dressed, I found myself agonizing over fashion details I ordinarily gave no thought to—which shade of stockings was "correct," how I should wear my hair (I'd been wearing it the same way since I was fifteen), what makeup and jewelry to choose. It wasn't just a question of wanting to look my best; I had to look perfect. Not out of simple vanity, either, I admitted to myself as I wiped off misapplied eyeliner and started over for the third time. I knew it was stupid and cruel and pointless, and part of me felt ashamed, but in truth, I didn't just want her admiration, I wanted to show her how much she'd lost by giving me up.

I wanted revenge.

I fussed over myself for such an insane amount of time that in spite of having started my toilette early, I ended up having to run all the way to and from the subway. Before entering the restaurant, I smoothed down my hair and gave myself a once-over in a mirror to make sure price tags weren't still dangling from my new suit. Then I made my grand entrance.

No Jeanne.

The only person in sight was a busboy setting tables. I took in the room's gilded-châteaux decor and instantly knew the food and clientele would both be rich—an odd selection of restaurants for Jeanne to have made since she knew I wasn't exactly rolling in money. Was she trying to impress me with her sophistication or was she downright inconsiderate?

"Oh, you're here already," she said unapologetically when she breezed in a few minutes later. It was an embarrassing moment since neither of us was able to come up with an appropriate greeting. The hug I'd given her in my fantasies seemed phony-intimate, a handshake between mother and daughter absurd. As we filled the air with chatter, I caught our reflections in a wall mirror and noted how peculiar we looked standing together. Mutt and Jeff, Abbott and Costello—a laughable pair. Because not only did our heights and coloring contrast dramatically, our clothing couldn't have been more dissimilar. I was wearing a tailored navy-blue suit, black flats, and tiny pearl earrings. Jeanne was wearing a white silk tent dress and huge quantities of oversize Mexican jewelry on her ears, wrists, and neck. We looked like we were attending two entirely different social functions.

"Unfortunately, ladies, we are not serving lunch for another thirty minutes," the maître d' said, swooping down on us with a disdainful sniff. I knew his kind. Two single women would definitely not make his A list. Even in an empty restaurant, he'd seat us in the back of the room between the kitchen and the dirty plate station.

Jeanne's forehead accordioned into rows of horizontal creases. I wondered vaguely if I'd end up with the same set of lines. "I thought you did brunch from eleven-thirty," she accused.

"No, no, no," he said, wagging his finger at her. "On Sunday, we never sit anyone before twelve-thirty, madam. But perhaps you like to relax at our bar and have ze drink, yes?"

"Let's go to the restaurant next door," I suggested, afraid of prolonging what might turn out to be an excruciating afternoon. After all, how much did we actually have to say to one another? How much couldn't we say?

"I've eaten there, and it ain't great," she said, looking doubtful.

"Doesn't matter. I'm not fussy."

Five minutes later, I understood her resistance to my idea. The neighboring place was the sort of trendy hangout that had nothing to do with food and everything to do with noise. As we stood in the crush of people waiting to be seated, a row of sad-eyed middle-aged men leered at us from the bar. I doubted a single one of them took us for mother and daughter.

"Let's split a bottle of red wine," Jeanne said the instant we sat down. She waved at the waiter as if she were drowning. I noticed tiny beads of perspiration gathering on her upper lip like a transparent mustache.

"I don't drink. I'll just have water," I told her.

"What?" she said, cupping her ear.

"I never drink alcohol," I said, raising my voice a few decibels.

"Why not? You have a drinking problem?"

Heads swiveled. The couple at the next table waited for my answer.

"I don't like what it does to me," I told my audience self-consciously. "I get foggy."

"Phillip could drink like a fish, you know."

My stomach tightened at the mention of my father's name, but I struggled to tamp down my resentment. After all, he was our main link, one of the few things we had in common, I told myself. Of course he was going to be the centerpiece of our conversation. Nevertheless, I hated having my memories of him corroded by her bitterness. Even the sardonic way she said his name set my teeth on edge.

I must have looked stricken because she quickly dropped the subject of Phillip and ordered Perrier water for me, a half bottle of Burgundy for herself. Then she turned and gave me a smile. Or rather, her mouth smiled. Her eyes were wary and sad.

We carefully made our way into the conversation. I started out with a few inane comments about the weather, how time flies, and what a small world it is. Jeanne took over and described the renovation she planned for her store. Suddenly, one of our neighbors let out a series of shrieks and invited another squawking couple over to join them. Once their noisy four-way conversation ensued, we practically had to shout across our table to be heard, and even then it was chancy. I missed half of what she told me about her store, and just kept nodding. Finally, the screamers evacuated and the room quieted down, but that only highlighted the fact that the lulls between our comments were getting longer and more frequent.

"That's a pretty dress," I told her, scrounging for something new to talk about.

"You think? It's very outdated," she said, looking down at herself.

"No, I like the way it sort of . . . floats around you." In truth, it looked like a cross between a wedding gown and a maternity outfit, but then, hey, why not? I said to myself. Wasn't it the perfect choice for today?

"I've put on so much goddamned weight, I have to stick to loose clothing. Not that it bothers me," she added, waving her nicotine-stained hand in the air.

I stared at her hand, wondering if I should tell her how I'd once followed a woman out of a store because her fingers had resembled mine. Would she think the story funny or pathetic? I decided to let it pass.

"Every time I stop smoking, I pick up five, ten pounds. Then I go back to smoking and I'm stuck with the weight."

"Why don't you join a gym or take up jogging?"

"Nah, it's impossible to get weight off at my age. I'm almost sixty, you know."

"A journey of a thousand miles starts with a single step," I heard myself say, inwardly cringing at my platitude. I sounded exactly like Ruth at her worst.

"Now, you're a different story," she said, eyeing my body enviously. "The way you're built, you can wear anything you want. You certainly picked the right genes."

"You make it sound like an accomplishment," I said, drawing invisible lines on the tablecloth with my fork. "It's not like I had much choice in the matter."

"Neither of us had much of a choice about a *lot* of things, did we?"

I knew she was waiting for me to agree, waiting for me to absolve her for having given me up. I struggled with myself. Part of me wanted to be kind and forgiving; but a tougher and angrier part of me refused to say a word.

I opened my menu and pored over the list of food as if it were the most fascinating piece of literature I'd ever read, even though my stomach was twisted in knots.

"Ready to order, ladies?" the waiter asked, rescuing me from a bad moment.

"I'm not very hungry. I'll just have a spinach salad and a plate of grilled vegetables."

"Rare steak and fries," Jeanne told him, closing her menu and studying me through narrowed eyes. "What, you live exclusively on rabbit food?"

"I'm not a vegetarian if that's what you mean. I just like greens a lot."

"I like greens a lot, too—in paintings. When I'm eating, I like real food."

I shrugged without answering. Food and mothers—a loaded subject at best—and in our case, an especially volatile combination. "Speaking of paintings," I said, "have you seen the contemporary Russian show at the Modern? I hear it's amazing."

"I'm not much of a museumgoer, especially when it's stuff that could have been painted by a bunch of demented six-year-olds."

I laughed uneasily. "What about the theater? Have you seen any good plays lately?"

"Nah. Tell you the truth, I hate live performances of any kind," she said, sipping on her wine. "I'm always worried the actors'll forget their lines or the dancers'll trip and fall off the stage. I get nervous just watching them."

I smiled thinly, unsure whether she was joking. It was sometimes hard for me to tell where her cynicism left off and her humor began. "So what do you generally do in your free time?" I asked, steeling myself for yet another wisecrack.

"What free time? I'm not like you teachers, I've got to work for a living. I'm in the store six days a week."

"That still leaves Sundays and evenings," I persisted, trying to ignore her jibe. "You must do something other than work."

"Actually, I've pared down my life quite a bit in the past few years. I work. I read. I play bridge. That's about it. You play bridge?"

"I don't know how."

"Oh yeah? That's too bad. Maybe I could give you a few lessons sometime."

I imagined the two of us huddled over cards, playing at mother/daughter. The band of pressure around my skull tightened. "I don't think so. Card games put me right to sleep."

"But bridge isn't like other card games. It's a real intellectual challenge," she said, biting into a piece of steak so undercooked I thought it might moo.

"But when I play cards, I never care who wins."

"I'm sure you'd feel different if you'd been exposed earlier."

"I'm sure I'd feel different about a lot of things if I'd been exposed earlier," I heard myself say.

There was a painful silence. To fill it, we both began talking. Then we broke off and there was another silence. Our conversation was dying a torturous death, and we still had to get through dessert and coffee, pay the bill, and say goodbye. My head throbbed harder.

"What do you think of the mayor?" I asked, shifting lettuce around on my plate to make it look like I was eating, a skill I'd mastered during childhood.

She rolled her eyes. "Oh, don't get me started on this city. If New York keeps spending money on all these special programs, we're going to go bankrupt." She tossed off a long string of statistics about unions and welfare payments and education and the homeless.

"I can't argue with your numbers," I answered, irked by her Ayn Rand politics, "but it's obvious we're either going to pay now through social programs or pay later in crime and mental illness."

"Oh no!" she said, screwing up her features in mock horror. "Not another bleeding-heart liberal!"

"It's got nothing to do with politics," I said, spearing an olive with my fork. "I'm basing this on what I see every day in my classroom. Since the federal cutbacks, my classes have gotten so crowded, students are practically hanging from light fixtures."

"That's because the U.S. government lets in too many foreigners. Over a million people came into this country last year. They're crowding the public schools, the jails and hospitals—"

"Immigration's another issue entirely. The point is, these people are here, and they need help."

"Help, shmelp. These social programs are wiping us out, especially in this town. Sure life's tough, so what else is new? There aren't any free rides—not even in God-bless-America."

"My students aren't looking for free rides," I said, beginning to boil inside. "They're just trying to learn enough English to get decent jobs."

"Oh, come on, there are plenty of jobs out there if someone's willing to work. New York can't baby-sit the whole world, you know."

"But you can't just abandon people like that!" I cried out, waving my hand so emphatically that I smacked into her water glass and toppled it over. Water splashed across the table and gushed onto her lap.

Cursing loudly, she jumped to her feet, grabbed her napkin, and swatted at the puddle as if it were alive. I apologized over and over again and offered my napkin. She mumbled incoherently and stomped off to the ladies' room, holding her soaking-wet dress away from her body.

I hunched over the table watching the waiter sweep up the shattered glass from the floor. I was miserable. The afternoon had been a complete failure, a disaster. I didn't merely dislike this woman, I disliked the prissy, cold, petulant stranger I became when I was with her. And worse than that, I saw with horrible clarity that it would always be this way. I'd never be able to replace the baby she'd given up: She'd never be the mother of my childhood. Rage and disappointment would shadow us forever.

Yet even as I thought all this, something else flashed into my mind.

It doesn't matter.

I sat up, startled by the thought. Was I lying to myself—using pop psychology to soften the pain? I began probing my feelings, testing the idea. . . . It was true, I suddenly realized. It didn't matter how I felt about her because I didn't need a mother. All I'd needed was to find her—and that much I'd done.

My despair lifted like a great black bird. I felt free, light, exultant. By the time Jeanne came back to the table, I was so intoxicated with relief, I'd even worked up a kind of perverse affection for her in spite of her prickliness. She was tough and thorny, difficult to handle, just like her cactus plants. But like them, she was a survivor.

And so was I.

"Here's the check, ladies," the waiter said, placing it between us.

I reached for my wallet. "How much is my half?"

"Put your money away," she instructed.

"But I want to split the bill with you."

"Please, Sarah," she said. "Let your mother buy you lunch."

I wanted to tell her I wasn't usually this cool and defensive, wanted to say how glad I was that I'd found her. But as we stood on the sidewalk in front of the restaurant in the brilliant midday sun, all I managed to squeeze out of myself was an offer to pay for the dry-cleaning of her silk dress.

"Nah, forget it. If I'm lucky, the cleaner'll tell me to

throw the damn thing out. It's time I bought myself a new dress, anyway."

"If you do get something new, maybe you can wear it the next time we get together."

"You want to get together again?" she asked uncertainly.

"Sure. I mean, if you do. I'll call you next week."

"That's what you said last time, but you never called."

"Well, actually, I was waiting for you to call."

"I did."

"I'm glad."

I leaned down to kiss her cheek just as she reached out to shake my hand. Flustered, I straightened up and extended my hand, but by then she'd withdrawn hers and was offering her cheek to be kissed. We stared at each other in dismay, then broke into nervous laughter.

"We're like an O. Henry story," I said, feeling all choked up.

"Maybe if we keep practicing, we'll get it right someday." She patted my arm and then, as if catching herself, pulled away. "Want to share a cab?"

"No thanks. I feel like walking for a while."

I headed south, struggling to sort out the strange mixture of competing emotions I felt. I didn't want to go home yet, so I decided to walk over to the Museum of Natural History to pick up a few posters for my office.

I cut across Eighty-third Street and got as far as Columbus Avenue before admitting to myself where I really wanted to go.

The thought of seeing Alex again made me light up

inside, not with sentimentality or romance, but with raw lust. I backtracked to the discount drugstore I'd passed on Broadway, bought a few necessities, then hurried over to Central Park West, imagining all sorts of raunchy scenes in my head.

Cornel was lounging in front of Alex's building, leaning against the car as he read the newspaper. I waved at him from the distance, but he didn't wave back.

"Is Alex home?" I asked, somewhat miffed he hadn't remembered me.

"Mr. Alex go upstairs one minute ago. They just come back from lunch party."

"They?" I said, blanching.

"He's with Miss Kasey. . . . If you want, I call up on car phone—"

"No no, don't bother," I said quickly. "I'll catch him some other time."

Still clutching my pathetic little bag of pharmaceuticals, I slunk away.

Chapter Twenty

An animal scurried out of the pile of garbage. I screeched and leaped back, nearly toppling over as an alley cat shot past my legs, its tail puffy with fear. I regained my balance and studied the sign hanging over the doorway, trying to decide if this was Doc's building. I knew his address well enough—God knows I'd written 106 Queen Street on enough forms and applications—but wasn't at all sure what these scratched-out numbers actually said.

The idea of apologizing to Doc had begun clanking around my hyperactive mind at around three-thirty in the morning as I lay in bed organizing my life. At that hour, my course of action had seemed astonishingly clear.

First, I had to get my hands on Alex—not an easy task since I faced two daunting obstacles: the Kasey person who'd insinuated herself into his life, and Alex, himself, who was probably still angry at me for trifling with his affections. Nevertheless, I was confident of prevailing in the end because I planned to throw caution and pride to the wind and do whatever it took to convince him of the rightness of us as a couple, something my astute and loyal friends had been trying to convince me of for an embarrassing amount of time. Also, I believed Alex's once-passionate feelings for me, although currently in remission, couldn't have completely evaporated, since he was a man with an essentially serious nature.

I hoped.

Of course, I'd have to hold off contacting him until Kasey, who'd probably installed herself in his apartment for the weekend (in fact, she was probably in his bed at that very moment, doing all sorts of things to him that I refused to let myself think about), crawled back to her own lair. The soonest I could call him was Monday evening. Unless they were living together, which would mean the end of the line. Aggressive I didn't mind being, but my scruples prevented me from following an anything-goes policy.

Lying in bed, I brooded over the possibility that Kasey was a permanent fixture in Alex's life, which made me hate her violently and unreasonably. Even worse, since I knew nothing about her except what Sam had said—that she was attractive and smart—I could find no flaws on which to hook my self-confidence. Dandruff. Cellulite. A nasal voice. She was the most vexing sort of rival, existing as she did only in my imagination. Well, you're not getting in my way for long, Miss Perfect. Back to the photo shop for you . . .

By dawn, I'd mentally polished off my rival and had started thinking about Doc. I felt guilty about the way I'd treated him, ashamed that I hadn't done for him what I would have done for almost any other student, namely track him down when he'd dropped out of the program and talk him into coming back to class. Which was why, when I got out of bed, I'd come down to Chinatown, and now found myself standing in front of a smashed-in door in a foyer that stank of piss at nine in the morning.

A single naked bulb hung overhead but no names were listed on the dented mailboxes. No one at NYAFS had seen or heard from Doc since the police had released him, and I wasn't at all sure he still lived in New York.

I waited around for a while hoping someone would show up, but the building seemed deserted. I was about to leave when I heard a faint noise, an eerie clicking sound that made me think of a Ping-Pong ball bouncing down a staircase. Suddenly, an elderly blind man appeared at the other end of the hallway, tapping out his path with a carved bamboo cane. His yellowish beard hung down on his chest like a soiled bib, giving him the look of an aged baby.

"Excuse me, do you know if Doc Chin lives here?" I asked.

"None English," he wheezed.

"I'm his teacher."

He paused for a moment as if impressed and tilted his head in the direction of a nearby doorway. Before I could interrogate him further, he slipped out the door, navigated around the pile of garbage, and disappeared.

I tiptoed over to the apartment he'd indicated, wondering if he'd really been answering my question or had just wobbled his head randomly. I strained to hear voices inside, but could only hear blood pounding in my ears. I imagined a gang of junkies opening the door and pulling me inside. Raping and torturing me. Tossing me off the roof like a rag doll . . . I ordered myself out of the building instantly, but watched in horror as my hand curled itself into a fist and rapped on the door.

"Who?" a voice asked.

I stepped back, ready to run. "Doc?" I whispered. "It's Sarah Bridges, from school."

Chains clinked, locks turned. The door flew open.

"Trouble?" Doc asked, rubbing his eyes. His hair was standing up like porcupine quills. A deep sleep crease cut across his cheek.

I let my breath out in relief. "No, I just want to talk to you. But I can come back later if you're sleeping—"

"Not really sleeping. Have just come home from restaurant. All-night party for owner birthday. Come in, please."

I followed him down a narrow hallway into a small room that was even more squalid than I'd expected. Two mattresses on the floor, a pair of lopsided metal chairs pulled up at a Formica table, cardboard cartons pretending to be furniture. A hairy green vegetable large enough to star in a science-fiction movie sat on a worn enamel sink. My eyes fell on something in the corner that looked disconcertingly like a dead body covered by a blanket.

"Swoye at work now. Doc try sleep one hour but cannot. Many nerves."

"But Al told me your legal problems are all settled."

"Yes, but when arrest, Doc lose job. Now find waiter job but work more hours less pay. You like tea?" he asked, hunkering down on the floor and placing a dented kettle onto an electric burner.

I nodded and sat down on one of the chairs, tilting crazily to the side. Doc sat across from me, clasping his hands in front of him. I stared at his delicate wrist bones, trying to shape my complicated feelings into sentences he'd be able to understand.

"Doc, I'm sorry I left you so abruptly the night you were with the police," I began.

He winced. "Not talking about arrest, please. Very shame."

"Is that why you quit school—because you were embarrassed?"

"No time for school. New waiter job in China restaurant have most business at night. Cannot come uptown for class."

"Why don't you take morning classes? Hunter has an ESL program."

"Doc also having morning job in bake company—"

A shrill sound cut into the air. Doc jumped to his feet and hurried over to the lump in the corner. He pulled off the blanket and uncovered a large ivory cage that housed an olive-colored bird about the size of a robin.

"What kind of a bird is that?" I asked.

"Hua mei bird from Guangdong Province," he answered proudly, holding the cage up for display. "Gift from parents of Lotus before leave. Very value. See white circle around eyes? Words *hua mei* mean painted eyebrow in Chinese. Suppose like Xi Shi, beautiful girl in ancient time. This hua mei is name Lotus. Very trouble taking care. Every day, she need two bath and big walk in Sarah Delano Roosevelt Park on Delancey or won't singing. Plus have special diet."

"What does she eat?" I asked, inspecting the bird more closely. She fanned out her tail feathers as if pleased with all the attention.

"She love alive cricket, but too expensive. Most time, she eat Big Mac like real American."

I laughed. "Well, now you have another reason for staying in school. You have to keep up with Lotus."

"I keep try study but is difficulty," he said, putting the cage down. "Every night, after home from restaurant, copy over one old composition from class." He poked through one of the cardboard boxes and pulled out a sheaf of papers and a slate board.

"That's great, Doc."

"Not so great. Mostly, head use blackboard for pillow instead of write," he said, handing me a stack of old compositions to look at.

I riffled through them, reading my comments at the top of each page. *Incomprehensible!* I'd written over and over again in red ink. It was true, too. His words had been incomprehensible to me, but not just because of his poor spelling and grammar. I hadn't *wanted* to understand him.

"Listen, Doc, I want to explain why I've been so jumpy around you. You see, your loneliness reminded me of my own loneliness—which was something I was trying to ignore. The truth is, I'm a terrible coward. I've been a coward my whole life."

"What you talking coward?" he said indignantly.

"Before this year, I never had the courage to face my own family situation—"

"No no no!" he said angrily, clapping his hands over his ears. "Cannot be true! You very courage lady. Never give up help students become real American—even dummy like Doc. If teacher Sarah have no courage, students have no courage and stop try."

I swallowed back my confession. "Right. That's exactly why I'm here. I'm not about to let you off the hook so easily."

"What mean off hook?"

"Escape, like a fish who swims away," I said, wiggling my hands. "It's admirable that you're studying on your own, but it's not enough," I said sternly.

"Nothing enough for Doc stinky English, not one hundred year study," he said, picking up a piece of chalk and writing *100* on the slate board. He paused, and then in a fury of concentration stood up and added more zeros until he'd run out of space. "Even if study this long time, Doc talk stinky English." He threw the chalk on the floor and crushed it with his heel. "Already be in New York three year, but when talk to customers in restaurant, they not understanding."

"That's probably because they get confused when you

refer to yourself as Doc instead of saying *I* or *me*. Remember how we talked about that in our conferences last year? You really have to break that habit."

"Difficulty," he said, frowning. "In restaurant, customer shout waiter bring food. In bakery, everyone speak Spanish, no talk English. Swoye live here only for sleeping, not practice conversation. Since Lotus leave from neighbor, no person say Doc name. Have shadow life. So Doc say name himself to make sure still alive."

"I know you're lonely. That's why you can't quit school now. You've got to learn how to speak properly so you can communicate with people more easily."

"School not possible," he moaned.

"Yes it is. If you can't afford to come back to class right now, I'll mail you the assignments and you can work on them at home. When you're done, you can mail them back to me for correction."

"School in letter go back and forth?" he said, brightening slightly.

"Exactly. And in the meantime, you can practice your conversational skills with your customers. Once you're speaking more fluently, you can find a job as a manager of a restaurant."

"You think is possible?"

"I *know* it's possible."

"If Doc manager, you come for dinner and will not cost you."

"That sounds great. I love Chinese food."

"And have very big party celebrate story of Chin family in book when is publish."

"I hate to tell you this, Doc, but I don't think there's going to be a book. No one wants to publish it."

His face crumpled in disappointment. "But book only grave Doc have for parents and little brother. Only chance for honor Chin family. You must get publish!"

"I don't know what else to do. I've just about given up."

"Cannot give up," he said fiercely. He thought for a minute and then opened a drawer and took out a small velvet box. "For you," he said, thrusting it at me.

I opened the box and studied the antique coin inside. "It's beautiful, Doc, but I couldn't possibly take it."

"Teacher Sarah must have *ba gwa* coin. Will bring good luck. You have give Doc—" He caught himself and started over. "You have give me hope, and I make promise for keep study. This give you hope, and you make promise for publish book."

Ceremoniously, he poured out two cups of tea. We clinked our cups in a toast and drank in silence, with the coin gleaming on the table between us.

Chapter Twenty-one

*B*efore beginning my full-scale campaign, I checked my calendar to make sure I had no early-morning appointments, then tucked my most seductive lingerie into a small bag just in case Alex offered an instant invitation. Thus prepared, I dialed.

When his answering machine clicked on, I had to make a quick decision. Should I come clean and tell him the truth—that my timing was abominable but I wanted to see him again—or should I just leave my name? I decided to do neither. All sorts of people probably had access to his machine, and I didn't want to embarrass any of us. I hung up.

I called again the next morning, hoping to catch him pre-office. This time I left my name and number with his Hispanic housekeeper, who asked me to spell *Bridges* three times. ("Lemme see I get this right, lady. P-R-I-G-G-E-F.") Lacking confidence in her phonics, I nevertheless checked my answering machine throughout the day.

Nada.

I advised myself to play it cool and let some time elapse before calling again, but I wasn't in the mood. All my mental tiptoeing around, all my equivocating and telling myself I didn't care had been consumed during my pursuit of Jeanne. Now that I knew what I wanted, I didn't feel like wasting time. I left my name and number on his answering machine and when I didn't hear from him, left it a second time. Refusing to be discouraged by his silence, I made up all sorts excuses for him. He was extraordinarily busy. He was traveling. He hadn't gotten my messages. His pride prevented him from calling. He didn't want to seem overeager. He needed time to ditch Kasey. I clung to my optimism with a tenacity fueled by romantic notions, and in that turned-on exalted state, I couldn't imagine anything but a lot of sex and a happy ending.

Finally, when all else failed, I called his office, something I'd been reluctant to do. I hated the thought that he might be watching the clock, worrying he was going to be late to his next business meeting while I was confessing my passion. It brought back a humiliating experience in college when, in the midst of going down on a boyfriend between classes, I'd caught him glancing at his watch.

Alex's secretary put me on hold, then immediately came back on and said in a haughty tone that Alex wasn't available.

"He's out of town?" I asked hopefully, trying to keep my spirits up.

"No, he's here."

"Well, I've left several messages for him already. Would you tell him it's really important. He can call me at home or at NYAFS."

"Oh, you're from NYAFS?" she said, her tone instantly softening. "You got the letter, didn't you?"

"Excuse me?"

"It went out a few weeks ago."

"Sorry, I'm not following you."

"About the increase in the VIP grant."

My brain spun its wheels. I couldn't process her words. Then the gears clicked into place, and my jaw dropped.

"The VIP foundation is *Alex's?*"

"Is something wrong?"

"Then he's been giving money to NYAFS for years!"

"I just started working here a few weeks ago, so I don't know all that much about it except that it's named for his aunt."

"Look, would you ask him to call me? Tell him it's urgent."

I hung up, my mind racing back to the night I'd met Alex in Ann's store. He'd been familiar with NYAFS, but I'd assumed his knowledge had come through the emigré grapevine. . . . My feelings for him expanded, tinged now with renewed admiration. Not only hadn't he used his philanthropy to impress or seduce me, he was still supporting NYAFS even though I'd treated him so shabbily. Then I remembered his recent grant increase and felt a spark of hope flicker in my breast, but the glow only lasted long enough to illuminate the ghastly truth.

He was never going to call me.

That I'd missed my chance with him was so obviously true, I couldn't believe I hadn't seen it before. I suddenly understood the verb *to swoon*. I was breathless with misery. Of course he wasn't going to call me back, not after the way I'd jerked him around. The fact that he'd upped his donation to NYAFS had nothing to do with me. Or maybe he'd done it because he thought I was such a screwed-up mess, he felt sorry for me.

I tried consoling myself in a variety of ways. First, I told myself that losing Alex was the price I'd paid for finding Jeanne.

You could have had both of them if you weren't such an idiot!

Second, I reminded myself that since I'd learned my lesson, I'd never suffer this kind of loss again.

That's because you'll never find anyone like Alex again!

Then I experimented with alternate salves.

I took up my old habit of jogging as a way of pumping endorphins into my aggrieved system. Each morning, I hit the path next to the West Side Highway with the other compulsives and ran for a solid hour. Ran, in a manner of speaking: I was so out of shape, I could barely keep up with the race walkers.

I made enough reeds to last a lifetime and practiced my oboe religiously, managing to memorize the entire Telemann Suite in A minor.

I arranged several different kinds of events with Jeanne, some more successful than others. As it turned out, success wasn't predictable: Our relationship was far too strange and fragile for predictability. We weren't bonded by love or friendship or a shared past, but by a shared absence that had left a crater-sized dent in both our lives.

So after some uncomfortable lunches and dinners, I finally figured out that lengthy conversations were risky since even the most innocuous subject could send our words coiling around us, strangling our good intentions. The safest bet was going someplace where we wouldn't have to talk very much. I bought a pair of tickets to a serious play. She fell asleep halfway through the first act and snored her way through the second.

Hoping a less intellectually ambitious production might do the trick, I bought tickets to a British shlepic-cum-slopera, the kind of nonplay I ordinarily avoided. She managed to stay awake this time but didn't seem overly enthusiastic. In the end, we settled into the routine of having a quick bite at a coffee shop and seeing a movie together every couple of weeks. It was easy, it was uncomplicated, and by sitting next to one another in the dark, we created the illusion that we were spending time together, without having to talk very much.

But even after several expeditions I still didn't feel like I knew Jeanne very well. Her personality was so heavily cloaked in cynicism and sarcasm that trying to have any sort of deep, emotional conversation with her was almost impossible. Even in the odd moments when she softened up a bit, her armor was only reduced to the weight of chain mail. So for the most part, I didn't try to pierce her defenses, and in turn, I kept my own guard up.

That's what had made our most recent outing such a surprise, especially since the evening had started out badly. Jeanne, who was generally an impatient person, made a mistake about when we were supposed to meet, and had to spend an extra thirty minutes waiting for me in front of the movie theater, about which she continued to grouse long after we were seated. In addition, the Woody Allen movie I'd chosen turned out to be about the search for an adopted baby's biological mother, which, of course, was a disastrous subject for us. That the woman turned out to be a ditsy prostitute did not strike either of us the least bit funny. Surprise, surprise.

We left the theater without saying anything about the film, but were both melancholic and subdued when we stopped for a cup of coffee at an overlit deli near the theater. As we began talking about inconsequential events in our lives, I felt the urge to pour out my whole tale of woe about Alex.

"They say you can't fix an egg once it's cracked," she commented when I'd finished, stirring three packets of sugar into her coffee. She'd recently stopped smoking and was using sweets as a substitute for cigarettes.

"I guess not," I said with a shrug, realizing at that moment that I was waiting—hoping—to hear her dismiss my story with a series of her typically acerbic and ridiculing wisecracks, thereby putting it into the proper perspective.

But to my consternation, she looked at me with an almost pleading expression on her face. "I'll tell you one thing, babes. If you care about this man as much as I think you do, it's worth everything to try to patch it up. He may be mad at you, but I'll bet he hasn't forgotten you."

"But there's nothing more I can do about Alex. It's hopeless."

"Nothing's hopeless till you're dead," she said, her voice reverting back to its usual biting tone. "Now let's get the check and get the hell out of here. We look so dismal, people are going to take this place for a funeral parlor."

The next day, in a last-ditch effort to cheer myself up, I agreed to go out on a date with one of my longtime colleagues, a recently divorced man who looked a little like Alfred E. Newman but who was nobody's fool. We had a perfectly pleasant evening during which he told me all about his marriage. I agreed his ex-wife was a monster. I could see he needed to fall in love with someone fast, but when he kissed me good night, I told him I had herpes.

My black mood persisted.

"What do you think this is, a party?" I yelled at Indi. "First you take fifteen minutes for lunch, then you leave to go to the bathroom, and now you want to make a phone call?"

"Is emergency. I must call my little boy," she explained nervously.

"No way!" I shouted, slapping a rolled-up newspaper against the palm of my hand. "Now get back to your desk and don't try any more of this monkey business."

"Then I will leaving," she declared defiantly.

"Not so fast," I said, wagging my finger in her face. "You signed a contract when you started here. If you break your word, I'll have you sent to jail and you'll never see your little boy."

Her eyes darted around the room for help.

"Tell boss you send *her* to jail if she sweetshop you!" Korn shouted.

"Slavery is illegal," Tamir coached.

"That's right," I said, softening my voice and dropping my role as Evil Boss, a part I played at the end of every semester to hone my students' survival skills. Thanks to my beastly mood, this term's performance had come easier than usual.

"Everybody, what's the most important thing to remember in a confrontation like this?" I asked, waving my hands as if conducting a symphony.

"Don't get scared," a chorus of voices shouted back at me.

"And don't let anyone—and I mean anyone—intimidate you. Not your boss, not a policeman, not your boyfriend or girlfriend. If you panic, you won't be able to think clearly and your English will get garbled and confused. . . . Now there's only a minute or two of class time left. I need a courageous person to demonstrate how Indi might have defended herself using the right words and the appropriate body language. No karate experts, please."

Hands waved wildly in the air to get my attention. I scanned the back row, where the shyest people habitually hid, looking for someone who hadn't yet spoken. I finally selected the man in the army jacket who'd been cowering behind the mountainous Hernandez twins all evening.

He took off his baseball cap and sunglasses and stood up. Alex.

I blushed disastrously as he strode to the front of the room. A million different thoughts ran through my mind. I was a mess was one of them. I tried remembering when I'd last used a comb. My hair—never what you'd call pin-perfect—always ran wild in damp weather. I glanced at my reflection in the window and saw that I resembled the leader of the Tree People in the Flash Gordon movie I'd seen recently at a Worst Films Ever Made film festival. But then, he probably hadn't come to admire my grooming habits.

He turned toward me and smiled as if waiting for me to start things up again. I tried to look calm and composed, but internally I was frantic. I glanced up at the wall clock, praying the bell would save me, but the wretched hands refused to move. I could see I was going to have to brazen it out.

"Okay, Mr. Astor," I croaked when I found my voice, "how would you handle a situation like this?"

He drew himself up to his full height and took a few steps toward me.

Instinctively, I backed up to get out of his way and managed to knock over my chair. By the time I righted it, the bell was ringing.

"Terrific class," he said when the last of my students filed out of the room.

"It's an enthusiastic group," I answered, gazing at his face. He was thinner than I remembered, but I couldn't tell if it was because his hair was so short or because he'd really lost weight. I hoped he'd lost his appetite from angst.

"You're too modest," he said, leaning against the blackboard. "From what I've seen, all your students are equally enthusiastic about you."

"You've been here before?" I said, aghast.

"Only twice. The night you moderated the debate on abortion, and the time you did your imitation of George W. You were very funny."

I groaned inwardly, remembering how I'd put on a cowboy hat and walked around the room smirking insanely while making inane political statements. It had not been a dignified performance, to say the least.

"You're very good at this, you know. I wish I'd had a teacher like you when I first got here."

It was on the tip of my tongue to say something playful, like: It's never too late to be a student, but a scene from a recent dream came back to me. I was on my way out of Alex's apartment, valise in hand, while Alex and Kasey stood in the doorway waving good-bye. I'd woken up feeling so humiliated, I still burned whenever I thought of it. So I just said something like: Have a seat, make yourself comfortable.

He perched on the arm of an all-in-one chair/desk and fiddled with his cap, bending the brim back and forth. He seemed uneasy, which slightly boosted my self-confidence.

"I see you're wearing native American garb tonight," I commented to fill the silence.

He looked down at his denim shirt, jeans, sneakers, as if he'd forgotten what he was wearing. "I never thought of it that way."

"When I was in Paris a few years ago, I loved seeing

Frenchmen who were trying to dress like Americans," I babbled on nervously. "They wore the right clothing, but their jeans were perfectly pressed and their shirt collars were pulled up at the neck for style. They never looked sloppy enough to be Americans."

He laughed. "As I recall, that's what you once said about my English—that it's not sloppy enough. I've tried to loosen it up, but I'm afraid it's hopeless."

"Maybe not. Maybe you just need some help. A bit of tutoring," I added recklessly.

He considered my suggestion for a long moment. Then he looked at me and shrugged. "I think the moment has passed."

My heart sank. It was all over.

But then, what was he doing here?

"You look very different with short hair," I managed to say. I was so distracted by my interior conversation, I was having trouble talking to him.

"My lawyer advised me to cut it."

"Your lawyer?"

"I had to testify in Washington about racketeering in the music industry, and she thought I'd be a more credible witness if I didn't look like a musician. Apparently, some of the more provincial Senators think long-haired people are trying to hide something."

"Are you?"

"Me?" he said in surprise.

His innocent tone provoked me. On an impulse, I picked up a piece of chalk and drew a heart on the blackboard.

Then I carefully printed *A.A.* and *VIP* in its center. "Good old Aunt Vera."

His jaw muscle jumped. "How did you find out?"

"A clerical error."

"Whose?"

"I'd rather not say—I don't want to get anyone in trouble. Why didn't you tell me you've been giving money to NYAFS?"

"I don't need to be petted by organizations, and I don't like the resentment a donation can cause."

"What resentment?"

"Large sums of money can have strange effects on people in both directions. I have an old friend—we met when we were both working down on Orchard Street unloading trucks. He's a left-wing journalist and automatically assumes that anyone who has money is corrupt. He makes no exception for me, you understand. We argue about this all the time because, as I frequently point out to him, the only reason he can remain so pure while living on the Upper West Side and sending his kids to a fancy private school is that his wife's family has money—" He stopped. "How did I get started on this?"

"We were talking about gifts. Money."

"Right. It's been my experience that anonymity often has its advantages."

"In any case, you've been very generous. We all appreciate it around here."

"Was that what you were calling me about?"

"No. Actually it was— Listen, another class is going to be

starting in here in a couple of minutes. Why don't you come home with me so we can have some privacy."

He studied me closely for a moment, then broke into a chilling smile. "You really are hell-bent on your mission, aren't you?"

"Excuse me?"

"Nina told me all about it. I mean your efforts to resuscitate your book."

"Oh, that," I said, giving him a sheepish look. "I guess it was pretty stupid of me. I promised a student I'd get my book into print somehow—"

"And you think I'm the somehow," he said sharply. "I assumed that's why you were calling—to get me in front of your tape recorder again."

I was stunned. "But that wasn't it at all."

"No?" he said doubtfully.

"There was something I wanted to tell you."

"Really . . . Well, now that I'm here, why don't you go ahead. I'm all ears," he said, crossing his arms on his chest.

"I just wanted to say—" I broke off, discouraged by the skeptical look on his face. "You're not making this very easy for me, you know."

He shrugged. "I've never pretended to be an easy man. I confess your messages had me going there for a while. I'd almost forgotten how convincing you can be. Or rather, how susceptible I am to your charm."

"And I'd almost forgotten how difficult you can be in spite of yours."

"You mean because I won't play your game?"

"Is that what you think I'm doing—playing games?"

"Frankly, yes."

Stung, I turned around and began erasing the blackboard in great sweeping motions, continuing long after there was anything left to erase. I was hurt, not only because he was rejecting me, but because he thought I'd been hustling him all along. In truth, I had fantasized about interviewing him and instantly selling the book as a result, but even in my worst moments, I'd never considered actually asking him for help.

Finally, I got hold of myself and turned to face him squarely. "I was calling to tell you that I found my mother. I don't mean I've located her geographically; I've gotten to know her. We've spent a considerable amount of time together."

His eyebrows shot up in surprise. "Congratulations."

"Thank you," I said coolly.

"I'm sure it wasn't easy."

"No, it wasn't easy. As you can imagine, it's not exactly the most comfortable relationship in the world. There are a lot of things we can't talk about—can't even go near. But it's okay. I mean, it is what it is. Better than nothing. You were right about that."

"Well, I'm glad everything worked out for you." He put on his hat as if getting ready to leave.

There was a tense silence. I desperately wanted to tell him the truth about how I felt, but the finality of his tone made it impossible.

"At least I've leveled the playing field," I said after a long pause, trying to gauge his reaction.

"Excuse me?"

"The ghost you wouldn't compete with is gone."

Without responding, he stood up. "I'd better get going now. I'm sure you have work to do. Nice seeing you again. Good luck with your mother." He crossed the room and then paused. "Oh, and I apologize if I disrupted your class tonight."

"You didn't disrupt anything. I was just surprised to see you."

"I assure you it won't happen again."

"No, no, feel free to come back whenever. After all, you have every right to see how your money's being spent."

"That's not why I came down here," he said, looking surprisingly injured.

"It doesn't really matter at this point, does it?" I put down the eraser and brushed off my hands.

"It matters to me, or I wouldn't be here."

His face was turned away, so I couldn't read his expression. He reached for the doorknob. "Sam says Kasey is a terrific woman," I blurted out suddenly.

He seemed taken aback. "She is terrific."

"She's a photographer, isn't she?"

"Yes. She's been helping me document some of my work. She's one of my closest friends."

I blinked a few times, taking in what he'd said. Relief surged through me. "She's a friend? I mean, she's not . . . you're not really . . . involved?"

A smile flickered across his lips. "You know, I'm having the oddest sense of déjà vu. Haven't we had this conversation before?"

"You mean at Sam's party—when I was talking about Stoddard?"

"I guess that's it."

"Except we seem to have switched roles."

He closed his eyes for a moment. "Now it's coming back to me.... What was that peculiar phrase you used to describe our kiss?"

"Uh . . . I believe I called it unseemly grappling."

He laughed. "That was it—unseemly grappling. And I said something pretty strange myself. About being in love with you."

"Ditto," I said so softly I wasn't sure I'd spoken aloud.

He gave me a quizzical look.

"Tsk, tsk, tsk," I said, shaking my head sadly. "I see you're still having a bit of a problem with American slang, Mr. Astor."

"That's true. I sometimes get my signals crossed. Do you have any suggestions?"

"Yes, as a matter of fact, I do. I think you ought to consider being tutored privately."

"Do you know of a good tutor?"

"Actually, I was thinking I might be the right person to help you."

"I thought you weren't taking on new students."

"I have room for only one."

"How do I sign up?"

"Well, by coincidence, I happen to be giving a special hands-on workshop at my apartment tonight. You can sign up there."

"It sounds interesting. But I have to warn you about something."

My heart lurched. "Yes?"

"I'm a slow learner. I think I'm going to need a lot of practice."

I smiled. "Let's hope so. I'm planning a very long course."

I picked up my briefcase and turned out the lights.

Time for my next class.